AN AMERICAN

First published in Great Britain 1993
by Mills & Boon Limited

This edition 1993

ISBN 0 263 78048 1

Masquerade is a trademark published by
Mills & Boon Limited, Eton House,
18–24 Paradise Road, Richmond, Surrey, TW9 1SR.

Set in 10 on 11½ pt Linotron Baskerville
04-9303-78680

Typeset in Great Britain by Centracet, Cambridge
Made and printed in Great Britain

CHAPTER ONE

'No,' said Sally-Anne McAllister dazedly. 'No, please, no,' and she struggled fiercely against the arms which held her—a man's, she noted, and that was enough to start her struggling even harder.

She would not be held by a man ever again. No, not at all, and then, even in her confused state, her mind shied away from the reasons for her distaste, and she found herself saying even through her pain and shock, 'I will not think about that, I will not,' and so saying she stopped struggling and sank back into oblivion once more.

The next time she returned to consciousness she discovered that the whole right side of her face was numb, and that was all she registered. The memory of being held in a man's hard arms had disappeared. Her eyes opened; she was on her back. Above her she saw a ceiling, grey and white, a plaster rose from which depended a gas-light inside a glass globe, engraved with roses.

She heard voices which at first made little sense, could not, for the moment, think where she might be or even who she was.

'Mama,' she said, her voice a thread, speech strangely difficult.

'She's coming round at last.' It was a man's voice, educated, a pleasant if cold baritone. An earlier memory returned. Was he the man who had held her? She did not want him to hold her again. She tried to sit up, but was pushed gently back, by a woman's hand this time.

'Oh, dear God, Dr Neil. Thanks be to Him she's conscious again. I thought she would never recover,' said a woman's voice this time. 'The second blow was a cruel one.'

'Stupid,' said the man's cold voice. 'It was stupid of her to try to intervene between Jem Higgins and his Poll.'

Sally-Anne opened her eyes, tried to sit up—a mistake that, everything reeled around her again; but memory had returned and she knew why she was in this room. . .and even why she had reached there, but not how.

And how dared the man standing between herself and the light so that she could not see him clearly speak so harshly of what she had done? It might indeed be stupid to try to stop a man from attacking a helpless woman. . .but. . .

'Someone,' she announced, her voice suddenly strong again, 'someone has to try to prevent poor women from being beaten by great strong brutes.'

'Oh, yes,' said the man drily, 'I could not agree with you more. But not young girls who could barely defend themselves against a schoolboy, let alone the professional bruiser Jem Higgins once was. How came you here, anyway?' And from what she could see of him, which was not much, he was giving her the coldest of stares. Her memory returned fully. . . She remembered quite clearly what she had been doing scarce ten minutes ago.

Sally-Anne McAllister—although that was not her real name—walked along Vetch Street in London's East End late on a hot afternoon in the early summer of 1903.

Not that summer did anything for Vetch Street; dust

motes hung in the warm air and the sunlight was pitiless, starkly revealing the cracks in the broken pavement, the decaying brickwork of the small terrace houses, and the larger tenements which stood among them, and the rottenness of the wood in the unpainted doors and window-frames. Here and there a larger house stood, once the home of some magnate now long gone, broken and rotten, a warren where different families lived in every room.

In all her short life Sally-Anne had never before encountered the squalor which she had seen in the few days since she had arrived in these poor streets in the hinterland between London Docks and Stepney. Although she was not aware of it she was, in her shabby white cotton blouse and her dark green skirt, with her blue-black and glossy curls drawn up and knotted simply on the top of her head, her face glowing and vital, the only touch of colour in the grimy street.

She carried a small basket in her hand containing food for her frugal evening meal, although the rancid smells around her were strong enough to diminish any desire to eat—she had not yet grown sufficiently accustomed to them to ignore them.

Later she was to think how little she was prepared for the simple events which were to change her life completely—indeed she would have said that so much had happened to her already that any further incidents must be minor, a judgement which could not have been more faulty.

She had been living in Crow Court off Vetch Street for nearly a week, and the narrow lives of the people among whom she found herself appalled her. What perhaps struck her the most was that, despite all, many of them appeared to be happy, while she, Sally-Anne, who could if she wished command the most luxurious life a woman could dream of, was most desperately unhappy, and had no idea of how she might become otherwise.

Her thoughts, which as usual these days were depressing, were disturbed by the noise of a fight, a fracas on the corner where Vetch Street met Millstone Lane. A man, a large man, was beating a woman, a little woman who seemed scarcely more than a child, and was trying to drag her into one of the tenements which lined the opposite side of the road.

A group of ragged children and some idle women were watching him with amusement rather than disapproval, half applauding him with their cruel laughter, and although one woman boldly cried, 'Shame,' most seemed to be enjoying the unequal struggle.

The little woman suddenly broke away from him, ran across the ill-paved road towards her, tripped on the broken pavement, fell on to her knees before Sally-Anne, and, face wild, looked up at her imploringly, wailing, 'Help me, missis, please help me. He'll kill me yet,' in a thin broken voice.

Sally-Anne, hampered by her basket, tried to pull herself free. The woman stank of neglect, her clothes were torn and filthy, and tears had made twin furrows down her face.

Pity rose in her. And anger—anger at the man, at all men. He had loomed up before her, had arrived to claim the woman again, pulling her away from Sally-Anne, his own face twisted with rage. He cuffed the woman on the head, attempting to drag her back into the doorway.

Sally-Anne was almost choking between rage and fear. She put her basket down on the pavement, held on to the woman with one arm, pulled on the man's huge arm with the other, said to him firmly, if more than a little fearfully, 'No, you are not to touch her again. Leave her alone.'

This came out with more bravado than Sally-Anne really felt, and had she seen him more clearly before she intervened she might not have said anything at all. The man was a bear, unshaven, face mottled purple, his eyes yellow and feral, his teeth broken, but his body, huge and strong, running to fat.

He paused to stare at Sally-Anne, face ugly. 'An' who might you be, to tell me what to do wi' mine?'

'Never mind who I might be,' said Sally-Anne firmly, trying to swallow her fear. 'Just stop what you're doing or I'll set the police on you.'

She might as well have saved her breath. The feral eyes glared cruelly at her.

'Leave go, missis, or it'll be the worse for you.'

It was impossible for Sally-Anne to obey even if she had wished to. The woman had sunk to the ground to avoid her tormentor, had clasped Sally-Anne around her knees, and was shrieking up at her, 'Oh, help me, help me, do.' She cried and wailed into Sally-Anne's skirt so pitifully that Sally-Anne's own fear of the brute before her was lost in sympathy for his wretched victim.

The watchers were now bellowing encouragement to each of the players in a game which had taken a new turn. They hallooed and shouted. Windows were thrown open, heads appeared.

The unequal tug of war continued, and something kept the man from actually striking Sally-Anne, although he rained blows on the woman, who was now giving vent to a low, keening moan. Emboldened, Sally-Anne cried to the watchers, 'Fetch a policeman. He could arrest this man for assault.'

Guffaws greeted her. 'Not likely, missis; it's only Jem keeping his Poll in order. No case for the Peelers.' And their cruel laughter was that of any mindless mob finding entertainment in violence.

By now Jem had almost succeeded in prising Poll free from Sally-Anne, with the result that Poll's wailing went up an octave. Almost dragged free, her hands had dropped around Sally-Anne's ankles, nearly bringing her, too, to the ground.

Looking up, eyes wild, Poll made one last supplication to Sally-Anne. 'Oh, don't let him take me, missis, please, don't let him take me. He'll kill me this time, for sure.'

'No,' said Sally-Anne, breathless. She fell on to her knees, held on to the woman, whose face was now on her shoulder. She looked up at Jem bravely. 'No, I won't. You, Jem, stop this at once. Shame on you for hitting a woman. I shall certainly set the police on you if you continue to go on as you are doing.'

This reasoned and ridiculous plea had no effect at all on Jem, other than to inflame him to further violence. He bent down, thrust his unshaven face and stinking breath into Sally-Anne's, put his great hands under her armpits and hauled her to her feet by main force, Poll still clinging desperately to her. 'You will have it, then, damn you,' he growled, and he struck not Poll, but Sally-Anne, hard in the face.

She saw the blow coming, but hampered by Poll could take no avoiding action other than to turn her head slightly on receiving it. All her senses stunned, she realised that he was about to strike her again, and this time, when he did so, oblivion took her, man, woman and jeering watchers all disappearing into the vacant dark. . .

And now, here she was, wherever here was, with a woman, short and comfortable, who possessed a kind face, and a man who was none of these things, judging by the coolly impersonal way in which he spoke to her. She could see little of him, only his tall body, lean against the light.

'How did I get here?' she asked, looking around a shabby but pleasant room, feeling so frail that she might have been made of china, china broken into a thousand pieces. She remembered Jem's first blow, but not his second.

'Dr Neil carried you in,' said the woman, who was now holding Sally-Anne's right hand with her own left hand, while gently wiping Sally-Anne's poor bruised face with a damp cloth held in her right.

Sally-Anne's returning senses told her that she was lying on an old-fashioned sofa with a high back at one end, and no sides. The man standing before her had earlier been on his knees on the opposite side from the woman. Painfully, looking up at him, she saw a good strong profile, sandy hair tipped with gold from the sun coming in through the lace-curtained window.

'Dr Neil?' she said questioningly.

'Dr Neil Cochrane,' he replied brusquely. 'What on earth possessed you to get involved with Jem Higgins? Suicidal, if I may say so. You have got off lightly, even if your face will be swollen and painful for some time.'

He looked hard at Sally-Anne, ignored her shabby clothes and shoes, looked instead at her hands and face, and all the signs of good care and feeding about her, so different from most of the women who lived around Vetch Street.

He was about to ask her what in the world she was doing in the East End when he was reproached by an angry Sally-Anne. Oh, she hated all men, did she not? Particularly officious, domineering ones. She had not pushed into, or invited, the fight; Poll had involved her.

But she would not defend herself, by no means, and she answered him in tones as brusque and hard as his own.

'I could not see such a large man mistreating such a poor little woman.'

'I can only say, Miss. . .? that if you are to defend every maltreated woman in London's East End you will spend all your days in such labour, to no purpose. The law does not like, or support, those who come between husband and wife.'

'Oh, indeed?' said Sally-Anne furiously to this supporter of wife-beaters—and if only he would move so that she could see him, and not continue to stand between herself and the light—'How typically male. Only a man could say such cruel things,' and then, belatedly, remembering her manners, which her mama had so often told her she was always forgetting, 'But I must thank you for taking me in. And my name is Sally-Anne. . . McAllister,' and she almost tripped over the last bit, but hoped he had not noticed.

She did notice that the nice little woman had gently squeezed her hand when Dr Neil was being at his most dictatorial over men's right to beat their wives.

Whether Dr Neil had noticed her hesitation or not, he said to the little woman—ignoring both Sally-Anne's anger over his cruelty, and her thanks—which just went to show, she thought crossly, that it was no use trying to placate the unpleasant creatures—'Matey, you will make us all a hot pot of tea, strong and sweet. It will restore Miss. . . McAllister a little. She has received quite an unpleasant shock.'

'Thank you, no,' said Sally-Anne impatiently; she needed no condescension from him or any man. Unpleasant shock, indeed. She hardly knew which was worst, Jem with his blatant nastiness, or this man defending it—implicitly, anyway. 'I will be on my way.

Drink your tea yourself. You seem to need it more than I do.' And how would Mama react to *that*? Oh, Sally-Anne, do you never think of what you are saying before you say it?—all in the most sorrowful manner, no doubt.

She swung her legs over the side of the sofa, which reduced her defiance to mere childishness, alas, since her head began to swim dreadfully, and also caused him to say impatiently—he really ought to meet Mama, at least he would agree with *her*—'Oh, do be quiet for a moment, madam. You are in no condition to go any where. Miss Mates will make us all some tea, give you some sweet biscuits, and only when I am fully satisfied that you are fit again shall I allow you to leave. While you are here, in my home, you are my patient. Perhaps some sweet tea will restore your temper a little—or are you always so pointlessly combative?'

Pointlessly combative! Only her spinning head prevented her from rising and leaving at once. She stared fierily at him. What was he doing in the East End? His voice was educated, his clothing good, if a little careless—a tweed suit, and a cream shirt, well cut, if his collar was a little frayed. She could still see only his profile, and when he moved away, into the room's shadows, she could not even see that.

He seemed to take it for granted that everyone would do what he told them. Miss Mates had already sped to do his bidding, giving Sally-Anne one last sympathetic squeeze of the hand before she left her.

Even in her dazed and painful state his imperious, if not to say imperial manner amused as well as annoyed her. Few people ever expected Sally-Anne to do as she was told. It was usually a vain hope. She had been independent since childhood and hoped to remain so. Thoroughly spoiled, her mama had said sadly, the last time she had seen her.

But suddenly the thought of her mama was painful to her, and to push it away she leaned back again, said, amusement plain in her voice, which, although she did not know it, surprised Neil Cochrane a little, 'Oh, I will be good, because in my present condition I cannot be anything else, I fear.' She could almost feel her absent mother's approval of her belated politeness.

Dr Neil turned away from inspecting his own bookshelves, said, apropos of what she could not imagine, 'You are not English, I perceive, Miss McAllister.'

'You are quick, Dr Neil,' she said, a little surprised in her turn. Her East Coast American accent deceived most people, it was so like, and yet in some ways so unlike, that of the society in which she had been living for the last six months. 'No, I am American, from the East Coast, but I have been living in England for some time.'

Neil Cochrane moved forward, sat down in an armchair facing her, and said, 'I am happy to see that you are prepared to rest a little, after all.'

But what he said had little effect on Sally-Anne compared with the sight of his face at last. She had already noticed that when he walked he limped more than a little, favouring his left leg, but his face had taken a greater hurt.

His left profile, first glimpsed, was that of a handsome man, but the right side of his face was a ruin. It was marred by a puckered scar which had destroyed his cheek, beginning just above the right-hand corner of his mouth, but, fortunately for him, narrowly missed his eye to disappear into his hair, twisting and distorting his whole face.

Neil Cochrane's mouth tightened when for the first time Sally-Anne saw his face plain, and reacted by controlling her own, so that the shock which she had received was only momentarily shown. He gave no other sign of distress, merely turned his head to greet Miss Mates, saying coolly, 'You are prompt, Matey, even without your kitchen help.'

Miss Mates was carrying a black lacquered tray with a delicately flowered china tea-set on it—Wedgwood, Sally-Anne noted—and a silver teapot. The elegantly shabby room in which she had found a haven was an oasis in the East End's desert, which could be glimpsed through the small bow window.

Sally-Anne took the tea which Miss Mates offered, and drank it gratefully. Full awareness was returning to her, her head had ceased to swim, and all that was left of her recent encounter was the pain in her face, and her consequent anger at every member of the male sex.

'What happened to Poll?' she asked, determined not to be silenced by Dr Neil Cochrane, and not to allow the ruin of his looks to create any pity for him. She did, though, wonder what dreadful accident had left him marked for life, and lame into the bargain. She tried to eat a small biscuit, grimaced a little at the consequent pain. This made her think suddenly of the pain which Neil Cochrane must have endured, so that she felt pity for him, after all.

'What do you think?' said Dr Neil, watching her. He had already noted in her favour that she did not avoid looking him full in the face as many did; nor did she flinch or stare when she did.

'Jem took her home, as he intended to.' He forbore to add that Poll might have earned a few more blows as the result of Sally-Anne's intervention, to prevent her from involving anyone else in future.

'And beat her again, no doubt,' said Sally-Anne acidly.

'No doubt.'

'You are annoyingly cool about it, sir.'

'Dr Neil, or Dr Cochrane, if you please,' he said, remaining determinedly cool—to reproach her, no doubt, for what he considered misplaced pity. 'No sirs. We cannot dance up and down about poor Poll; it would not help her. That does not mean that I approve of what Jem does.'

'But the police——' began Sally-Anne.

'Oh, the police do not care about, or interfere in, domestic matters. She is his wife, whether married in church, or what we call over here his common-law wife. That is, she lives with him, and that, I fear, is the end of it.'

'You fear!' she flashed at him. 'The wrongs of women do not concern you?'

'Oh, everyone's wrongs concern me,' he said, but his voice was as cool as ever. 'But I do not flatter myself that I can do anything about them. Except, of course, where they directly impinge on me, that is. You are a suffragette, I take it?' Sally-Anne could not tell whether he said this critically or not. His cold, impassive manner had not changed when he spoke.

'What decent woman would not be,' said Sally-Anne, waving her biscuit at him, 'given the way in which society treats us? It is not only East End bruisers who mistreat their women, by no means.'

She was fast recovering, Dr Neil saw; the pretty, wilful, if swollen and bruised face was vital, the springing blue-black curls were a sign of vigour and health. Miss Sally-Anne McAllister had always been well fed and well cared for, he noted professionally. She was also a young person well accustomed to having her own way—there was no doubt of that.

'And what is this decent, well-educated woman doing wandering around London's East End?' he asked.

Before Sally-Anne could reply—and fortunately for her, for she needed to consider her answer carefully—there was a knocking at the door, and Dr Neil was required there for a moment.

In his temporary absence, Miss Mates refreshed Sally-Anne's cup again, said gently to her, 'Do not mind Dr Neil's manner, my dear. He is the kindest of men beneath his brusque exterior. His patients swear by him. Do not let him frighten you.'

'Oh, he does not do *that*,' said Sally-Anne cheerfully; all her normal *brio* had returned, and she was not going to allow Dr Neil to put her down, and when he came back she gave him her most dazzling smile, and prepared to do battle with him, whenever battle was necessary.

Kind he might be, although it seemed improbable from what she had so far seen of him, but Sally-Anne wanted nothing from men, neither kindness. . .nor love. . .nor anything.

CHAPTER TWO

BUT when Dr Neil Cochrane returned to the business of Miss Sally-Anne McAllister who had so strangely arrived in his home he was as firmly pressing of her as he was before.

Miss Mates had brought in Sally-Anne's basket after Dr Neil had intervened to save her, and driven off a Jem Higgins who was by then a little fearful at having laid Sally-Anne so low. Dr Neil had seen her few poor items of food decently arranged upon a napkin in the bottom of the basket, and there seemed little doubt that she was actually living in the district—although why he could not imagine.

He sat down by Sally-Anne, his ruined cheek slightly averted, poured himself another cup of tea and began to question her again.

Sally-Anne stirred restlessly. He might have saved her from Jem, but did that give him the right to such a ruthless inquisition? She demurred a little when he said, picking up his teacup, and looking at her over the top of it, 'You never answered my question, Miss McAllister. What exactly are you doing here? I see by your basket and your dress that you are domiciled in the neighbourhood.'

Domiciled in the neighbourhood, indeed! What a pompous way of putting it. Amusement at that made her tone light. 'If you must know, Dr Neil, and I suppose I owe you that, I am looking for work.'

'Work?' he said, raising his eyebrows and looking at

her as though she had said drilling for oil or prospecting for gold.

'Yes, work,' she said sharply. 'One must eat. Money is needed to buy food. One is given money for work. What is so surprising about that?'

Dr Neil could have given her several answers, beginning with the beautiful hands lying in her lap which had visibly never done a stroke of work in their owner's life, but said instead, 'A strange place for a young lady like yourself to look for it.'

'Indeed not,' replied Sally-Anne, with all the fiery determination which her own family knew so well. 'It is hard for an unqualified and unapprenticed female to find any work in London, except in the East End where, I am reliably informed, there is casual labour aplenty, and unskilled work, too.'

'Yes, I know that,' he said, smiling a little at her charming vehemence. 'But how does a young American lady——' and he stressed the last word slightly '—come to be alone and seeking work in London?'

How indeed? thought Sally-Anne ruefully. Her fertile and inventive imagination came to her aid. She was frequently appalled at her own ability to lie convincingly, thought that perhaps she got it from Papa, one of the world's great tricksters—not knowing that on occasion her apparently innocent mama had the gift as well.

She had no alternative but to tell him a series of absolute whoppers, as her younger brother, Rob, would have said. The poser being, of course, that she could not tell him either the true reason she was here, or even who she really was.

She improvised wildly and skilfully, dabbing at her eyes while she spoke with a rather grubby handkerchief.

'My papa died after he lost all our money in the last

great depression. My. . .mama. . .had long gone.' Even an unscrupulous Sally-Anne could not quite kill her mama off completely—if he thought that her mama had bolted, well, so be it.

She gave a half-sob, added, 'I had to find work. An old acquaintance of the family needed a governess-companion for her little girl during a prolonged visit to Europe. She came from New York State, too—her husband was an executive in an automobile works there—and I thought my troubles were over.'

She heaved a great sigh of which she was privately rather proud, thinking that it added a touch of verisimilitude to the sad tale she was spinning. Later she was to wish that she had neither been so deceitful, nor so colourful, but at the time excitement and expediency combined carried her away.

'Unfortunately my employer's husband. . .' And she cast her eyes modestly downwards.

'Yes?' prompted Dr Neil with a grin—for some reason he did not believe a word of this farrago—to hear her reply in a low voice,

'He took more than a proper liking to me, and when I indicated that I was not interested in his advances he had me cast off. . .without a reference, so that I cannot find suitable employment.'

Sally-Anne was particularly pleased with the last bit, and saw by Miss Mates's sympathetic expression that she was swallowing every word. She was not quite so sure of Dr Neil, but she ploughed steadily on.

'I was left with very little money, came here to live in Crow Court, because it is cheap. I need employment to live, and in the hope that I can save my passage home again. I would do anything to earn a wage, however small—be a servant, even. I would not mind being trained, and I am not afraid of hard work.'

'A servant?' said Miss Mates, coming over and taking Sally-Anne's hand. 'You poor child,' and Sally-Anne swallowed a little at this, feeling ashamed of telling such a kind-hearted creature such whoppers. 'But the work is so hard, for so little. And you are so old.'

'Old?' said Sally-Anne a little indignantly, to Dr Neil's amusement as he watched the two women. 'Why, I am not yet twenty-one.'

'Oh, but one starts training housemaids and cooks at twelve and thirteen,' said Miss Mates gently, but at the same time she was thinking of her own problems in finding and keeping satisfactory girls, and Miss McAllister looked both strong and willing. A little high-spirited, perhaps, but hard work and long hours would soon cool her down.

'I learn very quickly,' said Sally-Anne submissively. 'And I really do need to earn my passage home. I meant it when I said that I would do anything. Perhaps you might know where I could usefully apply?'

Was it her imagination or was the man opposite her regarding her warily? Since Miss Mates had intervened he had said little, although he had had enough to say before that, goodness knew, thought Sally-Anne briskly. Strange how handsome he looked with the shadow concealing his ruined cheek a little. What a pity for him.

She thought that perhaps her manner was somewhat too bold for one who so recently had been only a governess, and now wanted to be even less. She smiled and bent her head. She must remember not to be her usual confidently aggressive self if she was offering to take up such a subordinate post.

'Are you serious, Miss McAllister?' Dr Neil asked. 'About becoming a servant, I mean. You do know how hard the work is, I hope?'

'Oh, yes!' exclaimed Sally-Anne eagerly. 'But I do

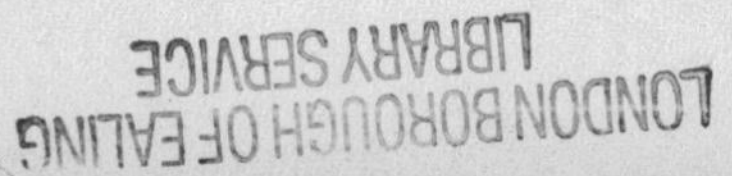

not intend to do it forever, and I am very strong. Papa says that most horses would envy me in that line!'

This frankly offered statement brought an almost unwilling laugh from him.

'Did he, indeed? Let us put Papa's notions to the test, then. I know that Matey here wants a maid of all work, and that the last two were highly unsatisfactory. You could hardly be worse, I suppose.'

Sally-Anne bridled a little at this. She liked to think that she was very efficient in all she did. From what she had seen of maid's work it was not very difficult. An idiot could do it.

What she did not know was that it was not so much that the work was difficult, but that there was so very much of it, and all tiring. Like most young ladies of her class she had no idea at all of the effort which went into making her own charmed life easy. She was not so much spoilt as totally unaware.

'I'm sure that I should be satisfactory,' she said stiffly. 'You could put me on probation, I suppose.'

'I have no intention of doing anything else,' said Dr Neil briskly. He was now all employer, coolly assessing Sally-Anne as a prospective slave about the house. 'I should be taking you on at a week's notice. Your wage would be five shillings and all found, one evening and one afternoon off a week—you can arrange all that with Miss Mates. To church on Sunday, with Miss Mates, of course. Oh, and no followers. I want no policemen hanging about the kitchen.'

He thought that if Miss McAllister was not serious that would be sure to put her off. He decided to inform her of her duties, said casually, watching her as he spoke, 'Your day would begin at six o'clock, finish at Miss Mates's bedtime between half-past ten and eleven, and you will have the attic bedroom. Miss Mates will show you to it.'

Sally-Anne was scarlet. Policemen followers, indeed! And her hours! She had genuinely possessed no idea of how long servants worked, and for how little. She suspected that the good doctor might be laying it on a little thick, but she would not be put off, and said in her stiffest voice, 'Yes, I understand all that, and I am prepared to work hard,' and she added for good measure, 'You need not worry about followers. I truly despise *all* men.' This came out in Sally-Anne's best manner.

'So very glad to hear it,' said Dr Neil Cochrane brightly. 'Now we all know where we are. You will not be flirting at the kitchen door with the milkman and the coalman, and Matey will not be chasing you for doing so.'

He was no fool. Despite being an East End doctor he also knew the great and wide world outside. There was something vaguely odd about Sally-Anne McAllister and the farrago to which she had treated them.

He did not doubt that she was an American, but as to her story—well, he was not sure. But he was a man who liked challenges and this wilful—child—for despite her boasted nearly twenty-one years, to Neil Cochrane she seemed little more—appeared to offer one.

And Matey badly needed help; indeed, she was looking at him with something like approval. She said to Sally-Anne, 'Well, I do need a maid of all work, that's true, but I never thought of hiring a lady. . .' And her voice trailed off as she surveyed Sally-Anne in all her proud and pampered beauty. Did she really understand what she was taking on?

'I *said* I was willing to work and to learn,' said Sally-Anne, exasperated by all this havering. Goodness, how the British went on. A good American would have had her in the kitchen with a flue-brush, or making pastry, by now. 'I'm an excellent cook,' she announced proudly. 'Mama made sure of that.'

'Well, that's certainly something,' said Miss Mates, overwhelmed by such artless eagerness, so foreign to any maid of all work she had encountered before.

'I could start immediately,' Sally-Anne roared on, striking while the iron was hot, just as Papa always advised—one maxim which she had not disdained to learn from him. 'Because I am running out of money,' she added, and she crossed her fingers beneath the light blanket which Miss Mates had thrown over her earlier and asked God to forgive her for such dreadful lies, and so many of them.

She brought her hands up, clasped them together, said impulsively, 'Oh, do say yes, Dr Neil, sir, Miss Mates—help a poor, lonely orphan,' and this last flew out without her even thinking, and certainly dissolved Miss Mates, even if Dr C, as she privately thought of him, looked a little sardonic.

Miss Mates, indeed, kissed her on the cheek, said, 'Oh, you poor thing,' which made Sally-Anne feel a little mean, even if it was the last copper-bottomed clincher—that was her Uncle Orrin this time, not Papa—which got her the job.

For good measure, she added, a trifle pathetically, 'I am a good girl, really truly, even if I can't give you any references, and I will work hard, I promise.'

'Oh, we shan't give you any opportunity to be anything else, Miss McAllister. You're sure you want her, Matey?' drawled Dr Neil, still sardonic, but his use of Miss Mates's nickname was the final sign that he was prepared to take her on. But for Miss Mates the 'really truly' was the icing on the cake, even if she had more doubts about Sally-Anne's stamina than her missing references.

'Perhaps you could start this evening,' she offered. 'If Dr Neil says that you are fit.'

Sally-Anne tried to stand up, found that she was still somewhat rocky, looked at Dr Neil, and said doubtfully, 'I don't think that I am quite fully recovered yet. I might be able to fetch my things from Crow Court where I am rooming a little later on, but as to work. . .'

'Oh, yes, work,' said Dr Neil in his rather hateful way, as though every word she said was dubious in itself, and, even though they were, Sally-Anne could not help feeling righteously indignant. 'I would not want to slave-drive you as early as this actual moment.' And he looked pointedly at his watch, a fine gold hunter which he pulled out of his pocket and cocked an eye at.

'Five o'clock,' he announced. 'I should think you might be ready at six-thirty,' and now the quizzical eye was cocked at Sally-Anne.

'Surgery at five-fifteen,' he said. 'Matey will look after you, and perhaps later on we can collect your traps from Crow Court. I take it that you will not need a pantechnicon?'

'You take it correctly,' said Sally-Anne, a little peevish, despite her pleasure at having found employment so easily, and in an area where she could observe and record the life going on around her. She must not forget the other reason why she had wished to find work here, and exile from her old life was not the main one for her presence in Vetch Street.

Miss Mates, who had removed the tea things, came bustling back, said to Dr Neil, 'Mind you are ready for surgery,' and brought him a plain black coat which he put on instead of the rather sporty Harris tweed one which he was wearing.

'You see, McAllister,' he said gravely, 'were it not for Matey I should never look presentable. I tend to forget what a proper doctor should wear. That's why it's so important that she has efficient help.'

He strolled off to the surgery, Matey still fussing about him. She came back, sat by the fireside, and said to Sally-Anne, 'The surgery's at the side of the house. I suppose you've seen it when you've walked by.' She sighed. 'He works too hard, but there, you can't tell him anything. He's always gone his own way. I've made another pot of tea for us. It will do your head the world of good. No restorative like tea.'

I wonder the British don't bath in it as well, thought Sally-Anne naughtily, but she was grateful for the extra cup, and for the sandwiches which Miss Mates brought in with it for them both. 'To tide us over. We usually have a bit of supper when Dr Neil's day is ended. Not that it ever really ends. Many's the night he's been called out in the small hours. . .' And Matey heaved another great sigh.

She spoke of him, Sally-Anne thought, as though he were still only twelve years old. She giggled internally at this, visualising tall and haughty Dr Neil wearing the black knickerbockers, funny jacket and cap of an English schoolboy.

The smile this brought to her face pleased the old nurse. 'Beginning to feel a bit better, are you?' she said kindly. She leaned forward, pulled the wrapper over Sally-Anne up to her chin. 'Have a bit of a doze, my dear. You've had a hard day, and by the sound of it not an easy life. Yes, have a little nap; it'll set you up for a day's work tomorrow. I'll leave you to go and wash the pots.'

She tiptoed out, leaving Sally-Anne to fall into a light sleep—but not before she felt a little mean, as she would have said in the USA, about deceiving the good old lady—and Dr Neil Cochrane, of course. Although she didn't feel so badly about *him*. He was only a man when all was said and done, and men—well, they deserved to be deceived.

But it was not a great deceit, after all, and perhaps one day she might be able to explain it to them, and apologise, but for the present matters could not have arranged themselves much better.

What a pity about Dr Neil's ruined face—and his suspicious manner, were her last conscious thoughts before sleep took her.

CHAPTER THREE

REALLY, the worst thing about being a kitchenmaid-cum-parlourmaid-cum-everything else, Sally-Anne ruefully considered, was all the scrubbing and the grate-cleaning which had to be done every day. It was not that she minded the hard work; it was what the hard work did to her poor hands.

The scrubbing was the nastiest, she thought despairingly, bad though blacking the grates, particularly the kitchen range, was.

She was down on her knees, finishing off the doorstep; an apron made from some coarse sacking was protecting her plain black dress, her legs were clad in thick black wool stockings and her feet were shod in heavy, much mended shoes—second-hand into the bargain, as was most of her servant's clothing.

And what a ritual the doorstep was. First the scrubbing, and then the almost religious whitening not only of the step, but their share of the pavement before the step. It had to be done every day, too.

What was worse, within minutes people would be walking all over her back-breaking work—it did not bear thinking of. She straightened up, and carried the pail, the soap, the brush and the swab, as Miss Mates called the cloth, to the outdoor drain at the back of the house. And she shuddered at the chore the whole thing would be in the winter—if she lasted that long—seeing that it was such a drag in the mildness of summer.

Her soft hands were so unaccustomed to such hard work that it became—temporarily, Miss Mates said, until they hardened—difficult for her to help with the fine sewing, and the darning and repairing needed in the little house. Which was a pity, Miss Mates also said, looking approvingly at Sally-Anne's neat and careful stitchery, done before her hands became ruined.

'Oh, Mama always made sure that I learned to do the practical stuff, as well as fine embroidery and canvas work,' Sally-Anne had said. 'She always said that bread and butter was needed as well as cake.'

'Your mama sounds like a sensible woman,' said Miss Mates. 'A pity that you had to lose her and earn your own living.'

'Needs must,' lied Sally-Anne, who was beginning to wonder whether she would ever be able to tell the whole truth again. That was the worst thing about duplicity, she was beginning to find. That and having to watch what you were saying. Keep it simple was a good motto.

She returned to the present, replaced the cleaned pail, the soap, the brush and the swab beside the pump in the lean-to outhouse at the back—it stood in a small soot-encrusted yard where a few fearless London sparrows frequently gathered—and returned to the house to clean the surgery.

She had already thrown yesterday's damp tea-leaves on to the parlour carpet, and when she had finished in the surgery would take a small, hard hand-brush and, down on her knees yet again, would painstakingly sweep them all up into a dustpan, to remove the previous day's dirt and dust, Miss Mates said, and purify the air.

Sally-Anne liked the surgery. Small and cramped although it was, it reminded her a little of Papa's office back home: a room where a man obviously worked. She briefly envied Dr Neil and Papa—so easy for a man to do useful and purposeful work. On the other hand, she conceded, someone had to do the kind of menial tasks she was at present condemned to—but why was it always women who did them? And for such a poor reward, too.

She knew what Papa would say to *that*. 'Now, Sally-Anne, men do menial work, a lot of it, and harsher often, than women's. They go down the mines, herd cattle, tend sewers—you must admit that.'

She knew what Papa would say because he had said it a few years ago when she had begun to reproach him and all men for their oppression of women. He had not denied it—he had explained it instead, which was worse, she had once said angrily.

Her eyes filled with tears. Oh, she did miss them so, both Mama and Papa. But she would not crawl home for comfort, defeated. Twice defeated now, and the second one so bitter. . .and so irrevocable. Humpty Dumpty could never be put back again. . . No, she would not think of that—no, never that, and she began to wield her feather duster with such angry vigour that Dr Neil, coming in, was amused at her bright energy which even the ever-lasting drudgery which she performed could not dim.

'You are supposed to be suppressing dust, McAllister, not raising it and spreading it about,' he said cheerfully to her back.

Sally-Anne could not get used to being known so abruptly by her surname. She had never queried such a thing before—indeed, had taken servants, their duties, and how one addressed them for granted, after the fashion of all wealthy and pampered girls, she now supposed. She would never do so again.

She stopped, turned to face Dr Neil—as everyone, she found, called him, even his poor patients as well as Miss Mates—and said cheekily, 'Oh, come, Dr Neil. If

I am dull and slow I am reproached, and now it appears that being vigorous does not answer, either.'

Dr Neil put his head on one side and said gravely, 'You must learn not to be impudent to the Master, McAllister—it really will not do,' but she knew by his manner that he was not serious, and she thought again what a pity it was that the ugly scar so spoiled and distorted his face.

And he minded that it did; Sally-Anne knew that. She was not so young and giddy that she had no understanding of the desires and problems of others. Besides, living as she now was in a small house on top of two other people, and Dr Neil's surgery boy, and seeing at close hand the wretched people who frequented his surgery, was giving her insights into the motivations and behaviour of the people around her because she had to consider them, whereas always before, in the past, other people had been compelled to consider *her*.

What pity she had possessed for others had been diffuse and impersonal, for women as a mass rather than for individual women such as poor, defeated Poll whom she saw daily, the marks of Jem's fists on her face.

Dr Neil was now seated at his desk and she lingered a little. For some reason, even though he was often sharp and rather short with her, however kind he was to his poor patients, she had begun to like being with him. Perhaps it was because he did not defer to her, flatter her, praise her beauty and her charm, admire her ready wit, as all the men she had known before had done, when what they really liked and deferred to was the knowledge of her father's immense fortune and the certainty that she was sure to inherit a great part of it.

Miss Mates worshipped him. She had been his nurse when he was a little boy, she had told Sally-Anne when they were preparing dinner for him one evening. Sally-Anne remembered the carrots falling into small red-gold coins as she cut them while Matey talked.

'He was a soldier, you know,' she had said, podding peas so rapidly that Sally-Anne was full of awe for such expertise, pea-podding being difficult, she had discovered. 'Sent into the army at eighteen, as younger sons always are. And then, when he was doing so well, he was badly hurt in that nasty Africa.' Africa was always nasty to Miss Mates because it had maimed and nearly killed her treasure.

'When he came home he had to leave the army, you see. He was ill for a long time. He still limps, as I suppose you have noticed.'

Yes, Sally-Anne had noticed.

'Well, he said that he wanted to do something useful with his life, seeing that it had been given back to him when he hadn't expected it. Africa had changed him, you see, and he still only in his early twenties. He said he wanted to be a doctor, and his papa, Sir Hanley, agreed in the end to him becoming one—not a thing for a gentleman to be, he said, but Dr Neil insisted, even when Sir Hanley said that he didn't want an apothecary for a son.'

He had called Neil a damned snivelling apothecary, Miss Mates remembered, but she had never used, or repeated, such language.

'So, here we are,' Miss Mates had finished. 'He said that he didn't want to be a fashionable doctor. He owed his life to his men, he said, and he had been horrified to discover the conditions in which they lived at home, particularly in the towns—he being a gentleman, you see, and always living in the country in comfort. Goodness, child, do hurry up. You work carefully, but you must learn not to be so slow.'

'I shall be better with more practice,' Sally-Anne had said humbly. She had thought that she was doing rather well, but that appeared to be a fatal thought to have. Whenever she felt *that* it nearly always turned out that she was wrong. Another lesson she was learning.

'Pay-day today,' said Dr Neil suddenly, watching her whisk the duster over the windows and the drapes—she must remember to call them curtains while she was in England.

'So it is,' said Sally-Anne, struck. Friday had come round so quickly again—such a contrast to her old life when the week had often seemed boringly endless.

'Might as well pay you now,' he said, and pulled a little tin box out of one of his desk drawers, opened it, and began to count out her meagre wage.

Why was it, Sally-Anne thought when she went forward to take it, that this pitiful sum seemed more precious to her than her huge allowance which she could claim any day she wished? Perhaps it was because the shining pennies were a reward for her hard work, some recompense for her sore knees and the work-reddened hands which took the coins from Dr Neil.

Her pleasure was written so plainly on her face that Dr Neil wondered again about the true nature of his new and strange housemaid. Looking into her great eyes, their blue so dark that it was almost black, he was uncomfortably aware that having Miss Sally-Anne McAllister in the house was a most disturbing influence on a man who had not only denied himself sexually for some years, but who had rarely mixed with young women at all since he had left the army. He had been a bit of a gay dog before that, he remembered, enjoying himself freely like all young men of his age and class. Certainly he had not been in such close proximity to a pretty young girl for as long as he could remember.

He had forgotten how pleasing a woman's soft voice was, the faintly suggestive noise her skirts made, and the delightfully pleasant scent which accompanied McAllister everywhere, so different from Matey's sensible Lifebuoy and carbolic.

Was the scent essentially McAllister, or was it some subtle perfume she chose to wear? As he had passed her in the little hall this morning a tendril of her silky black hair had brushed his ruined cheek, and the smell of it had been so distracting that he had feared for his composure.

Good God, what was he coming to, that his previously monastic life should be tottering, if ever so slightly under the impact of a pretty minx who had invaded his chaste home?

And a pretty minx who was an accomplished liar, and who doubtless had some ulterior motive, though God knew what, in choosing to live in a milieu so unlike her usual habitat. There was no doubt that, disguise it as she might, McAllister reeked of wealth and privilege.

And he, Neil Cochrane, really did know about such Birds of Paradise, for had he not been loved and betrayed by one, and learned his bitter lesson—never to love or trust a woman again?

To check his wandering thoughts he started to ask her to resume her labours elsewhere and finish the surgery when he had completed his own tasks in it——Only to find that she was hopping gently from foot to foot, and was bursting to ask him a question.

Dr Neil sighed. He decided that temptation would have to be removed later rather than sooner. He could not snub the child so openly. He mentally called her a child to avoid admitting that she was very much a woman.

Sally-Anne's question was, for her, a very important

one. It was one which she had been longing to ask him ever since the night on which he had come home so late, just before she had turned off all the gas-lamps. He had arrived grimly silent, his face old and drawn, the great scar livid and prominent. He had told a worried Miss Mates that his patient had just died having her twelfth child. The child had survived, but it was deformed.

Sally-Anne had been horrified. Twelve children! Even she knew that there was no need for this. . .that there were ways and means. Single girls of good family were not supposed to know of such things, but Sally-Anne, if not an active suffragette, knew about Miss Annie Besant, and those who said that women should not be tied to endless childbearing and that there were practical ways of avoiding it.

'Dr Neil,' she said bravely, her dusting finished. She must ask him, she must, however forward he might think her.

'McAllister?' he said, looking up, surprised, to impress on her that maid servants, even American ones, were not supposed to quiz the Master when he was at work—should not even originate a conversation with him.

'May I ask you a question, please?'

'Yes,' he said, his mouth quirking a little, despite himself. McAllister's perfect manners, running in tandem with her fiery, impulsive nature, made a mix which had begun to amuse him, and added to her disturbing charm.

'That woman. . .the one who had *twelve* children.' She trod on the word in her horror. 'You're a doctor. Why don't you tell them?' Somehow, in her mixed anxiety and embarrassment, this was coming out all wrong. Perhaps Mama was right. She should think more before she spoke.

'Tell them what?' he said, genuinely puzzled, admiring against his will the pretty, ardent face opposite him.

'Tell them. . .it's not necessary. . .to have twelve children. That there are ways. You could. . .instruct them.' Sally-Anne was suddenly rosy red at her daring, but she had to say it; it needed to be said. Women were *dying*.

Dr Neil came down to earth with a bump. In all his thirty-three years no single woman had ever addressed him after such a fashion, or spoken of such a delicate matter.

'It's not my business, McAllister,' he said stiffly. 'Nor yours, either.'

'Not your business? I suppose it's your business to watch them die having their deformed babies! How dare you be so cool?'

Dr Neil was not cool at all beneath his impassive exterior. He had grieved over the dead woman, and Sally-Anne had put her work-reddened finger on something which had frequently troubled him in his slum practice.

'Come now, McAllister. You are talking about matters between a husband and a wife.' He had never thought to find himself discussing such a thing with a single young woman, but he had heard of American girls' frankness, and he supposed that this was a sample of it.

'But even you, a man, must agree that the whole business is so unequal. What chance has any woman, rich or poor, against the tyranny which her husband exercises? As a doctor, you know that such suffering is not necessary. Is it not your *duty* to do something about it, to help such victims? If not you, then who?'

Sally-Anne was by now in full flow, and when she paused for breath Dr Neil said, as drily as he could, 'I will only say to you what I told you on the day when you arrived here: it is useless to take the world's burdens on your shoulders. It is not a simple matter of informing people what to do as you seem to think. No, wait,' he continued, when she opened her mouth to speak again. 'Think. Since you seem to know whereof you speak I will only say that you must know that the burden of restraint by means of the. . .mechanism. . .employed will, of necessity, fall upon the man. Think back to Jem Higgins and ask yourself of what use it would be for me to preach your message to him.'

It was just like arguing with Papa, thought Sally-Anne with some disgust. He was so reasoned, and there was so much truth in what he said. But against that was the suffering endured by women which she saw all about her in London's East End. Not simply the women dying of too many children, but the women who were compelled to sell their bodies because that was all that they had to sell.

She might have said no more, except that, unluckily for him, Dr Neil felt impelled to continue. 'You see,' he said kindly, 'it is one thing for someone like yourself who has always had an easy life—up to now, that is—to speak glibly about suffering women, and think that there is an easy way out——'

He was violently interrupted by a Sally-Anne almost incandescent with rage. Not know how a woman could suffer! How dared he? He knew nothing, nothing, of what Sally-Anne had had to suffer at the hands of one of the monsters who controlled. . .what were his weaselling words?. . .the mechanism. How would he, a man, know anything? And why should she expect him to change a system which benefited men so greatly?

'Oh, yes,' she said, waving her feather duster at him with such violence that the end tickled his nose. 'Do nothing. That is the way, I see. Why not do something?

Publicise, make the ability to control birth available to the poor women in the East End as well as to their rich sisters in the West End. It may be indelicate of me, but I think that women will only be truly free when someone invents a. . .mechanism. . .which women can control. That would be even better and more useful to poor women than the vote, desirable though that might be.'

Dr Neil could not but admire her. However mistaken he thought that she might be, and that her vision of life was based on a charming naïveté which took little account of the cruel realities of existence, it was, to him, admirable that she should care about such things, and in such a practical way when all was said and done.

The simple demand for the vote, the be-all and end-all of most suffragettes, was truly seen by McAllister as a minor step compared with relieving poor women's social and economic disabilities, a measure which had little to do with suffrage.

He gave a half-smile which was immediately interpreted by Sally-Anne as patronising contempt. 'Oh,' she said, 'I see that for all your fine words you are much like the rest,' and there were tears in her eyes when she turned away from him. She should have known better. Despite the cool way in which he had always spoken to her she had thought him different from other men.

For some reason which she could not understand a feeling of desolation swept over her. She groped blindly for the door-knob, her glossy head bent.

Long suffering had made Dr Neil sensitive to the feelings of others. He stood up, walked round his desk, put a hand on Sally-Anne's arm, and said gently, 'McAllister, look at me.'

His voice was so unexpectedly kind that Sally-Anne's anger drained away. She looked up at him, mouth quivering a little.

'I did not mean to patronise you,' he said. 'Even if I thought that you were mistaken.' He paused. 'It is hard enough for me to run my practice here, seeing that I am that strange animal, a gentleman. If I started trying to come between husband and wife, and that is how it would be seen, I could hardly help anyone at all. I must have these people's trust, the men's as well as the women's.'

Sally-Anne nodded mutely. Perhaps he was not just another male ogre, after all. She would like to think so—even if he did defend the status quo, just like Papa.

Dr Neil put out a hand. He suddenly did not want to lose her respect. Woman she might be, but she was displaying a genuine compassion rarely seen among rich young girls.

'Come,' he offered, 'shake hands on it, McAllister.'

Something else occurred to Sally-Anne. Almost for the first time in her life she checked her wilful and impulsive self, even questioned a little a previous action or speech.

'Dr Neil,' she said, and her manner was almost shy, 'I hope you do not think the less of me for raising such a delicate matter.' Goodness, she thought, is this really me speaking? And she looked down at her work-worn shoes, half afraid to meet his eyes.

Dr Neil looked down at the bent blue-black head, and some idea of the enormous concession she was making to him struck home.

'No, indeed,' he answered gravely, although he had been a little shocked if truth were told. 'Not at all. On the contrary, I think it admirable that a gentlewoman should think seriously of such matters.' And suddenly he, too, thought, Is this really I, Neil Cochrane speaking? What can be coming over me? For despite having an open mind in many ways, his attitude to women and their problems had always been the conventional one of the young aristocrat he had once been.

He held McAllister's hand for a little longer than propriety might demand, and the pair of them stood for a moment, rapt, until the surgery boy, who ran the doctor's errands on his bike, delivered prescriptions and generally did a great deal of donkey work, knocked on the door before he came in, saying excitedly and importantly, 'You're wanted, Dr Neil, sir. Carrie Jackson in Vincent's Buildings is having her tenth and her ma has sent for you. She says it's urgent. Things going wrong.'

Her tenth! Sally-Anne was indignant all over again. Dr Neil dropped her hand smartly, picked up his bags, and was out of the room in a flash.

Miss Mates, who had followed young Eddie into the surgery, looked sadly after her departing treasure. 'He never thinks of himself these days. Only lives for his work, and now he's bound to miss breakfast. What he would do if I weren't here to look after him, I'm sure I don't know.'

The surgery seemed empty without Dr Neil Cochrane in it. On impulse Sally-Anne went to the kitchen and picked up a jam jar which she had earlier filled with sweet peas brought by a grateful patient who owned a little garden. She carefully carried it through, put it on his window-sill. She hoped that he would not find the jam jar too utilitarian, but he appeared to possess few vases. After all, despite his backward views about the wrongs of women, he really did work very hard for his poor patients!

CHAPTER FOUR

'OH, SHOOT,' said Sally-Anne disgustedly when the candle flickered and almost went out—again. She was in her tiny attic bedroom, sitting up in bed, propped up against a hard and lumpy pillow, sitting on a hard and lumpy mattress. Opposite her was a small washstand with a coarse crockery toilet set on a fake marble top. A roller towel hung on the door.

Beside the washstand was a closet—cupboard, the English said, containing her few clothes. Side by side hung her coarse morning working outfits, made out of casement cloth, which she had had to buy herself, much of it second-hand to save money, and two afternoon ones—a white cotton shirtwaister, black skirt, lacy cap with streamers and lacy white pinafore. Her afternoon shoes, slightly better than her morning ones, were ranged neatly beneath them.

By her bed was a chest of drawers which contained her underwear—several pairs of cheap directoire knickers, vests, petticoats, and corsets, plus black stockings of wool, cotton, and one precious silk pair which she had brought from her old life.

She was busily engaged in writing in a penny exercise book. It was already eleven-thirty at night. Through the gap in the curtains, also casement cloth, a romantic moon shone down on her, but Sally-Anne had little interest in romance or the moon. She was bone-weary from a day's back-breaking labour, but it was essential that she finish what she was writing, for she had a deadline to reach and that deadline was the day after tomorrow, her half-day, and she had barely begun her task.

The candle flickered again, so badly that it almost flickered out. There was nothing for it. She would have to go downstairs to find and fetch a new one from the store cupboard in the kitchen.

She threw back the covers, slipped a light shawl around her shoulders above her coarse calico night-gown, thrust her bare feet into her felt slippers, and crossed the room, avoiding the small oak bureau by the door, which she opened cautiously.

The whole house was quiet and she told herself that she must be careful not to awaken the two other sleeping inhabitants. Outside, for once, the East End was quiet, too. She crept downstairs, holding the green enamel candlestick high above her head so that she didn't lose her footing on the narrow wooden stairs.

The stair carpet didn't begin until the floor below the attic—another discovery she had made about the life-style of servants. She would have to pass through the parlour to reach the kitchen, an arrangement which had shocked the pampered girl she had been, but it was obviously designed to conserve space in the small house. Even so, Dr Neil's modest home was larger and better appointed than most around Vetch Street, and was vast compared with the one stifling room she had briefly occupied in Crow Court.

The hall at the bottom of the stairs was a tiny square, a door on one side opened to what had been designed as the best parlour, but was now converted to a waiting-room for the surgery, which was a lean-to structure at the back.

The door opposite gave access to the parlour where Dr Neil and Miss Mates lived and ate.

Sally-Anne's own preserve was the kitchen, where she

ate either at the kitchen table, or, when that was full, at a small card table which was folded up and put away when she had finished. A wooden Windsor chair, with a hard cushion, was provided for her when she was allowed to rest, which wasn't often, given the quantity of work which keeping even a small house clean necessitated.

She pushed the parlour door open and tiptoed in. It was dark and quiet. The candle she carried gave one last flicker—and expired.

'Oh, shoot,' she whispered again, trying to avoid bumping into the large oval dining table which stood in the window.

Someone, something, moved in the dark shadows by the empty fire-grate, filled in summer with a copper jug stuffed full of artificial flowers. 'Who's there?' said a blurred voice. 'Matey?'

Sally-Anne jumped and said falteringly, 'It's only me—McAllister. Come for a new candle.'

The someone, who was, of course, Dr Neil, struck a Swan Vesta to light the oil-lamp which always stood on a side-table where he usually kept the book which he was currently reading. He had a small but good library, much of it kept on shelves on the first landing.

The lamp's dim yellow light showed him to be seated, or rather slumped, in his big armchair. His tie was pulled loose, his shirt unbuttoned, and his hair was tousled. His face, too, was also blurred, only the scar on it was more livid and sharper than usual.

The reason for his blurred face and voice stood on an occasional table before him—a whisky bottle and a shot glass. She had never seen either him, or Miss Mates, take a drop of alcohol before in the weeks which she had already spent in Vetch Street.

'McAllister,' he said. 'And why do you want a candle at this hour? You should be asleep.'

'So should you be,' said Sally-Anne, greatly daring.

'*Touché*,' he said lazily, not at all put out. 'But you haven't given me an answer.'

'I don't like being up three flights of stairs at night without a candle. This one,' she said, setting the candlestick down on the table. 'isn't satisfactory. As you must have seen, it died on me a moment ago.'

'Fair enough,' Dr Neil replied, and by the careful way he spoke he had drunk quite a lot of the whisky from the half-empty bottle. Sally-Anne had seen drunken and half-drunken men before in Washington and London. American legislators were not noted for their abstemiousness, and nor were the denizens of London Society.

'If you will excuse me,' she said politely—no single woman ought to be talking alone with a man at nearly midnight—'I will collect a new candle from the kitchen and retire again.'

'No, I will not excuse you, McAllister,' was his answer to that, made with a kind of growling good nature. 'I require entertainment, and it is a good servant's part to do the Master's bidding. Sit down, McAllister, and entertain the Master.'

He had made no move to rise. All his polite gentlemanliness which he particularly observed with his poor patients, Matey and herself, was quite missing.

On the other hand, it did not seem likely that he was prepared to do anything improper, such as jump on her. Sally-Anne was very conscious that she was wearing only a nightgown and a light shawl, and the fear which she sometimes felt these days in the company of men, and had felt ever since—no, forget that—was threatening to overwhelm her.

Nevertheless she thought it best to humour him and sat down on the side of the table away from him and put her clasped hands on its polished top. She took them off again when she remembered that it would be she who would have to Ronuk it again if Matey saw its shine marred.

'How shall I entertain you, Dr Neil?' she enquired, and then regretted what she had said—it might bear the wrong meaning.

But he made no double-edged comment in return, simply said, 'Tell me of America, McAllister. Of your old home. I have never visited America and probably never shall.'

Well, that seemed innocent enough and it was probably best to humour a drunken man. She had overheard Papa say that once to Mama about a particularly notorious senator whom he was compelled to entertain.

'My home?' She thought for a moment, then decided to tell him of the little house in Washington where she and Mama had lived before Mama married Papa—— She wondered briefly what Dr Neil would have made of *that* story.

'We lived for a time in Washington DC,' she said slowly. 'We weren't rich, only comfortable.' And that part, at least, was true. 'We had a frame house with a garden around it, quite small. There was a picket fence, and a small gate. I have seen nothing quite like it in England. We were not in central Washington, you understand, but in a new suburb. Mama worked as an aide to a senator. . .' She knew immediately that she should not have said that.

Dr Neil picked her up immediately, saying, 'And your papa, McAllister—he did not object to your mama working? What did he do?'

Sally-Anne's fertile mind provided an answer which

had a kind of truth in it, or at least made a passing gesture in that direction.

'Oh, Papa was an accountant then. But after he inherited a little money and set up in his own business Mama stopped working, and then she had my little brothers.'

And that piece of undeniable truth was, perhaps, a mistake, too, for Dr Neil was not so drunk that he did not ask, without a pause, 'And what happened to them, McAllister, when you lost your parents and your fortune?'

This was a bit of a poser, but Sally-Anne, never at a loss, said, thinking of kind Uncle Orrin who would surely look after her and her three younger brothers if anything happened to Papa and Mama, 'An uncle took them in, but he said that he wasn't prepared to keep a great girl, and that I must fend for myself, and find employment, which I have done, ever since.'

'So, you didn't take to drink, McAllister, when you were disappointed in life and love.' And his voice had a note of self-mockery in it which surprised her.

'Women usually don't,' she said. 'That's a man's privilege.'

'Oh, *touché* again,' he riposted, the laugh in his voice genuine this time. 'You have a sharp and perceptive tongue, McAllister. Are many American girls like you? If so, you all reproach me with your cheerful resilience.'

'I suppose,' said Sally-Anne. She had never thought herself as part of a mass called American girls. She was Sally-Anne. . .McAllister.

Dr Neil picked up his glass, filled it from the bottle, waved the bottle at her, and asked, 'Do liberated American girls ever drink spirits, McAllister? Am I being inhospitable?'

'Some do.' Sally-Anne gave the matter as grave a

consideration as though he were asking her her opinion of the latest exhibition of Japanese art, or Beerbohm Tree's newest play. 'But not the kind that I am likely to know.'

Dr Neil gave a crack of laughter at that. 'And that should teach me not to ask ridiculous and impertinent questions,' he remarked, and his normal cheerfulness seemed to have returned, which was a relief.

Sally-Anne thought that Dr Neil might be a man, and therefore to be hated, but he was a good and caring doctor, and really shouldn't be abusing himself with alcohol. Papa said that it was a good servant, but a bad master, and he never joined in temperance rant.

'Should you be drinking so much?' she asked, greatly daring again.

'Probably not, McAllister, probably not. But tell me, can you think of circumstances where one might get drunk to reduce pain? Either physical pain—or that induced by unwanted memories?'

Oh, he had struck home harder than he knew. Sally-Anne had one pain, one memory of which she dared not even think for fear that she would lose all command of herself, one memory which she always pushed away when it tried to attack her. She pushed it away now. Would spirits dim that pain? Had he a pain like that? If she joined Dr Neil and his bottle, would she feel better?

Dr Neil had seen McAllister's face change even as he spoke so carelessly to her. He knew that in some way he had hurt her. He regretted it. The man who had endured great mental and physical pain always, when in command of himself, tried to avoid inflicting it on others.

But the demon which had driven him to drink that night, after months of abstinence, had him in its thrall. Perhaps—no, not perhaps, but because McAllister, with all her youthful ebullience and charm, was in his house, she had revived something in him which he did not want to feel and he had called up the demon to assuage it—no, to kill it.

'So,' he said, when she did not answer him, and the beautiful mouth quivered, ever so slightly, 'even pretty little McAllister has her secrets. Not so young and green, after all.'

'Oh,' said Sally-Anne, rising, 'you are hateful like this. You will not respect yourself in the morning. And I don't think that you own me after my day is over, Dr Cochrane. Pray excuse me. I will return to my room, and dispense with the candle.'

Her own memories were so strong that she feared that she would burst into hysterics before him, and that would never do. She had vowed never to give way to that. The lonely dark was preferable to staying to be taunted.

She made for the door, but as perforce she had to pass him he put out a hand and caught her by the wrist. Not hard, not tightly, but gently, a warm, almost loving clasp, but when he spoke his words were far from loving—they were jeering, even.

'Oh, come, McAllister. What's your game, eh? Tell me that.'

'My game?' echoed Sally-Anne, her heart suddenly bumping now that he was holding her, acutely aware of how little she was wearing. Besides, she had been caught like that by a man once before.

'Yes, your game, McAllister. You are playing a game, are you not? What are you doing here? Is it a bet?'

'A bet?' Scalding anger at him consumed her. 'Of course it's not a bet! I. . .need the work.'

'You do?' His voice was hatefully mocking, and whether it was the drink talking, or his resentment of all women because of what one beautiful woman had done to him, Dr Neil did not know. 'Now, why don't I believe you, McAllister? Entertain me even more. Tell me the truth for once. That would make you a pearl among women, and no mistake.'

Sally-Anne tried to wrench her wrist away, but to no avail. His grip tightened.

'No, indeed. You are not to go. The Master will not have it. We may face the black night together for a time. You may tell me why a young lady who, whatever she says, has never done any work in her life before, has come to the East End to find it.'

'I told you,' said Sally-Anne, exasperated by his probing, annoyed that he had seen through her whoppers. 'And,' she added a little triumphantly, 'if my performance as a parlourmaid doesn't satisfy, then have the goodness to dismiss me, not bully me in the middle of the night.'

One word in this impressive little speech was unfortunate.

'Ah, yes, performance,' he murmured, taking another great gulp of whisky from the glass in his left hand, still holding her tightly with his right. 'What a good word, McAllister. I have never, in all my life, known such a diligent, hard-working, uncomplaining maid as you are. As good as a play. Real maids are quite different, moaning and wailing and kissing the local bobby between the dustbin and the outhouse. I shouldn't complain, I suppose. Matey and I get the benefit of your. . .performance. No, don't pull away. The Master commands you to stay. Don't you know that a really submissive maid soon learns to please the Master in every way. . .every way, McAllister? You take me, I'm sure. I most desperately need entertaining, as you can see.'

He was playing with her, teasing her. He had no real intention of assaulting her, however great the temptation which she presented to him. But he felt that McAllister had to pay something back for all the fairy-tales which she had told Matey and himself, and which Matey had so gullibly swallowed.

He was not to know that a real fear was beginning to overwhelm Sally-Anne. Oh, it could not happen again. God could not be so unkind. She began to tremble, tried to compose herself, to appeal to the coolly aloof Dr Neil of the day, not the drunken midnight man slouching in the great armchair.

She tried to control her voice, and was pleased that it was as steadily calm as she could have hoped.

'Please release me, Dr Cochrane. I am sure that you do not really wish to frighten me. I know that drink makes men. . .irresponsible. I am not so young and green that I am unaware of that. And if you let me go I will forgive you for the way in which you have just spoken to me.'

Dr Neil, thus so firmly rebuked, closed his eyes. He heard the calm voice, but could feel the trembling body which gave it the lie. He released the small hand, and said, his voice suddenly pleading, 'Don't go, McAllister. I didn't mean to frighten you. I. . .would rather not be alone. Stay, if only for a little while.'

'And you should not ask me that, either,' said Sally-Anne, head erect, carriage proud, refusing to be won over. 'We should not be talking alone, down here, in the middle of the night.'

And then, free of his grip, she recovered her courage and her gallant spirit to say to him, 'And you really ought to stop drinking. At once! What would Miss Mates think if she found us here like this?'

'The worst, I suppose,' said Dr Neil, somewhat wryly.

'You recall me to common sense and my duties, McAllister. A parlourmaid beyond compare. You are right to rebuke the Master when he forgets himself so.'

He sat up, corked the bottle, picked up his glass, pushed it away, cocked his head on one side, and said in a pathetic, slightly injured voice, as though he were the victim, not Sally-Anne, 'There—will that do, McAllister? I promise not to offend again, although I cannot promise that I will keep the promise.'

Sally-Anne struggled to repress the laughter which suddenly swept over her—relief after tension, she supposed. 'Oh, you really are too ridiculous. You owe it to yourself to behave properly, not to me.'

'A female Solomon,' said Neil, sighing, and then he gave her the most charming grin, and through the ruin of his face she suddenly saw what Matey must have known—the handsome soldier-boy he had once been. 'And even female Solomons must have their proper rest. Goodnight, McAllister; take the lamp. I can find my way up in the dark, or fetch a candle from the kitchen cupboard for myself. Here——' And he handed her the lamp, which had been designed to be portable. 'Be careful on the stairs, mind. I should not like my playing the Good Samaritan to end in a flaming holocaust.'

Sally-Anne could not demur. She took the lamp from him. At least she would be able to finish her article now.

'Goodnight, then,' she said, 'and thank you.' She could not prevent herself from saying in a doubtful voice, 'You will be careful when you go to bed, won't you?'

Dr Neil laughed a little at that. 'I may be overset,' he said, his voice and manner that of the daylight man again, 'but I am still quite capable,' and he gave her his charming smile.

She took the memory of it upstairs to bed with her,

but all the time that she wrote she could see him sitting there as he had been when he had first lit the lamp, his face full of an old pain.

Daylight brought the prosaic world back again, and a Dr Neil who was exactly like the man she had always known—it was as though she had imagined the improper advances of the night hours.

'You're dreamy today, McAllister,' said Miss Mates accusingly, making Sally-Anne scrub the kitchen floor all over again, the first effort not being deemed sufficiently satisfactory. The fact that she was basically a kind soul did not mean that she was soft on Sally-Anne or herself.

'You must try a little harder. We are having company this afternoon. The teapot, milk jug, sugar basin and tongs will require cleaning with Goddard's powder before midday, so that all will be proper, and the visitors will not be able to say that this house is a slum inside, even if there is one outside.'

'Who are we expecting, then?' said Sally-Anne, who, like all good servants, was beginning to identify herself with her employers, and was one reason for her surprising success as a maid of all work.

'Mrs Teresa Darrell,' said Matey, making a little of a face. 'She is a kind of cousin of Dr Neil's. She was married to Dr Neil's captain who was killed in nasty Africa, as poor Dr Neil nearly was.' She paused. She did not feel that she could tell McAllister that Mrs Darrell had designs on Dr Neil, and that she, Matey, was not very happy about the idea that Mrs Darrell might become Mrs Cochrane.

To begin with, Mrs Darrell did not approve of Matey. She thought that it was Matey who had encouraged Dr Neil to become a doctor and take up an East End practice. 'Not at all the thing for a Cochrane to do,' she had said more than once. 'After all, he is still poor Stair's heir, poor Stair never having married.'

Stair was Alastair, Neil's older and only brother, and was usually called 'poor Stair' because he had drunk, gambled and wenched away the small remains of the Cochrane estate, most of which his father had already dissipated before him.

Matey thought unkindly that Mrs Darrell rather liked the idea of becoming Lady Cochrane when Stair went to his last rest, which at the rate he was living might not be long.

Sally-Anne knew that Neil was Stair's brother; she had met him, and had not liked him much. He had been a friend. . .of. . .him. Neil's origins made his presence in the East End even stranger—and he had the impertinence to quiz her for her presence, when his own was just as odd.

Dressing for the afternoon, she wondered what Mrs Darrell was like, and whether she was worth all the tohu-bohu of preparing a slap-up tea, and being formally 'At Home', which had resulted in even more work for McAllister, as Sally-Anne was increasingly beginning to think herself when she was being a maid of all work.

Prompt at four o'clock, Dr Neil, complainingly dressed in his best suit at Matey's request—'Do I have to?' he had said, rolling his eyes at McAllister—Matey in a bottle-green velvet gown which McAllister had not seen before, McAllister in her best sateen skirt, white blouse, and small lacy cap with streamers, were all sitting in the parlour when the doorbell rang.

At least Dr Neil and Miss Mates were sitting; McAllister was standing at the kitchen door, and moved sedately forward to answer the urgent bell. Not promptly enough, apparently, for the bell rang again, peremptorily.

Mrs Darrell was in her middle thirties, was tall and statuesque and had been a bit of a beauty in her day. She was not, McAllister thought, very tastefully turned out, being inclined to the upholstered look, with a remarkable array of feathers in her hat above a maroon walking dress, trimmed with black. Her hat was nearly extinguished by the feathers.

She had brought along her companion, Norton, a thin, harassed-looking woman, whose drab grey attire set off her employer's brilliance.

McAllister took their hats, boas, parasols and wraps into the waiting-room, there being nowhere else to take them, after showing the visitors in.

'Well, my deeah Neil, you are looking positively deevy. So much bettah,' said Mrs Darrell in what McAllister recognised as an imitation of the society shriek affected by those around His Majesty King Edward VII. She kissed his cheek, managing to avoid the scarred one by some contortion recognised by both her victim and McAllister, who had taken an instant dislike to her. Why, she could not think.

'Do sit down, Tess,' requested Dr Neil. 'Yes, I am feeling better these days. I must say that you look in health.' Doubtless so rosy because of all the rouge on top of papier poudré, thought McAllister nastily. She had taken up her post by the kitchen door, standing there, hands neatly folded over her spotless apron.

'I see that you have a new gel, Matey,' remarked Mrs Darrell. 'Bit elderly, ain't she, for a maid?'

Dr Neil avoided looking at a bridling McAllister, particularly when Mrs Darrell went on to say, still in the same shriek, 'Hope she's honest, Neil. The last chit I hired not only got herself—well, you know, with the coachman, but made off with some of my best lace when I turned her away. Oh, servants, servants!'

'Just as well I have so few of them,' said Dr Neil. He still dared not look in McAllister's direction, for Teresa Darrell, frequently calling on Norton for support, continued her diatribe about the servant question.

I really should not be surprised by this, thought McAllister, fuming. As I well know, the servant question is a constant subject for conversation in every drawing-room, so why do I resent it so much now?

Because I have spent the whole day since six o'clock this morning working, and working hard, and this. . . painted maypole has done nothing all day long and will do nothing tomorrow, except complain about those who do work. Does she think that I have no feelings, or have been struck deaf because I stand by the kitchen door, silent?

'Tea, McAllister,' said Matey, to stem Teresa Darrell's flow. This, diverted, now turned into a recital about every distant relative Neil Cochrane possessed, all of whom, apparently, had only one wish—to see him back in polite society again.

She had not finished exhorting Dr Neil about this when McAllister, who could hear every word in the kitchen, returned with the tea-tray, staggering under its weight. By the time that she had balanced the tray on a small table, the silver teapot carefully placed where Matey could preside over it, Mrs Darrell had embarked on an attack on Dr Neil and the profession which he had taken up.

It was all done so genteelly that it set McAllister's teeth on edge. She was busy handing around cups and saucers, damask napkins, silver knives and cake forks, setting out the cake-stand, circulating plates of cucumber sandwiches, little patties and everything else considered appropriate for an afternoon tea in 1903.

'And I have no appetite, no appetite at all,' shrieked Teresa Darrell at Dr Neil, and consuming her fourth sandwich while she spoke. 'Now, if you set up a decent practice, somewhere in Belgravia, instead of this. . . slum, you could come and treat me. Think of the fortune such a charming creature as yourself could make. No one would mind calling in a doctor of your social standing.'

'Now, Tess, I have told you often enough that I have no wish to set up in Belgravia, Harley Street, or Wimpole Street,' said Dr Neil quietly, refusing the sandwiches which a servile McAllister was handing him. 'There are plenty of medical men to do that, and few to practise here, where the need is so great.'

'Oh, but you are a saint, Neil. We all know that. He is a saint, is he not, Norton, and Matey, my dear? But you should think of yourself a little; a halo is all very well. . .' And she burst into tinkling and self-approving laughter.

And what sort of halo does a drunken man at midnight, threatening to assault his parlourmaid, wear? thought McAllister nastily. And how could Dr Neil, who was such a man of sense, tolerate such a. . . nodcock?

Teresa Darrell waved for the cake-stand. McAllister took it round to her, at the point where she began again on the necessity of Dr Neil to rejoin polite society. This went on for some time, with Dr Neil fencing politely, Matey looking grim, and Norton sighing in counterpoint to la Darrell.

The climax to the whole tasteless display came when tea ended, and McAllister was required to take everything away. Balancing the tray, to which Mrs Darrell had kindly added the plate containing those cream cakes which she had not managed to devour, she heard her say to Dr Neil, 'You really ought to go into society again, my dear. You must surely have recovered from your shyness over your unfortunate injury. After all, we all know what you look like by now!'

Rage, pure and delightful, exploded inside McAllister. She could look neither at Dr Neil, nor at the tasteless harpy who was tormenting him with her tactlessness. The rage incited her to the most positive and extreme action.

A small tuffet stood between herself, Mrs Darrell and the kitchen door. With the most artfully devised deliberation she managed not to avoid it, tripped spectacularly in such a fashion that she fell forward, the contents of the tea-tray, cups, saucers, dregs of tea, milk, sugar and cream cakes, all cascading neatly into Mrs Darrell's lap, with McAllister herself, purple in the face as a consequence of stifling a dreadful desire to laugh, landing gracefully on her knees at the good lady's feet.

For a moment the noise was indescribable, much of it contributed by McAllister, who set up a keening cry, and, in endeavouring to make matters better by dabbing at the debris on Mrs Darrell's lap with a damask napkin, made them worse.

Inside McAllister, who was enjoying her own performance as a clumsy hoyden, a wicked devil was laughing itself stupid, until she felt strong hands under her armpits and Dr Neil hoisted her clear of her victim.

He set her on her feet, and said in a voice which she hardly recognised, 'You will go immediately to the kitchen, McAllister, to await further instructions, but only after you have apologised to Mrs Darrell, at once!' And his voice rose on the last two words.

Dr Neil knew perfectly well that what had been done

was no accident. He had seen McAllister's face just before her trip and something had alerted him, even before everything had landed in Teresa Darrell's lap.

'No,' said Mrs Darrell violently to McAllister, who was dipping a curtsy, and beginning a stammering apology, but only because Dr Neil had asked her, not because she was sorry for what she had done. No, indeed. It was no more and no less than such a creature deserved. 'No, you wicked gel. I don't want your apologies. You have quite ruined my gown. I demand that you turn her away, Neil. You surely cannot wish to keep such a clumsy thing.'

'No,' said McAllister in her turn, face white, and trembling as though to lose her post would be the tragedy which it would have been to the servant she was pretending to be. But she did not wish to lose her place, hard though her life as a servant was; such an outcome would be a failure which she could not endure. 'It was an accident; please don't turn me away.' And the slight wail in her voice was genuine, as Dr Neil could tell.

'Go to the kitchen, McAllister!' he commanded. 'Matey, you must help Tess and Miss Norton to clean Tess's ruined gown. I am truly sorry, my dear cousin, but the girl is new, not yet trained.'

'From what I have seen of her, she never will be trained,' snapped Teresa Darrell. 'An insolent little piece. You ought to turn her away. But there, you were always soft-hearted.' And she suffered Matey to lead her upstairs to try to repair the ravages which McAllister had wrought.

Left alone, Dr Neil walked to the kitchen to find a strange scene. McAllister sat in the Windsor chair, her head bent, crying. It was the very last thing he had expected to discover given McAllister's fiery and impetuous nature. He had fully intended to tell her exactly what he thought of her disgraceful conduct, for he had no doubt at all that what had been done had been done deliberately.

But the sight of her in tears disarmed him in the strangest way. Crying women had always annoyed him, and he briefly wondered why McAllister's tears should affect him so differently. She was crying with an almost fierce abandon. One might have thought her heart was broken.

'McAllister,' he said gently. 'Why did you do it?'

McAllister looked up. She did not know what had come over her. Always before, after similar wickednesses, she had felt almost gleeful triumph, but this time, although she was not truly sorry for what she had done to Mrs Darrell, she felt something like remorse. And to be turned away as well!

'Do what?' she sobbed. 'I tripped.'

'Tell the truth, McAllister,' said Dr Neil, still gentle. 'I saw you, immediately before you fell. I know that you tripped, but you tripped deliberately. Why?'

McAllister dropped her head. Why did she feel so strange, so. . .ashamed? Almost as though she had let Dr Neil down, rather than defend him, as she had meant to, by punishing a tactless fool who was hurting him.

Why did she mind his being hurt so much? For once, she must tell him the truth, never mind that he had behaved so badly last night.

'Yes,' she said into her sodden handkerchief. 'It was deliberate.'

'But why?' he repeated, genuinely puzzled. He was hardened to Teresa Darrell's tactlessness. She had been practising it on him for years.

'I didn't like her,' said McAllister stiffly. 'She deserved it.' And then, with a flash of her usual impetuous spirit, 'She was horrible to you, not once but again and again.'

'She doesn't mean to be,' said Dr Neil perceptively. 'She thinks that she is helping and encouraging me.'

'That makes it worse, not better,' burst out McAllister. 'What a fool!'

Dr Neil sighed. Like McAllister, he wanted to know what was coming over him. He wanted to comfort naughty McAllister, not punish her.

'It was a very unkind thing to do, McAllister,' he said. 'Was it right to criticise her for being, as you thought, unkind, and then be even more unkind yourself? Teresa Darrell is a most unhappy creature who lost her young husband shortly after their honeymoon, and I am one of the few people left who can remember and mourn him.'

McAllister began to cry again, dreadfully. It was as though all that had happened to her in the past year was suddenly before her, and all her own shortcomings into the bargain had landed on her in a heap, and were destroying her.

She had been almost unnaturally brave for so long, and now it was as though she had been given licence to cry over everything.

Worse, Dr Neil was being so kind, when reason told her that no one would blame him if he turned her away for what she had done. It was plain that he was not going to.

Suddenly, as much to his own surprise as McAllister's, Dr Neil went on his knees beside her. He pulled out his own spotlessly white handkerchief, which McAllister had laundered and ironed earlier that week, and said urgently, 'Oh, do stop crying, McAllister. It is not like you at all. I am not going to ask Matey to turn you away. Suppose I suggest to you that we stop part of your wages to help pay for the damage to the china and to Mrs Darrell's dignity, and you promise to be good in future?'

'Oh, dear,' said McAllister tragically. 'I have promised that so often in the past, and it has never answered yet!'

Dr Neil gave a shout of laughter. 'Come, that's better!' he said. 'You remind me of myself last night. We are a sorry pair, are we not?'

McAllister stopped crying, said shyly, 'Not promising to keep the promise, you mean?' She wielded his handkerchief with her customary vigour.

'Something like that. Now I must go to say goodbye to Tess Darrell, and apologise for half-trained servant girls. You will behave yourself in future?'

There was such an appeal in his voice that McAllister felt really ashamed, and then when he had left her, refusing to take his hanky back, saying, 'You need it more than I do,' she also felt something else—a kind of purging, a relief. She knew that she would probably be naughty again, because that was the way she was, but never again would she be quite so prone to take such instant action.

And she also knew that Dr Neil was well aware of why she had done what she did, and she knew something else—he was not only sorry for McAllister, but was even sorrier for Mrs Darrell, as well, a widow who had lost her husband in the most cruel circumstances, and for whom he knew that he would never offer, despite his pity for her.

And that was why she had done a wrong thing, and that her thoughtlessness was selfish—a new idea for the spoilt and pampered girl McAllister had so recently been.

But had it not been to rid herself of her aura of wealth

and privilege which had created her feeling that she was the darling of the gods—although the same gods knew how brutally they had treated her—that she had come to the East End to work, and to live as though she really needed to, and to survive on the pittance which she had earned, without bolting back again to luxury and comfort?

She would be more careful in future, consider others a little more. She could not, must not fail in her self-appointed task so soon after beginning it.

CHAPTER FIVE

'UP WEST?' said Matey, handing Sally-Anne the china from the small dresser in the kitchen, which had been scrupulously washed that morning and was now being replaced by Sally-Anne who was standing on a small stool to reach the top shelf. 'You are thinking of going there this afternoon?'

'Yes,' said Sally-Anne. It was her afternoon off in about twenty minutes. 'I thought I might like to window-shop. I can't afford anything this week, of course.' And she cast her eyes down modestly at this reference to her pay being docked for yesterday afternoon's fiasco.

'I suppose you could take the bus,' allowed Matey. It ran from the end of the road, pulled by a rather weary horse which had a habit of stopping suddenly to the dismay of its passengers. As usual Sally-Anne was not quite telling the truth. Her real destination was Fleet Street and the offices of the weekly *Clarion Cry*, but she could hardly inform Dr Neil or Matey of that interesting fact—it didn't quite fit the sad picture which she had drawn of the friendless, abandoned orphan without employment—not that the money which she earned from the *Clarion* would have kept her.

Dr Neil had been kind and friendly to her when she had served him breakfast. Despite himself he had been touched by her fierce defence of him, and although he frequently entertained Mrs Darrell he only did so because she was the widow of his dead friend. He was quite aware of her marital designs on him, but she was very much part of the life which he had rejected, even if she refused to recognise that fact, and tried to reclaim him for it.

Eating his bacon and eggs, 'Sunny-side up,' Sally-Anne had once said when she put his plate before him, drinking his coffee—he preferred it to everlasting tea, he said—he looked much better than he had done the day before; no midnight drinking, Sally-Anne thought.

Mental transference of some sort must have taken place because, putting down his napkin and rising, he had said to her when she had begun to remove his breakfast china, 'McAllister.'

'Dr Neil?' she said, turning and bobbing at him like a proper servant, a manoeuvre which amused him, so that his lips twitched at the unlikely sight—it was so much at odds with her determined personality.

'About yesterday—and the night before. . .' He hesitated, then gave her his unexpected smile again. 'If you keep to your promise—to behave yourself in future when I have guests—then I shall try to keep to my promise. Fair's fair, after all.'

'Oh, how splendid!' exclaimed Sally-Anne warmly, and with Matey safe in the kitchen, unable to hear, added, 'No more whisky at midnight!'

'And no more tilting tea-trays,' he said. Above all things he wanted to see McAllister's bright and bubbling face, and she had been unwontedly shy and subdued this morning.

She rewarded him with such a beaming smile that he took the memory of it into the surgery with him, where it stayed all morning, brightening the day for him. His unlikely American maid-of-all-work was beginning to occupy his thoughts more and more. . .

Sally-Anne took the horse bus. She was wearing her servant's clothing—a bottle-green cotton skirt, a white cotton shirtwaister, a light black shawl, black stockings and heavy shoes. She was carrying a small tapestry bag which contained her rather crumpled manuscript. But she did not ride on the bus all the way up West, leaving it instead where its route crossed Fleet Street.

She walked briskly by St Paul's Cathedral, along Ludgate Hill, to reach her destination. The *Clarion's* offices were small and dingy, but despite this, and the fact that it only appeared once a week, the magazine had a large and growing circulation because of the crusading character of its editor, J. D. O'Connor, who had been a leading journalist with the *Morning Post* before he had struck out on his own, financed by money left to him by his land-owning father.

Sally-Anne had met him at a party; he had long been settled in England, and he had been impressed and amused by her fiery conversation and her obvious intelligence. He knew that her mother had been a well-known journalist on the *Washington Gazette* before her marriage to Jared Tunstall, Sally-Anne's father and a Yankee millionaire, who as the result of his fame as one of America's so-called robber barons, and his friendship with King Edward VII and his circle, was nothing if not notorious.

Half seriously, half as a joke he had asked her to write a short piece for him on what she had termed in conversation with him 'wasted women'. By this she meant society women who were compelled by their roles as wives and hostesses to live empty and meaningless lives.

He had thought that that would be the last he would hear of her, but a few days later she had sent him her first piece, and he had been so impressed by it that he had printed it and asked her to write more for him.

'A weekly column,' he had suggested, and when some

weeks later, looking pale and rather ill, she had visited him and suggested a series of articles about the stunted lives of women and children in the East End, to be written from the inside, she had said, not the outside, he had rapidly agreed.

Her first piece, written before she had joined Neil Cochrane's household, from the viewpoint of a privileged outsider, had been even better than he could have hoped, and had caused favourable comment. To preserve her anonymity they had agreed on the pseudonym Vesta, and if at first he had thought a few days in the East End might dampen her enthusiasm he had been proved wrong.

Sally-Anne approached the cubbyhole giving admission to the building with some trepidation, rightly so when the commissionaire had sniffed at her, and demanded to know why she sought admission—her clothing and general appearance were not those worn by other visitors to the editor.

She produced O'Connor's card, with the words, 'This lady is to be admitted to my office on demand', written and signed by the great man himself, and mounted some uncarpeted wooden stairs to his somewhat grimy sanctum. O'Connor was in his shirt-sleeves; he rapidly assumed his jacket and pulled out a chair for her, first wiping it with a none too clean handkerchief.

'Pray sit, Miss Tunstall. I trust I see you well? You have something for me?'

'Two pieces,' said Sally-Anne, sitting down, grateful that her clothes were utilitarian, rather than the exquisite gowns which she had formerly worn. 'One is on the general treatment of poor women, the other is more particular. It is called, 'An East End Doctor's Surgery', and tells of his morning with his patients, their problems, and the difficulties of giving adequate medical care to those who can barely afford it—even when the doctor is good-hearted—as this one plainly is.'

She handed the two pieces over, and O'Connor began to read them rapidly, looking up at her occasionally while he did so. He had already recognised that she was wearing poor clothing, and it was also obvious that she was taking her work seriously enough to sacrifice her privileged lifestyle and live among those of whom she wrote. He was filled with sudden admiration for a professionalism which he had not suspected she possessed.

He put the papers down when he had finished them and looked at her long and steadily. He had noticed that she did not identify the doctor, calling him Doctor X. Sally-Anne experienced a sudden dismay. Oh, no, never say that he did not like them, after all her hard work and the writing of them in the small hours after her demanding duties as a dogsbody had already tired her!

She clasped her hands together, and cast a look of entreaty at him—which he correctly interpreted.

'Have no fear,' he said gently. 'Your work is excellent, written from the heart, but skilfully so. I could do with you on my permanent staff—but I think that these articles will hit home, cause a stir, such a stir as Henry Mayhew created some time ago when he, too, wrote of the cabined and confined lives of the capital's poor. No, it is not these articles which cause me concern, but you.'

'Me?' said Sally-Anne inelegantly, then added, 'I don't understand.'

'Miss Tunstall,' he said. 'Does the American Embassy, does the ambassador, know where you are living—and, more to the point, what you are doing?'

Sally-Anne flushed a little, and said, 'Uncle Orrin? No, I thought that. . .' She paused.

'That he might stop you,' said O'Connor, amusement on his face. 'Yes, I'm sure that he would have done—the East End is not the safest place for a beautiful and rich girl of good family to live.'

'Oh, I'm not a fool,' said Sally-Anne spiritedly. 'No one knows that I am that—rich and of good family, I mean.'

O'Connor looked at the glowing and vital face opposite him, and thought wryly that Miss Sally-Anne Tunstall, society beauty and heiress, carried her pedigree on her face and in her carriage.

'You are,' he said, 'presumably living in this doctor's household. By your appearance you are posing as a servant. You must find the work hard—which makes the writing of these articles even more commendable. At least let me know of your address, even if you feel you cannot tell the Ambassador, your uncle, or his wife where you are. Then, if I hear concern expressed about you—that you have disappeared. . .'

Sally-Anne thought all this a great to-do about nothing. 'Oh, no,' she said confidently. 'Yes, I will give you my address, but they think that I am touring with my friend Laura Parslow and her family. Laura and I arranged everything between us. *She* thinks it all very romantic—she does not know what hard work being a servant is—and nor did I, for that matter. I shall write you a piece on that, too. It is quite unbelievable. Even the kindest of souls, and the housekeeper for whom I work is certainly that, have no idea of the magnitude of the demands they make on one. It's a good thing I'm very strong—otherwise I might have dropped dead, like an over-worked horse, after a week of it. I shall never feel the same about cosy coal fires again; I have heaved too many buckets about for that. You have *no idea* of how much coal is needed to keep a small grate going so that one might cook.'

This heartfelt confession had its effect on her hearer. It's a good thing I'm not a womaniser, he thought, or else Miss T would be in danger; she is so attractive in her *joie de vivre*—and when that is added to beauty! I wonder what the good doctor and his housekeeper make of her—and what story she has concocted to explain her presence there?

But he said nothing of this, merely noted down her address, sighed a little at it, and made his latest recruit promise to visit him once a week with her piece. 'Without fail,' he said sternly. 'And if you are too tired to write you must come to see me in any case, and then I shall know you are safe. I have a good mind to ask you to serve full-time on my reporting staff, but I am selfish enough to want you to go on writing for me these exposés of low life, particularly the way in which such misery afflicts women. You are doing your sex a service, you know,' he finished.

That did it! That just did it! Sally-Anne could have jumped up and down for joy. She thought of all the wretched women in the East End, and aye, in the West End too, not excluding her own maltreated self, and thought that at whatever cost she would carry out the task she had set herself—to find out how the under-privileged lived, and to strike a blow for suffering womanhood while she did so.

Waiting at the stop for the horse bus to take her back to Vetch Street, Sally-Anne heard a voice she knew. After her interview with J. D. O'Connor she had mitigated her whoppers to Matey and Dr Neil by moving on to the West End, where she walked along Oxford Street, entering Mr Gordon Selfridge's store, gazing as raptly at its wonders as though she were truly the poor girl whom she pretended to be, the whole place seeming quite different now that she no longer had her papa's bottomless purse at her command. But she did make two purchases from the hat and the dress departments with the money which J. D. O'Conner had given her for the two articles which she had written for him.

She turned to see the maid-of-all-work from St Jude's Rectory, whom she had met after church last Sunday, staring at her. Rose Bailey had a sharply pretty face with the knowing expression of the East End urchin which she had so recently been. 'Why! If it ain't McAllister, from the doctor's. Bin up West?'

Rose's cockney accent was so strong that Sally-Anne could hardly understand her. Rose, for her part, thought that McAllister talked funny, and when Sally-Anne had told her that she came from the United States of America she had stared at her as though she had said that she came from the moon.

'Yes,' Sally-Anne said, 'I've been window-shopping. I had my pay cut this week for being naughty at a tea party.'

'Garn,' said Rose, staring at her, and revising her opinion that Sally-Anne was a bit prim and proper. 'Yer never! I've bought some nice ribbons, from a barrer off Oxford Street—cheap, they were.' And she fished a small parcel from her pocket, and showed Sally-Anne her treasure just as the horse bus finally groaned up—or neighed up, thought Sally-Anne irreverently. She had never thought that she would ever travel on such a thing, although she could not tell Rose that.

'Like to come wiv me next week?' offered Rose, the bus slowly bringing them nearer home with each plodding step. 'Could do wiv a pal, since my friend Lottie went into service up West. Call for me at the rectory, why don't yer? We could 'ave tea at Ma's, and then go up West in the evenin' fer a bit of all right.' And she closed one eye in a grotesque wink, leaving Sally-Anne to guess what the bit of all right was—a visit to a music hall or a theatre, she assumed—wrongly, for she still had a lot to learn about the ways of the aliens among whom she lived.

Innocent that she was, for all the sophistication conferred on her by the great world in which she had once lived, she readily agreed to Rose's suggestion, and when they had parted Rose took care to remind her of her promise.

She thought that McAllister would be an added attraction for any nobs they might meet—she was so much prettier than Lottie had been, and knew how to wear her clothes, looking better in her drab outfit than Lottie did in her furs and feathers. She began to look forward to the following Wednesday—— Who knew where they might end up?

Sally-Anne, feeling that with Rose's offer of friendship she was entering more and more into her new life, was humming 'Marching through Georgia', and had just reached Atlanta, when she let herself into Dr Neil's.

The house was quiet, no sign of Matey's bustling presence, and when she walked into the kitchen, taking off her shabby black hat, pulling the hat pins out of her abundant hair, she found Dr Neil, sitting at the kitchen table, his tea before him, quite alone.

He cocked a sardonic eyebrow at her. 'Well, well, if it isn't McAllister! Two wonders to consider: first of all it's your afternoon off, and secondly I was debating whether or not you might have tired of your games here and retired back to the place from whence you sprung.'

'Oh, indeed,' riposted Sally-Anne, eyes flashing and giving off all the danger signs which her family would have recognised. 'Now, why should you think any of that? I can surely do what I like on my day off, not be reproached if I choose to come home early because I feel tired, and secondly, as I said before, I am not playing games. I take my work here *very seriously indeed*.'

'So there. . .' said Dr Neil wickedly. 'I think your answer really needed that at the end to make it truly effective. Or perhaps a tongue stuck out would be even more so. Learning bad habits down East, are we?'

'If I am,' said Sally-Anne, glaring at him, 'it must be catching. You seemed to have learned plenty, I must say—baiting poor servant girls being one of them.'

'Ah, but we're not a poor servant girl, really, are we?' said Dr Neil, his head on one side again, the scar presented to her; it was a sign that despite his mockery he had accepted her, for with those of whom he was unsure, or not used to, he always attempted to shield them from its sight. 'So all that piff-paff won't serve, will it? And if you really mean to be a good servant you should have noticed that the Master's tea is cold, and the pot needs—refreshing, I believe, is the Yankee word.'

'I am off-duty,' said Sally-Anne awefully, 'and I am bound to tell you that although I am here I am not here in the sense of waiting on you.'

'Not just waiting on me, McAllister,' he answered—he seemed to have an answer for everything, she thought. 'I was about to suggest that we eat tea together, and, that being so, you would not mind a fresh pot. However——'

'Well, that's an artful way to get me to wait on you,' interrupted Sally-Anne frankly, 'and I suppose, since you are so cunning, and I am dying for a drink, you might have your way—perhaps a bonus on my wages might be an idea, seeing that I shall be doing this *out of hours*.'

Dr Neil thought that the way she occasionally trod on

phrases when she spoke was charming rather than irritating, given that it enlivened and illuminated her forthright nature. He was forthright back.

'Spoken like a true Yankee,' he said approvingly. 'Always on the chase for the Almighty dollar.'

Sally-Anne's laugh was robust in the extreme. 'The Almighty dollar! Land sakes! You are talking of a few pennies' pittance added to my weekly wage. Papa would think that an odd way to describe the Almighty dollar. And, come to that, why shouldn't I bargain for doing something extra? You'd dock my pay soon enough if I didn't do everything you and Matey ordered me to do in my waking hours.'

She had forgotten that her papa was supposed to be dead, and had spoken of him in the present tense, a fact not wasted on Dr Neil, who made no comment, but asked politely, 'And does all this stockmarket bargaining mean that you are going to make me a cup of tea, or not? I see that I must do a little bargaining on my own behalf. I am hoping that you will observe that I have fetched in enough buckets of coal this afternoon to spare you having to carry them in tomorrow. Now, what do you say to that, McAllister? Quits?'

Sally-Anne had finished putting her things down, and was feeling enormously hungry as well as thirsty—Papa had once said that she had an appetite as indecent as his own, and the wonder was that neither of them ever put any weight on!

'Not surprising,' her mama had said gently, 'seeing that neither of you ever sits still for a moment, nor ever stops talking, either.' She would have been surprised to learn that observant Dr Neil was thinking the same of her and her abundant energy.

'Quits,' she said cheerfully, and carried the copper kettle to the brass tap let into the front of the water tank which sat in the big iron stove alongside the kitchen fire, and ran the hot water into it before she set it not on the fire, but on a small gas ring in the corner, lighting the gas with a match from a box of Swan Vestas.

After that, watched by her amused employer she emptied the pot of cold tea, scrupulously dried it, and set it to warm on the hotplates beside the fire, then placed a tea-caddy, ornamented with the features of King Edward VII and Queen Alexandra, a souvenir of their coronation, on the table, ready to spoon the required amount into the pot.

'So, our Yankee maid has learned the ritual of tea-making,' Dr Neil said with a naughty grin.

'How could I not,' said Sally-Anne, 'with Matey hard on my trail? You may tell her when she returns how well I have learned my lesson.'

'Oh, yes,' said Dr Neil, watching her lay a place for herself, putting out the china, cutting fresh bread, buttering it from a clay crock, and spooning home-made jam lavishly on it. 'Eat like that, McAllister, and you will grow fat.'

'Not so long as I am working for you.' And her blue-black eyes on him were merry. 'I shall grow thin rather, with exercise, and all the knee-bending I perform when I clean the carpets and scrub the floors.'

The kettle began to boil, and she completed the ritual of tea-making, finally standing the pot on a porcelain plate with Windsor Castle painted on it, mounted on sterling-silver trivets, and crowning it with a tea cosy knitted by Matey back in the days when she had lived in the Cochranes country house, now almost derelict since Stair's expensive debauchery had impoverished the estate.

Sally-Anne sat down, and began to eat the bread and

butter, home-made scones and Victoria sponge cake as though she had not eaten for weeks.

'You did not treat yourself to a snack in an ABC or Lyons, then,' said Neil, gratefully drinking his own fresh cup of tea.

'No, indeed,' said Sally-Anne, mouth now full of currant bun. 'My pay does not stretch to that, especially after the moths got at it yesterday.'

'But you are making up for that today,' said Dr Neil gravely, his mouth twitching, particularly when she looked at him, a question on her pretty face, her mouth being too full for further speech. 'By eating so much of your and Matey's baking,' he explained. 'Can we afford such an appetite, I wonder?'

Sally-Anne was too busy eating to want to spar with him further. It occurred to her suddenly that she had rarely enjoyed herself so much as she was now doing, seated in Dr Neil's kitchen, dressed like a skivvy and eating a huge meal, rather than languidly nibbling at it, as she would have done at one of Aunt Nella's 'At Homes'.

And how come Neil Cochrane was amusing her so easily without even trying? He was now leaning back in his chair, having completed his own frugal meal, contemplating her while she polished off the final remains of her own large one.

'And tonight, McAllister,' he said, at last. 'What are you going to do tonight?'

'Why,' she said sweetly, rising and picking up her clothes, and her bag, now empty of the articles which she had given J. D. O'Connor, 'tonight I am going to turn in early, read and rest—such a change after all I have done since this time last week. And you,' she added, greatly daring—but, since the Master was quizzing her so relentlessly, why should she not quiz the Master? 'What will you be doing tonight, after surgery?'

'You forget, McAllister,' he said lazily, 'no surgery on a Wednesday. And that is why I am wondering whether you would favour me with a game of chess before retiring to your boudoir?'

'Some boudoir,' she replied, inelegant again. 'Are you serious?'

'I am always serious about chess, McAllister,' he replied, eyes mocking her. 'It is the only way to treat it. Do you play?'

'Papa taught me,' she said. 'But I am not his equal. Few people are—at chess, or anything else.'

'Does that mean that you will give me a game?' His voice was sardonic again—he had noted the present tense when she had spoken of her poor 'dead' papa!

Sally-Anne nodded at him, to hear him say, 'Right—leave the pots, McAllister. Your duty tonight is not to wash up, but to allow the Master to slaughter you on the black and white field—unless you play a game as wicked as Papa's—in which case you may finish off what the Africans began on me!'

Well, he was certainly in a good mood, and no sign so far as she could see that he had been drinking what Matey called 'his nasty whisky', so she prepared herself to play him. It was some time since she and Papa had played one of their fierce games; he never gave quarter to anyone, but she thought that she could remember what he had taught her.

'You are sure I am up to it?' she remarked a little naughtily; it would help if he underrated her—another of Papa's precepts she had found worth following.

'If you're not,' said Neil grandly, 'then the Master will teach you. What are servant girls for, but being taught by the Master?'

He took her arm, and the contact, for both of them, was startling. A mixture of fear, at being touched by a man at all—and something else, quite different—swept through Sally-Anne so that she began to tremble as he walked her through to the parlour.

For Dr Neil the feel of her, so soft, the scent of her hair, and of McAllister herself, was so wild and sweet and struck him with such force that his breathing grew a little ragged and his body reminded him of how long it had been since he had satisfied it. Unwanted emotions overcame him, too, not helped by her trembling, so much at odds with her usual fierce, unflinching pride. It surprised him a little; he would not have thought her so easily affected by a man's touch.

Sternly, he told his body to behave itself, and his face reflected the power of his feelings, so that Sally-Anne, looking up at him, was a little daunted by his expression—goodness, was that the effect the prospect of playing a game of chess had on him?—and resigned herself to a grim half-hour.

But it wasn't like that at all. Dr Neil sat her down in a chair opposite to his, and drew out the permanently set-up board on which she had frequently seen him working out problems. His expression lightening a little once he had let go of her, he pulled a penny from his pocket, and said cheerfully, 'We'll toss for white. Agreed, McAllister? No favours for the fair sex. I always play to win.'

Sally-Anne was delighted by his changed manner; he always looked so charming when he smiled—even the scar seemed to disappear a little, and as she was always ready for fun herself—a trait she shared with her papa—and the game looked like being fun, she said, eyes shining, 'Oh, I play to win, too, but a good servant always does what the Master commands,' and she cast her eyes down in the manner of a stage domestic registering submission.

'At last, some proper respect!' Dr Neil tossed the penny up, she called 'heads'—and won. 'So,' he said, leaning back in his big armchair, his expression enigmatic, 'let battle commence.'

Oh, it was a battle, and no mistake, thought Sally-Anne; it was almost like playing against Papa—only Dr Neil played more slowly; but he was just as cunning. As she looked across at him during the game to see him, chin propped on his hand, his whole face a mask of concentration, but paradoxically, at the same time, as relaxed and self-forgetful as she had ever known him, it was plain how handsome he must once have been. Living so close to him, she understood; she was beginning to see not the disfiguring scar and limp, but instead the essential Neil, who was so kind to herself—for all his teasing of her—and to Matey and his poor patients.

Neither of them spoke, and if Dr Neil was a little amused to see how playing a highly competitive game silenced McAllister, so that the whole of her vital spirit was directed towards winning, he did not betray it.

She had been well taught, and after making the odd minor mistake during the opening moves she soon recovered herself, and began to play with a concentration and a ferocity which was also a surprise. He wondered a little at what the unknown papa who had taught her so well was like, if this was the kind of game he had favoured.

Time was magic, Sally-Anne thought; it stretched or contracted according to one's pleasure. In one sense the game took no time at all, in another it seemed to last forever, and there in the quiet room, opposite the quiet man, she began to feel a kind of peace. The clock above the fireplace chimed out its message, but it was lost on them.

Once, his bishop slaughtered in an exchange of pieces, Dr Neil looked up at her and said, 'It's a good thing that the Master didn't underestimate you overmuch, McAllister. You play a wicked game—if reckless.'

It was his only comment after an hour's play, and she gave him her flashing smile, remarking, '"Dare all," Papa used to say, "and the game will reward you—always provided that you cover your back."'

This brought one of Neil's cracks of laughter and the comment, 'A wily gent, I see,' and then silence took over again, and lasted for a long time, until the front door opened, and Matey returned from the sewing circle at St Jude's Church Hall, and stared at them, sitting there in the dusk, hunched over the board, rapt.

She did not speak—she knew better—but walked into the kitchen, thinking furiously, among other things, that her treasure had not looked so happy and fulfilled for years as he did sitting opposite to his American servant girl—and what could that mean, and did she approve? She was not sure.

'Cocoa?' she offered, coming in a little time later, carrying a small tray with three enamel mugs of steaming beverage on it, and a plate of Marie biscuits. She could see that the game was drawing to a close—nearly all the pieces on the board had disappeared—and although she had no idea who was winning she thought that the gladiators needed sustenance.

Sally-Anne sighed, yawned and stretched, not at all ladylike, and said joyously, 'Stalemate! What a happy conclusion. No one wins, and no one loses. Oh, I did enjoy that!'

'Spoken like a true woman,' said Dr Neil, staring at the board, empty save for a few pieces clustered round a pair of kings in one corner. 'I cannot agree with you. We men like to win, and it is quite improper for the servant to be so impudent to the Master as not to allow him to win.'

'Papa always said that only fools did that,' proclaimed Sally-Anne cheerfully. 'Throw a game, I mean.' She took the proffered mug from Matey's hand. 'Unless you did it to gain some advantage, of course.'

'From all you say of Papa,' announced Dr Neil naughtily, 'I'm astonished to learn that he went bankrupt. That sounds like a fate reserved for his competitors.'

Oh, dear, thought Sally-Anne, there I go again. I really must watch what I say—he has a mind like a knife; but aloud she said, doing her best to look distressed, 'Oh, he had a run of bad luck——' an explanation that hardly seemed to convince her hearer.

All three of them drank their cocoa with pleasure. Neil was astonished at how pleasant the evening had been; he had seldom enjoyed a game of chess more, and, thinking this, said a little slyly, 'Another game, another night, perhaps?'

Sally-Anne, her heart thudding in the strangest way when he asked her this, as though he had said something much more intimate, and then suddenly understanding by the ambiguous way in which he had spoken that he had offered her other games than chess, and his wicked expression betraying that he had seen her confusion, flushed, and he added softly, so that Matey could not hear him, 'Come, McAllister, give me your answer—you surely wish to please the Master in every way possible,' the last bit in a fake American accent so bad that she laughed out loud.

'Oh, I will play you at chess any time you like,' she informed him demurely.

'Pity that,' he murmured. 'There are other games master and servant can play, you know.'

'Yes, I do know,' she said, rising to collect her things from the kitchen where she had left them, 'but I have no intention of obliging the Master further, either now, or in the future.'

He watched her go, his smile crooked, heard her say goodnight to Matey—her manners were always impeccable—then followed her into the kitchen to pick up her candlestick and light the candle for her; it had grown dark while they had drunk their cocoa and eaten their biscuits.

'At least let me be your linkboy,' he said. 'I will escort you up the first flight of stairs, but I shall observe the proprieties by leaving you to look after yourself on the second landing.'

Sally-Anne saw Matey's face, half approving, half disapproving of Dr Neil's boldness, and said in reply, 'Thank you, sir,' in a neat parody of every servant who had ever lived. And they set off, Dr Neil behind her, holding the candle high, so that it threw strange shadows on the walls and ceilings.

There was a small old table on the second landing. He put the candle-holder down on it, then turned towards her, and before she could stop him he gave her a kiss so gentle that it hardly registered, and she stared at him, wide-eyed, put her hand to where he had saluted her, and said huskily, 'No,' although what she meant by that neither he nor she knew.

'Goodnight,' he said. 'Sweet dreams, McAllister. Stalemates in life are not as satisfactory as those on the chessboard, you know.' And then he was gone down the stairs, running lightly, for all his limp, and the last which she saw of him was the sandy-blond head before he turned the corner of the first landing.

CHAPTER SIX

'HELLO, Rose,' said Sally-Anne briskly. She was at the rectory kitchen door a week later, meeting Rose as she had promised, for tea with her ma and a trip up West in the evening.

She had been reviewing the previous week on her walk to the rectory. It had been hectic, to say the least. Dr Neil had been busy with a small epidemic of low fever which had fortunately missed Vetch Street, and Matey had decided to do some summer cleaning, spring cleaning having been missed out, due to the deficiences of Sally-Anne's predecessor.

Such a carry-on Sally-Anne had never seen, and all of it exhausting. What with hauling carpets in and out, cleaning the wallpaper with a loose dough—a trick Sally-Anne found oddly satisfying, if messy—washing every curtain, sheet, blanket, cushion-cover, piece of crockery, floorboard, door and window-frame, ceiling—you name it, Sally-Ann cleaned it—by Sunday she felt quite stunned and had gone to sleep during the rector's sermon, only to be prodded awake by Matey, to a smiling Dr Neil's amusement.

'Heathen, are you, McAllister?' he had murmured during her fervent singing of 'All things bright and beautiful'. 'Which Amerindian tribe do you belong to, Huron or Apache? And is the Great Manitou the God you worship?' Which had made it difficult for her to stifle her irreverent giggles, particularly with Matey's severe stare on her.

Afterwards they had gone out into the brilliant sunshine of mid-June, the English summer being fine for a change, and Matey had introduced her to her other, lesser treasure, the curate Mr Julian Sands. She called Sally-Anne, 'My new help,' which sounded more dignified than maid-of-all-work, somehow, McAllister had allowed.

Mr Sands, a pale, shy young man, had taken one look at Mr Cochrane's vivid servant girl and had fallen promptly into a deep and worshipful love for her, a fact written on his ingenuous face. He had even felt compelled to shake hands with a girl whose like he had never seen before. He held her hand a little longer than he should have done, and had stammered at her, 'I—I have a cousin in Florida, Miss McAllister; I wonder if you have run across her?'

Sally-Anne had to stifle more giggles—by his conversation Mr Sands thought that the USA was roughly the size of Wales. Nevertheless she was her usual polite society self with Mr Sands—she had learned in her papa's home and at the embassy how to put people at their ease—and all in all the sight of his skivvy doing the gracious afforded Dr Neil another bout of inward sardonic mirth, however it delighted young Mr Sands, who thought what a splendid creature she was, and a great pity she was only a servant—she had so much presence.

He had invited her to join the ladies' sewing circle, and even suggested that she might like to attend the Tuesday evening Bible readings which he ran—he was sure that 'dear Miss Mates' would release her for the hour and a half the readings usually took.

'Oh, I'm sure we could let you out for that, McAllister,' Dr Neil had said, only for Sally-Anne to murmur modestly that since she was already well treated for time off she could not possibly ask for more.

'What a hard working treasure you are, to be sure,' Dr Neil had said, walking his two women back to Vetch Street, tipping his soft hat to those who were happy to greet the young doctor.

'Not at all,' said Sally-Anne, 'and before you plead for me with Matey let me tell you that you will have your tea salted and your eggs sugared every breakfast if you do any such thing. If you are so enthusiastic about Bible readings, why not attend yourself?'

'Ah, but I am not a pretty young skivvy,' said Dr Neil wickedly, 'and dear Mr Sands does not wish to see me walk through the door. What a conquest you have made, McAllister, and think what a triumph it would be for a maid-of-all-work to become a curate's wife. You could hardly have dreamed of such a possibility. It beggars belief.'

Sally-Anne could see that the good doctor, as she had naughtily begun to call him, was going to take a great deal of delight in mercilessly teasing her about Mr Sands.

'It would beggar belief even more for me to attend a ladies' sewing circle, or a Bible reading for that matter,' she replied, hardly able to keep amusement out of her voice. It occurred to her that in any other circumstances the only description for what she and Dr Neil constantly did was flirting.

She looked sideways at him; the ruined cheek was away from her, and this morning he was hardly limping. His crooked smile was very much in evidence and Matey could have told her that since her arrival Dr Neil had been happier than she had seen him for a long time—there had been fewer backslidings towards the 'nasty whisky' since McAllister had appeared in his life to provide him with such rich amusement.

To her astonishment, Sally-Anne, who for two dreadful months had hardly been able to bring herself to be near any man, however young and apparently innocuous, wanted to stroke the corner of his mouth—more, she wanted to smooth the scar away—or, rather, since that was impossible, to run her hand down it and tell him that it did not matter, such a thing could only disturb those who were themselves already disturbed!

Whatever was coming over her, to think any such thing? Especially of a man whose extreme scepticism about herself and her doings was daily expressed. She shook herself inwardly, said severely, Control yourself, Sally-Anne Tunstall; remember what happened when you had such soft thoughts about a man before, and the sudden dreadful memory this evoked hit her so hard that she stopped dead in her tracks, gave a stifled wail, and went so white that Dr Neil, hearing her, and looking at her, saw that her pallor was so extreme that he thought her on the verge of fainting.

'Good God!' he exclaimed. 'What is it, McAllister?' And he went to take her by the arm, for he feared that she might fall—only for an even worse horror to grip Sally-Anne, so that she pushed him violently away, quite unable to control herself, stammering, 'No—no. . .' The bright day was ruined, and the peace that the last few weeks had given her shattered.

For one agonised moment she thought that Dr Neil was going to insist, to touch her again, and she could not bear that—no, no, not that! Such a strange thought when a moment ago she had fantasised so cheerfully of touching *him*! It was a thought that made her breathing grow even shorter, and blackness was on her, and everything disappeared, to reappear a few moments later.

She was now seated on the ground, propped up against the wall of one of the grimy tenements they had been passing; someone had brought water, and Dr Neil was gently wiping her face with his damp handkerchief.

A look of relief passed over his own face when, the dreadful malaise gone, she croaked at him, 'Oh, dear, what happened?'

'You fainted,' said Dr Neil, looking at her keenly. 'Do you,' he said—and he was suddenly hesitant—'know of any reason why you should?' He was being very much the doctor, Sally-Anne noted, even through her distress, which was growing less by the minute as she regained the self-control which she had so suddenly and disastrously lost.

She must not let that happen again, she must not, and with Dr Neil looking at her so sharply—and why was that?—she was just able to turn her thoughts away from the unthinkable into whose pit she had just fallen.

And then it suddenly struck her what he must be thinking, and she remembered Aunt Nella fainting like this in the early days of her pregnancy with Cousin Lawrence. Did he think she was hiding in the East End because of *that*? Something between distress and amusement struck her this time. Of all things she knew that *that* was not true.

She tried to stand up, only to find that he would not allow her to do so, and Matey was saying, sharply to her, 'Sit child, sit.'

'No,' Sally-Anne cried vehemently. 'It is not what you think, Dr Neil. No, not at all, no, *never*.'

And the 'never' came out so wildly that he was surprised again, and, his eyes still watchful, he said, 'I thought not, but you must see, McAllister, I had to ask you—for your sake.'

Her answer was as cool as she could make it, with her head held high, even though holding it so steadily erect made her feel dizzy. 'I think it must have been coming from the cold of the church into the warmth, or, perhaps—' and she made a wan attempt at humour—'it might have been the thought of attending the ladies' sewing circle which overcame me!'

She could tell that Dr Neil was looking at her most sceptically, although he was touching her so gently that the black fear which she had felt before she had fainted did not return—and pooh to his suspicions! He could have no idea at all of what was really wrong with her; Sally-Anne was sure of that.

'Well,' he said finally, helping her to walk with Matey's assistance, 'I have heard of the ladies' sewing circle accused of many things, but never of bringing on a swoon. Resisting them, rather, is the usual belief.'

He was being kind, she could tell, and not probing further, so she rewarded him with a rather watery smile, and said sententiously, 'There's always a first time for everything.'

And what on earth Papa would say of that banal piece of wisdom she could not imagine—and why was Papa, whom she had parted from in a high old anger, so much in her thoughts these days?

Dr Neil registered how withdrawn she was, and once they were back home hot, sugary tea was poured down her in a constant stream, and then, despite the warmth of the day, Matey put a shawl around her shoulders and made her sit near the fire.

Normally Sally-Anne would have rejected such molly-coddling, but she did feel dreadfully cold, and said so to Dr Neil who said quietly, 'It is the usual consequence of shock, McAllister, and for some reason you were suddenly very shocked. You would not care to talk about it with Matey—if you do not feel you could confide in me?'

Sally-Anne tossed her head at this, and repeated that

it was all nothing—'And really you should not make such a fuss over so little'—but all the same she was happy to let Matey help her up to bed; she felt strangely weak, and the thought of Sunday lunch and washing up, and all the work to be done before the day was over, made her feel worse than ever.

She sat up, cheeks flaming. 'Oh, I do hope they don't think I did it to get out of doing my chores; that would be *too* bad.'

But neither Dr Neil nor Matey thought that, and when Matey said hesitantly, 'You don't think it's the obvious. . .?' Dr Neil shook his head, and said firmly.

'No, she said not, and although I think that virtually everything she has told us about herself is a pack of lies I don't think she's lying about that.'

Sally-Anne did not know of this conversation, of course, and by the next day she was her usual bouncing, energetic self, and it being Monday not only was it wash-day—oh, dear—but summer cleaning also began again, with everything being put back, and the whole place was shining and sweet-smelling, so that, Wednesday having come round, McAllister had sunk down into Dr Neil's big armchair with a great, 'Phew, I'm glad that's all over!' amusing Matey, whose soft spot for the girl who seemed to be making Dr Neil more reconciled to his lot grew greater every day.

How it would all end Matey could not imagine. She was nearly as sceptical as Dr Neil about the reason for McAllister's presence in their life, but she was such a good, hard-working creature, despite her decorative appearance, that Matey could not quarrel with her.

And when, after lunch, she came downstairs in her new outfit, bought from Selfridge's last week with the money which J. D. O'Connor had paid her for her articles, and with her next two articles in her bag, ready to be handed in to the great man himself before she returned to the rectory to pick up Rose Bailey, whose time off did not begin until four-thirty, both Dr Neil and Matey thought that she looked enchanting.

Her frock, which had cost far less than one of her hats in her old life, was a short-sleeved model in navy blue, with a sailor's collar in navy blue and white silk, and had anchors embroidered around the hem of her skirt. With it she wore an imitation of a sailor's hat—if one could imagine a sailor's hat with a broad brim and long navy blue streamers—and she looked extremely desirable in her cheap finery.

Dr Neil felt quite a pang. No one like himself, a partial cripple, with a badly scarred body—his limp was paining him this week—and with a ruined face into the bargain could hope to aspire to such a Bird of Paradise; he could only imagine what she looked like in the clothes she normally wore.

He wondered again what her game was in Vetch Street, and what rich young fellow was waiting for her, back in her real life. He was sure that there was a rich young fellow—no one who looked and behaved like McAllister could be without one.

'Will I do?' she asked Matey, in her charming, half-joking manner, for Matey to reply in like vein,

'Delightful, my dear. Have a good day, and be careful, mind.'

'Oh, I will,' said McAllister gaily; every day she spent in Vetch Street she felt more and more like McAllister, Dr Neil's unconventional parlourmaid, and less and less like Miss Sally-Anne Tunstall, American beauty and heiress. Miss Tunstall had not possessed work-reddened hands and knees. And if, at first, she had had to remind herself to be careful not to be found out, deceit was becoming second nature to her.

Yesterday she had gone to the dingy little newsagent at the corner of the street to pay the paper bill, and to buy Matey a writing pad and envelopes, when she had seen on the counter a pile of postcards depicting society beauties.

To her horror the top one was of herself. It had been taken when she had been presented to King Edward VII and Queen Alexandra earlier in the year. The presentation had been quite an unnecessary proceeding, as she and Uncle Orrin Tunstall had agreed, seeing that she had met and known both the King and Queen since she was ten years old and had first visited England with her mama and papa.

Her papa, Jared Tunstall, the senior senator for Nevada, was a personal friend of the King, and Sally-Anne had first met him when he was the Prince of Wales. The Prince had loved children, had been very kind to them, and Sally-Anne had been delighted to see him gravely encourage two four-year-old boys, the twin sons of an old friend, to race pieces of bread, butter and jam up and down his expensively trousered leg.

When Sally-Anne, dolled up in ostrich feathers and pearls, had gravely made her elaborate curtsy to him at Court, he had put out his hand to lift her, and after she had replied, 'My thanks, Your Majesty,' he had twinkled at her, using the famous charm which had somehow made one ignore his years and his obesity, and said,

'Oh, I hope I shall always be Kingy to you, Miss Sally-Anne,' making it clear that he included her in the charmed circle of his friends.

While she was standing in the grubby little shop, this incongruous memory had flashed into her head at the sight of her face. How the printers had got hold of her photograph she did not know, but they had, and now it was being sold all over London, along with ones of Lillie Langtry and other noted belles. Beneath the photograph was printed not her name, but a sobriquet, a common practice—Mrs Langtry was always know as 'The Jersey Lily'. Sally-Anne had been christened 'An American Princess' soon after her arrival in London, and the name had stuck.

She thought that the photograph neither flattered, nor was very like her, but suppose Rose, or, worse still, Dr Neil or Matey saw it?

Rose had entered the newsagent at that very moment, and Sally-Anne, acting with characteristic speed, had swept up her photograph and one of Mrs Langtry, and, putting the second one on top, she had handed them over to buy them with her hard-earned pennies.

Her friend—for she and Rose had become quite close—had sniffed at Mrs Langtry, and said kindly, 'I 'ear as 'ow she's a right fat cow these days,' and fortunately had not asked to look at the other one she had bought. Sally-Anne had already checked that this was the only one of herself in the pile.

Now, ready to leave for her afternoon and evening's fun she thought it unlikely that she would meet anyone she knew in Fleet Street, or even up West with Rose, and anyway it was a chance which she was prepared to take, for she intended her little excursion to be the basis of yet another article. Her only regret was that Dr Neil did not buy the *Clarion Cry* so that so far the only piece of her work which she had seen in print was the one which she had written before she had arrived in the East End.

Dr Neil wanted to tell her to be careful, that she really had little idea of how hard and cruel the world was outside the privileged fastness in which she had previously lived, but he contented himself with saying instead, 'Have a good time, McAllister. Don't miss the last bus back.'

He was intending to go up West himself that evening, but hardly expected to meet McAllister when he did so, seeing that, for once, he was going out with his disreputable brother Stair, and God knew where they would end up—nowhere respectable, that was for sure.

So troubled was he for a girl who, after all, was of age, high-spirited and clever, that after she had gone, and Matey had answered reflectively when he had asked her if she knew where McAllister was going, 'I don't know. With Rose Bailey from the rectory, I believe,' he felt compelled to reply, a little worried,

'With Rose? Are you sure?'

He had met Rose, recognised what she was, and guessed why she was going up West, and what for, and he was suddenly certain that while McAllister might be a member of a sophisticated society she knew little of the world that Rose Bailey lived in.

'You ought not to have let her go with Rose,' he said reproachfully.

'Whyever not?' said Matey, looking up from her mending, surprised at the urgency in his voice.

What could he say? Matey's knowledge, too, was circumscribed, and she had no idea of the bold way in which Rose looked at him, and the unmistakable invitation in her eyes. He did not like to think of McAllister alone with her, but that was stupid—McAllister was no concern of his, and surely did not need a battered doctor to look out for her.

But all the same he wished that McAllister were not going up West with Rose that night, and wondered what was coming over him that such a fly-trap could fill his waking— and his sleeping—thoughts!

* * *

Rose was waiting for McAllister at the rectory. She was wearing a bright red dress, shiny black boots, and despite the heat of the day a black feather boa to match the huge feathers in her large picture hat. In street clothes she looked very flash, not at all as she did in her neat black and white servant's uniform.

She had run to the door after seeing McAllister walk up the front path, and greeted her with a wide grin, brought on by the sight of McAllister's sailor outfit.

'Cor,' she shrieked, 'yer'll 'ave the mashers after yer tonight, an' no mistake!' Which surprised Sally-Anne a little, mashers not having figured in her plans.

The two girls, so near in age, but so different in their experience of life, walked briskly through the mean and dirty streets. On one corner they were hooted after by a group of young men wearing brown bowlers tipped over their eyes, and then they grew particularly bold, following them along the cracked pavement, Rose turned and screamed after them, 'Does yer muvver know yer art?' A witticism which convulsed herself and the recipients of it.

'Give as good as yer get, is my motter,' she informed McAllister. 'No p'int in takin' up wiv them as 'as no blunt.'

Rose's ma lived with five of her children on the ground floor of one of the tenement buildings about three-quarters of a mile from Vetch Street.

'Ere we are,' said Rose, and pushed McAllister through an unpainted door, along a grimy passage into a smelly room facing an interior courtyard. The table was already set for high tea, with ham, bread and butter and a very yellow cake. There was no cow's milk provided—it went off so quickly in hot weather, with nowhere cool to store it—and a tin of Nestlé's condensed milk stood beside a jam jar full of sugar. A saucepan full of water was hissing on a tiny range, a miniature of the one in Matey's kitchen.

Rose and her ma exchanged smacking kisses, and 'Ere's McAllister from the doctor's, ma, come to 'ave tea wiv us,' Rose announced.

Ma Bailey wiped her hand on her dirty apron and extended it to Sally-Anne. 'McAllister?' she said. 'Ain't she got annuver nime?'

'Sally-Anne, please,' said the Tunstall heiress. 'McAllister reminds me of scrubbing floors and cleaning ranges.' This was not strictly true. McAllister, she felt, was reserved for Dr Neil.

'McAl—Sally-Anne,' said Rose, reading her ma's stare correctly, 'is a Yankee; that's why she talks so funny. Don't mind that. She's a bit of all right.'

One thing, thought Sally-Anne, looking around her, after Ma Bailey had set her down in one of the few chairs the room possessed, was that no one here had ever done any summer cleaning, nor spring, autumn nor winter cleaning either. There was a bed in one corner still unmade, although it was five o'clock in the afternoon.

Three or four dirty children arrived for tea; she and Rose were the only clean persons in the kitchen—for so Sally-Anne supposed the room—and while Ma, Rose and Sally-Anne sat down at table the children all stood, and wolfed the food down mannerlessly, fighting among themselves while they did so.

The ham, which everyone ate avidly, and which Sally-Anne forced down, was off and the butter was so rancid that she almost choked over it. As for the tea! Matey had already told her that most of the tea sold in East End grocers was collected from the leavings of the West End, dried, repacked and sold again. Drinking her tea at Rose's ma's, Sally-Anne could well believe it.

Afterwards she helped to clear the table and to carry the pots through into a lean-to kitchen, the room in which they had eaten being the best parlour.

'Don't bovver wiv 'em,' said Rose, but,

'At least let me wash them up,' replied Sally-Anne determinedly, and, Rose giving way, she discovered that the water had to be fetched from a tap in the inside court, there being none piped into any of the surrounding buildings, and the privy was a common one, also standing in the yard.

Outside, running the water into the misshapen saucepan, Sally-Anne found the stench indescribable, so much so that she began a desperate burst of coughing to prevent herself from vomiting.

She was about to commiserate with Rose on her unfortunate circumstances when Rose proudly said, 'We're ever so lucky to be'ere Sally-Anne, wiv the 'ole grarnd floor to ourselves—not like them upstairs what only 'ave one room.'

'Them upstairs' were obviously of an inferior race, and their habits were disgusting, Rose said. Sally-Anne also made the mistake of assuming that Rose's ma was a widow, only for Rose to stare at her, burst out laughing and say, 'Ow, there weren't no Mr Bailey, and me dad 'opped it long ago and 'is name weren't Bailey; he was only 'im as lived wiv 'er.'

''Er' was apparently Rose's ma, and it seemed likely from Rose's hints and sniffs that all the children had different dads, which, looking at Ma Bailey, fat, defeated and unlovely, Sally-Anne found difficult to believe.

How could any man want to lay a finger on her, never mind father her children? The youngest of whom, she discovered, was only six weeks old, and was brought from the bedroom in an elderly bassinet to be fed, not mother's milk, but some patent milk powder made up with the dubious water from the outside tap.

It was one thing for Miss Sally-Anne Tunstall, pampered beauty, to contemplate the horrors of poverty from the relative comfort of Vetch Street, but to see it in practice, that was quite another thing. All the loose women Sally-Anne had previously met in both English and American society had been particularly lovely and tempting creatures, not gross and depressed objects who looked like unmade beds—as Rose's ma did.

Just before six o'clock they finally left for the West with Rose's ma's warnings ringing in their ears. 'You be careful, mind, our Rose, and you too, miss.' Rose's ma, even more than her daughter, had appreciated what a strange creature had arrived in their meagre lives.

How fortunate I am, thought Sally-Anne, running with Rose to catch the horse bus. How can people live like that? And are there those, as Rose suggests, who live even more straitened lives? She shuddered—for if there were she really must find them out and write of them, or her articles could not be considered authentic.

She did not reflect that only a few weeks ago she would have thought it impossible that she could have lived the life of a servant, let alone bear eating and drinking in the den in which Rose and her ma lived, but she did know one thing—she would never take her comfortable life for granted again. And what she did not know was that she had even more lessons to learn—and that some of them might not be pleasant.

CHAPTER SEVEN

NEIL COCHRANE was not enjoying himself. Dressed as he rarely was these days, in evening togs and carrying an opera hat, a white silk scarf around his neck, he was, at ten o'clock at night, completely sober, although the group he was with, headed by his brother Stair, and Havelock, usually known as Havvie, Marquess of Blaine, heir of the Duke of Innescourt, whose stag party night this was, were all three-parts drunk.

Stair, who usually ignored Neil since his brother had given up his privileged life and become an East End doctor, occasionally felt that he had some sort of duty to him; he was, after all, his heir. His idea of duty took the form of inviting Neil to join him in the nightly round of enjoyment which made up Stair's life. Neil refused most of these invitations, but had accepted this last one—the temptation to indulge himself, since he had stopped his midnight drinking, was suddenly great.

But the sight of their debauchery stifled his own, and the knowledge that they were going to end the evening at Madam Rachel's select brothel, just off the Haymarket, far from exciting him, disgusted him. Havvie Blaine disgusted him most of all. He was marrying one of America's richest heiresses, who was, Stair had drunkenly informed him, 'As ugly as a pug dog,' solely for her money, and was proposing to bed Madame Rachel herself as a preliminary to his marriage at St Margaret's, Westminster, the following morning, the biggest society wedding of the year.

For very form's sake, and because, after all, Stair was

his brother, he had stayed with the party through one act of a musical comedy at the Gaiety Theatre where they had made so much noise that their departure at the first interval must have pleased the audience which they had left behind, had gone to Quaggers—Quaglino's—to dine—which meant drink—in a private room, and were now on their way to crown their evening's pleasure by 'Pushing the boat out for Havvie', Stair's witticism.

For whatever reason, Neil, who had almost looked forward to relieving his body's urgent demands—he seemed to have been continent for years, and McAllister's arrival in Vetch Street had most inconveniently revived his dormant senses—found that he was disgusted with himself most of all.

Stair thrust an arm around him, laid his head on Neil's shoulder, and said, 'Let me treat you to a good 'un at Rachel's, Neil,' which completed the destruction of any desire Neil might have had to treat himself.

How he was to avoid patronising Madame Rachel's girls without offending Stair he could not think. They were by now in Piccadilly Circus, which was as bright as day, and were surrounded by the crowds streaming from the theatres, cafés and dives which populated the area, painted ladies of a certain character being prominent among them—as well as the enthusiastic amateurs who had come up from the East End to make a few pennies, or even be given supper, as a price for their favours.

It was only because it was so rare that Stair ever troubled with him at all these days that Neil felt compelled to go along with him, willy-nilly. He had a brief memory of McAllister's bright face, earlier that day, and the thought of enjoying himself with one of Madame Rachel's girls did not attract.

Salvation came suddenly. Another crowd of gilded aristocrats and gentlemen, also out on the town and also half cut, recognising Stair's party, and Havvie Blaine in particular, decided to enliven his celebrations by staging an impromptu rugger game. Forming a scrum, they attacked Stair's party, and one young fellow who had brought along a hunting horn blew blasts on it to encourage his fellows.

The whole group, locked together, whirled around. Stair, turning to see what was happening, was borne away from Neil, who was himself carried down the Haymarket by a shouting throng—the rugger match had triggered off an impromptu riot as well. It's an ill wind that blows nobody any good, thought Neil platitudinously, as a large bruiser pushed him against one of the pillars of the Haymarket Theatre—I might get my nose broken, but at least my virtue looks like remaining intact!

He dodged away and took the opportunity to walk rapidly in the opposite direction from the one in which Stair's lot might be, towards Pall Mall, passing the narrow courts and alleys which led from the brilliantly lit main street.

Halfway down the Haymarket, now quite a distance from Piccadilly Circus, Neil paused, breathless, and afterwards wondered what kind god had arranged for him to be where he was. To his left from the dark street came a frightened female voice, shouting in a despairing manner, 'No, please, no!'

Neil, who never thought of himself as in any way a Galahad, or a knight errant in shining armour, saving virgins under attack, nevertheless felt compelled to investigate, particularly when the cry came again, more despairing than ever.

He ran the short distance down the side-street as fast

as his gammy leg would let him. He saw that a tall young man, dressed in the uniform of a lower-class masher—check trousers, brown bowler, shiny brown boots, and huge moustache—had a girl pinned against the wall of one of the office buildings, and was attempting to kiss her—or worse.

The girl was trying to fight him off, was kicking his shins vigorously, trying to hold her face away from his, and was giving vent to muffled shouts, which were, of necessity, growing feebler and feebler as her strength ran out. It was quite apparent that her resistance was not token, but real. The chivalry towards women which gentleman were supposed to possess—but often didn't—was a very real part of Neil's nature, and, having seen what was happening, he could not stand by, or walk away, telling himself that it was no business of his.

'Let her go,' he said, hoping that the masher would not see what a useless cripple he was. He was carrying Stair's silver-topped cane, given to him to look after because in his drunken state Stair could no longer remember to keep it with him. The masher turned his attention from the girl to Neil and moved towards him menacingly. Neil responded by lifting the cane high, ready to defend himself from a man who he saw was bigger, and probably stronger, than himself.

The masher dodged round Neil, lifted his fists, and said in what Neil could tell was by no means a confident manner, 'Throw that away, and put up yer dukes like a man!'

The only sensible response to this, Neil decided ruefully, was to keep hold of the cane, and continue to threaten the bully with it, and for a very short space of time they circled around one another—neither man, it soon became plain, really wishing to do more than threaten.

The masher's intended victim was not quite so indecisive; far from taking the opportunity to run off, leaving St George to fight the dragon on his own, she had taken the opportunity once her attacker's attention had been diverted from her to remove her right shoe, and she now proceeded to attack him from the rear, pounding him first about the head and shoulders with the shoe, and then with her handbag shrieking, 'Take that, you cowardly bully, and that,' leaving him open to any attack Neil might care to make.

Assailed from both sides, the masher decided that the game was not worth the candle, and, dodging by Neil, to the latter's great relief, he scuttled off towards the Haymarket. Neil dropped his cane, and turned towards the victim, now transformed into her attacker's Nemesis.

Her hair down and around her shoulders, her dress torn, her right shoe in one hand, and her bag in the other, the light of battle in her eye, McAllister stared at her saviour, Dr Neil, and he stared back at her. 'Good God, you idiot,' he said romantically, 'what on earth are you doing here, and where is Rose? Have you taken leave of your senses to end up being attacked in a back alley off the Haymarket of all places, by a man you don't know?'

'Oh,' said McAllister furiously, remembering something which she did not like to remember, 'you mean it would have been perfectly in order for him to attack me if he'd known me?'

All the anger she felt for the wretch who had assaulted her was transferred to Dr Neil who had arrived to save her.

'I might have expected such an answer from you, McAllister; it fits in with the general picture,' said Dr

Neil angrily, picking up his cane. 'I suppose that you will be gracious enought first to tell me how you arrived here, and secondly to allow me to take you home before you end up in another alley. Thanks I don't expect.'

Enormous relief at being saved, and delayed shock, hit Sally-Anne together. For one dreadful moment she had thought that God was going to play yet another ghastly trick on her, and one which she had not invited—any more than she had invited her previous one.

'Oh,' she almost wailed, 'I am being so thoughtless. Not to thank you, I mean—and Rose—oh, dear. . .' and her face crumpled, but the steely resolution which lay beneath her outward charm prevented her from giving way to the hysterics which she knew would take her over if she allowed herself to show any weakness.

Compunction struck Dr Neil. After all, the poor child was probably still in shock compounded of shame at being so discovered, and relief at her salvation.

'Let me help you to put your shoe back on,' he said gently, 'and I must thank you for coming to my rescue. The princess certainly helped her saviour tonight.'

Princess! The irony of the description struck Sally-Anne hard. She allowed Dr Neil to sit her down on a doorstep and help her to replace her shoe, and he guarded her while she tidied her hair, and pulled her torn dress together.

'I didn't ask for this,' she said. 'I. . .think I had better tell you what happened; I wouldn't like you to entertain any wrong thoughts.' She looked up at him, the enormous blue-black eyes wide and shadowed by her recent experience. She was wise enough to understand, now that her fear was leaving her, that it was Dr Neil's very real concern which had made him so sharp with her when he had found out who it was he had rescued.

'As for Rose. . .' she shivered, and Dr Neil, seeing her face change, said abruptly,

'When did you last eat, McAllister?'

Sally-Anne stared at him, surprised by this strange request. 'At Rose's ma's,' she answered. 'We had tea there, before we came up West.'

'I thought so,' said Dr Neil kindly. 'You are suffering from both shock—and, knowing your appetite, from hunger as well.' His eyes twinkled at her as he added, 'Would you allow me to buy you supper before I take you home?'

'Oh, yes, please,' said Sally-Anne fervently, realising that yes, hunger was succeeding shock, and the thought of food and drink was a pleasant one.

By now they had walked some distance along the Haymarket, and were on the edge of Piccadilly Circus where Dr Neil was relieved to see that Stair's party had disappeared and the crowds there had grown less. He turned to Sally-Anne who was clinging to his arm, and said, 'I know a small chop-house near here, and when you have eaten you may tell me what happened, and how you came to be on your own, under attack.' He hesitated. 'I blame myself a little. You know nothing of the world in which you have come to live, and I should have warned you about Rose, only I did not know that you were going out with her until after you had gone, and then, of course, it was too late.'

Both of them realised that he had abandoned all pretence that Sally-Anne was an ordinary young woman come to work in Vetch Street, but neither of them pursued the matter, Dr Neil from delicacy, and Sally-Anne because she could not tell him the real truth about herself—he would undoubtedly immediately send her back to the embassy, and she did not want that at all—it would be failure.

Only when they were sitting down in the chop-house and Dr Neil had ordered them soup and rolls, followed by lamb chops with seasonal vegetables, and a glass of red wine each—'Good for your shattered nerves,' he said gravely—and they were waiting for the soup to arrive did Sally-Anne have time to look about her.

She had never been in such a place before, and she saw at once that most of the men had girls with them who were certainly not their wives, or the kind of girl one took home to mother. The whole day had been a strange one for a young lady like herself who had never been allowed to go out on her own, had been carefully looked after and protected at all times from the impact of the world in which most people lived.

The soup arrived, a rich broth, and rolls and butter and a carafe of wine as well. Sally-Anne attacked her food with vigour, and when she had drunk her soup, buttered and eaten her roll, Dr Neil prompted her gently, 'Talk to me about it, McAllister. It will make you feel better.'

'Oh,' said Sally-Anne, wiping her mouth with her napkin, 'it was all such a surprise, the evening started out so well. 'We went to the theatre where Marie Lloyd was singing. I had never been to such a show before—not at all the thing that well-bred young ladies are supposed to attend—but she made me laugh. . . We went upstairs—Rose called it the gods, because we were so near to heaven, I suppose, and the stage was so far away.'

Her expression was wistful, reminiscent, as she recalled how, once they had gone up endless stairs and were seated on the hard wooden benches, an attendant had come along and pushed them all closer and closer together so that as many spectators as possible could be packed in.

At first she had disliked this, but Rose's amusement, and the joking of those around them, had infected her, too, and she had found herself giggling and laughing with the rest as they were shuffled along.

'And then,' she said, 'after the show was over, and we were outside again, Rose said, "What about a bit of supper?" And, oh, how stupid I was.'

She remembered how she had looked at Rose in some surprise, and said, 'Yes, that would be swell, but I haven't enough money with me to pay for supper.'

Rose had put her finger by her nose with a look of infinite cunning, and replied, 'Nah, Sally-Anne, yer ain't as green as that, surely. *We* don't need to pay. Watch.'

By now they were in Piccadilly Circus, anonymous among the largest crowd Sally-Anne had ever been in without some sort of companion to protect her, or to look out for her. A rich young girl of good family was seldom, if ever, on her own.

Rose had moved back a little to stand in front of one of the shop windows, scanning the crowd with knowing eyes. Two young men, superior artisans probably, out for a night on the town, dressed in an imitation of their betters, their brown bowlers tipped over their foreheads, their eyes searching the crowd for likely partners for a bit of fun, had attracted Rose's attention, and she had made sure that she attracted theirs.

Sally-Anne never knew precisely how she did it, but the next moment the shorter one was speaking to Rose, and the taller one had his wandering eye on a shrinking Sally-Anne, who was too confused to do more than understand that the Mashers were agreeing to buy supper for Rose and herself—in exchange for what? But she was suddenly sure that she knew!

'No,' she said, 'I want to go home,' only for Rose to ignore her plea, and say,

'Come on Sally-Anne; never say die!' And before Sally-Anne could do anything about it the tall young man was tucking her arm in his, and walking her briskly along at such a pace that she was horrified to discover that Rose and her companion were gone, lost behind them as fresh crowds emerged from yet more emptying theatres and dance halls.

Panic-stricken, she tried to pull her arm out of his, but her companion ignored her struggles, saying, 'Come on, ducks, no need to bovver ourselves with supper; let's 'ave our bit of fun first,' and pulled her along into the alley where Dr Neil had found her.

Their lamb chops had arrived as she finished telling him this sad story. 'I had no idea,' she informed him earnestly, 'no idea at all what Rose had in mind, or I would never have gone with her. She was going to sell herself—she *has* sold herself by now—and would have sold me—for supper. Just for supper!'

Dr Neil decided that McAllister's education in life needed adding to a little.

'Ah, but it isn't just for supper for Rose, is it? Rose could never afford for herself the sort of supper her young man will provide for her, and she's fly enough not to get herself dragged into an alley and done out of it. She probably managed to make him pay her a little more before she agreed to do what he wanted—and altogether earned for herself in one evening more than she does in several days of being a parlourmaid.

'Your partner probably recognised you as the innocent you are—and tried to take advantage of the fact. Eat up your lamb chops, McAllister, before they grow cold, there's a good girl. I don't like to waste good money, or good food either—and I promise to respect your virtue when you've finished.'

Oh, it was good food, Sally-Anne thought gratefully, tucking into it, beginning to enjoy herself now that her ordeal was over, and was happy to sit there with Dr Neil who was also enjoying his supper, by his expression. He poured her another glass of wine from the carafe which stood between them on the table. She thought that he looked nicer than ever in his evening dress, and sounded nicer now that he had dropped his brusque, cold manner with her again.

'You didn't recognise what Rose was?' he asked her.

She shook her head vigorously. 'No. I was foolish, I suppose.' It was dreadful to her to think that Rose was an amateur tart earning such a pittance in her legitimate work that she was ready to sell herself for so little. She should have realised the truth when she had met her mother and seen her wretched home.

Another awful thought struck her. How many of the young men and women of her own world were doing exactly the same as Rose? And the fact that they were doing it for a great deal more money, like Havvie Blaine, rather than for supper and a few pence, didn't make it any better.

She had finished her lamb chops, and they were really top-hole, or she was so hungry that anything would have seemed like ambrosia, the food of the gods. She looked across at Dr Neil; the overhead light was making a golden aureole around his sandy head, and she thought again that even with his dreadful scar he was an extremely attractive man. He intercepted her candid gaze, said gravely, 'Some apple pie, McAllister? Surely that monstrous appetite isn't yet satisfied?'

'Oh, yes, please!' returned Sally-Anne, and then caught her breath again, when he turned his head, presenting her with his beautiful, undamaged profile—he must have been an absolute stunner before he was disfigured. Not only did he order the apple pie and cream, but he also poured her yet another glass of wine—somehow she seemed to have drunk the other already!

'Should I really?' she said, looking at the wine glass doubtfully, speaking as much to dispel the strange feeling that was coming over her every time she looked at him as to reassure herself over the wine.

It was a feeling which she had never had before, not even with Terry or Havvie, both of whom she had thought herself in love with. This feeling was quite different; in some strange way it seemed to reach into her very soul. She wanted to protect him, and for him to protect her—it was as though her identity was bound up with his. And yet it was physical as well. She wanted to lean over and touch him, and, fearful though she was of men, and she shrank at the thought, she wanted him to touch *her*—gently, of course.

Surely she could not be stupid enough to be falling in love, be bowled over by a man's charm again, and so strongly this time? The mere idea made her feel faintly sick, as well as excited, but not sick enough to refuse the apple pie and cream when it came.

And Dr Neil, staring at her wine glass as though it were a bomb, said, 'Trust me McAllister; alcohol will do you nothing but good after your adventures tonight—you will sleep well, and I have already given you my word that I will behave myself.'

So he had, and Sally-Anne knew that, above all, Dr Neil was a man of his word. She ate her apple pie, which was excellent, and finished off her glass of wine, only for Dr Neil to look at her quizzically and say,

'Cheese and biscuits, McAllister? Surely you will not refuse cheese and biscuits?'

'Oh, I must,' she said gaily, but she accepted the offer of coffee, and, waiting for it to arrive, said, 'Now it is my turn to quiz you. What is Dr Neil doing in the West End, dressed up like a toff?' A word which she had learned from Rose.

Dr Neil leaned back in his chair and appreciated his maid's pretty face. She was quite the most attractive thing in the café now that the colour had come back to her face and she had regained her normal cheerful manner. More than one man had looked enviously at him.

'Oh, my brother Stair—I am sure that Matey has told you about Stair—invited me out tonight to the stag party of one of his friends; I used to know him slightly. He is marrying a rich American heiress tomorrow and is spending his last night on the town as a free man. I am sorry for the poor girl if her bridegroom chooses to behave as he did tonight, and, knowing him well, I cannot imagine that he will be any better behaved when he is married to her than he was before.'

'A rich American heiress,' said Sally-Anne thoughtfully. 'I wonder if I have heard of her?'

'Perhaps,' said Neil. 'Her name is Maybelle Foy—Stair says that she is not very pretty, but is enormously rich.'

For once, Dr Neil, engrossed in drinking his coffee, did not notice that McAllister had gone very still. She picked up her cup, and said in a voice as cool as she could make it, 'Yes, I have heard of Miss Foy, and what you say of her is true. What lucky man is marrying her?'

She thought that she knew who the lucky man might be, and it took all her strength of mind not to betray the dreadful emotions which merely thinking of him aroused in her.

'Havvie Blaine, old Innescourt's heir. That family is as poor as church mice, and Stair told me that Havvie had already managed to snare one Yankee heiress, but she got away, and now he has caught another—not quite so rich, but rich enough. They will be restoring Dunblaine Castle—unless Havvie spends the lot on loose women, drink and gambling—begging your pardon for being frank, McAllister. The Havvie Blaines of this world ought to wear a sign warning decent women off—and he's as handsome as the devil, which doesn't help.'

So he ought, thought Sally-Anne, and so he is, and, desperate to change the conversation, to steer it away from dangerous ground, she said, as brightly as she could, through numb lips, 'Shan't we miss the last horse bus home if we don't leave soon?' thinking how fortunate it was that Stair had not told Dr Neil the other heiress's identity—Sally-Anne Tunstall might have been a dead give-away; she really ought to have changed her Christian name.

Dr Neil, who had just called for the bill, pulled out his watch, and said cheerfully, 'Oh, we have already missed it, McAllister. If you can trust yourself to me in a cab we can travel back to Vetch Street in style, and if Matey is up try to think of an explanation that will not involve Rose, or men who trap young girls in alleys, or how I, fortunately for you, became separated from Stair and rescued you. We don't want her thinking that you and I made a secret assignation in Piccadilly Circus. No, by good fortune we met, after you were accidentally parted from Rose, and I saw you chastely home. Oh, and by the by, I want you to promise me that you will not go out on the rampage with Rose again.'

'No, indeed,' said Sally-Anne with a shudder. 'I can think of nothing that I would like less.' She took the arm he offered her, and they left the café together. Somehow Dr Neil's touch did not seem to affect her as badly as that of most men, even though in the cab home sitting so near to him nearly brought on the kind of faintness which she had felt on the walk home from church.

She managed to control herself and fortunately Dr Neil was as quiet as she was, and when they reached Vetch Street Matey had already gone to bed. Dr Neil lit the gas-lamp in the tiny hall and the one in the parlour and fetched their candles for them.

'Good night, McAllister,' he said. 'If your evening began well and had a bad middle, I hope you enjoyed the end.' As once before he leaned over and gave her cheek a gentle, passionless kiss. It was almost as though he recognised that she would not—no, could not—accept more.

Sally-Anne took the kiss and the last sight of him standing in the parlour in his beautiful evening clothes up to bed with her, and agreed with him—for really the end of the evening and their happy supper together had been the best thing of all.

CHAPTER EIGHT

'SURPRISINGLY I enjoyed going to the ladies' sewing circle, with Matey,' wrote Sally-Anne in her journal. It was five-thirty in the morning and she was already dressed for the day. She had recently found that she was waking with the dawn—or even slightly earlier—and she used the opportunity either to keep up with her journal or to rough out a column for J. D. O'Connor who grew increasingly pleased with her work.

She closed her book; her papa had given it to her before she left for England and she blushed a little on remembering how short she had been with him when he had handed it over to her. Somehow, since being at Vetch Street, working so hard, and living a life so different from her old one, many events in her past had taken on a different colour.

She rose from her chair at the little antique bureau which stood in the attic window space, bent down and fumbled for the catch of the secret drawer which she had found there. She had recorded in her journal everything which had happened to her since she had arrived in London and she wanted no prying eyes to read what she had written.

Not that she thought Matey, or Dr Neil, would come poking around her room, but she was changing rapidly from the trusting and innocent girl she had once been to someone more cautious—she, Sally-Anne, more cautious! How pleased Mama would be!—and she no longer took things for granted as she once had.

Six o'clock found her downstairs at the kitchen grate,

readying the little house for the day. She could hear stirrings upstairs and assumed that Matey, who often rose early when she could not sleep late, was on her way down to start her chores alongside McAllister.

Matey might not work so hard as McAllister did, or perform such menial tasks, like scrubbing the kitchen floor and whitening the front doorstep—which was next on McAllister's list of duties—but she did her share and was never idle, even in her spare time—hence her membership of the ladies' sewing circle and her encouragement of her housemaid, McAllister, to accompany her to it.

Only, it wasn't Matey who walked into the kitchen as McAllister began her blackleading, but Dr Neil, yawning and fastening the buttons of a rather natty grey coat which she had never seen before.

'Good morning, McAllister,' he said; his manners to all those society considered his inferiors were always punctilious. 'Would you leave off what you are doing for a moment? The Master would like a cup of coffee.'

McAllister put down her brush, placed her hands on her hips in the manner of every recalcitrant servant and said aggressively, with the hint of a twinkle in her eye, 'And what would Miss Mates say if I neglect my early morning duties?'

Neil sat down at the table and placed his newspaper on its gaudy oilcloth cover. 'Never mind what Matey might say——' and he was almost short with her '—I'll square her for you. It's the Master speaking, McAllister. Jump to it!' And he picked the paper up, not at first to read it, preferring to look over its top at a bustling McAllister instead.

She was so neat and quick in all her movements, and Matey had made her careful. Sally-Anne had never before understood the necessity to be absolutely precise in everything she did, and Matey's training, designed to make her a good maid, was beginning to affect her habits in every other part of her life. She found that she was bringing more and more discipline to her writing for the *Clarion*, and thinking of this she noticed that it was the *Clarion* which Dr Neil was reading, or pretending to read, for her new awareness told her that, too.

Finally the coffee was steaming in its pot, as hot as good coffee should be; the cream had been fetched from its place on the cold stone slab in the pantry and poured into its jug, sugar cubes had been decanted into a tiny flowered porcelain bowl which matched the pot and the jug, together with a matching cup and saucer. Lastly a small plate of Nice biscuits was added, and the whole was arranged on a round tray which McAllister had polished the day before with the rest of the silver, beneath Matey's stern eye.

McAllister placed the tray on the table before Dr Neil and performed the parlourmaid's traditional bob after she had done so. He put down the paper, said, 'Thank you, McAllister, most commendable,' and then added, 'And now you may fetch another cup and saucer and drink with me.'

'No,' said McAllister, for Sally-Anne was trying hard to be a real maid, not a pretend one. 'That would not be proper.'

Dr Neil banged his fist quite gently on the table, and said in his most severe voice, 'McAllister! The Master commands. Jump, girl, jump!'

He had no idea why he was behaving in such a flighty way. After rescuing McAllister just over a fortnight ago, he had told himself firmly, This must stop! and himself had refused to listen. After Angela Deverill's cruel treatment of him he had vowed never to have anything to do with women again—other than to slake certain demanding bodily appetites—and then even the appetites had disappeared until McAllister had revived them.

He looked covertly across the table at her, at the vital face, the dark eyes, the generous, amused mouth, the blue-black hair loosely knotted on to the crown of her head, so that curls and tendrils clung around the perfect oval of her face. No, it really would not do. She was his servant, whatever she had been in her previous life, and she was ten or more years younger than himself, and what a battered old soldier he was, to be hungering after such a fresh young girl.

More, she was passionate and wilful, exactly the sort of creature a man badly damaged by life and love ought to avoid—only, he could not avoid her. He and Matey had employed servants before, even quite attractive ones, and he had felt no temptation at all, they had left him cold, but McAllister. . .

McAllister sat herself down opposite him and poured out two cups of coffee—he had refused to drink his own until she had joined him. McAllister could not prevent her eyes from straying to his newspaper. She had several almost overwhelming desires. One was to see her own column—for so J.D. called it—in print, another was to know whether or not Dr Neil had read it, and still another was to know what he thought of it—and none of these desires seemed likely to be satisfied.

She took one of the biscuits; they were Nice biscuits in the pretty floral tin today, quite her favourite; she preferred them to Marie.

'You make good coffee, McAllister,' Dr Neil said; he had noticed her eyes stray to his newspaper, now neglected on the table.

'Thank you, sir,' said McAllister primly, 'Americans usually do. English coffee invariably tastes of dishwater.'

And she added, without thinking, 'Even in the best houses.'

'But this is not a best house, is it?' said Dr Neil with a grin. 'And in the best houses master and servant do not sit drinking coffee, or anything else for that matter, together in the kitchen. And I suspect that the best houses would not allow the *Clarion Cry* inside their sacred boundaries.'

'I am a little surprised, Dr Neil,' said McAllister prim again, but managing to sneak another biscuit—she really did feel hungry and breakfast would not be served until Matey came down at about seven-thirty—'that you have seen fit to buy it.'

'I have my duties,' replied Dr Neil, assuming a pompous voice, 'and one of them is to know what is happening in the world. For that, *The Times* is not enough. I am informed that the *Clarion Cry* is the thing to read if one wishes to be in the know.'

'Then perhaps I ought to read it,' was McAllister's somewhat impertinent response to this statement.

'Not at all. It contains matter not fit for a delicate young lady such as yourself.'

'But I am a servant now,' said McAllister incontrovertibly, 'not a delicate young lady. And, as you frequently remind me, I do not know enough of the wicked world in which I live—so one might consider the *Clarion Cry* a useful means by which to educate me.'

'Touché again, you disrespectful minx,' said Dr Neil. 'Why do I ever argue with you, I ask myself, McAllister? I never seem to win. Did that remarkable papa of yours instruct you in logic-chopping, as well as in how to play a wicked game of chess?'

'Oh, Mama had a nice line in that, as well as Papa,' said McAllister, remembering for once to use the past tense when speaking of her parents. She eyed the biscuit plate and the *Clarion Cry* simultaneously—surely he would not mind if she took another biscuit?

'You are, I see, determined to be naughty,' announced Dr Neil. 'For not only do you wish to read this disreputable rag, but, according to your wolfish expression, you are yearning for another biscuit. Go on! Eat the whole plateful! Why should I stop you? And if Matey complains about their rapid disappearance you may tell her that I have developed a passion for them!'

'Oh, thank you,' said McAllister, seizing the plate before he could change his mind. 'All these chores are making me so hungry that it is, as I said before, only fair that you feed me properly in order to keep me going.'

'The problem is not keeping you going, McAllister, but getting you to stop. Such energy!' He picked up the paper. 'Shall I read you something decorous while you gorge yourself? If I can find anything, that is. Ah, I see that there is a column written by a lady, if we can trust the name above it, which is Vesta. I doubt me that many ladies write for old J.D.—a dubious proposition, that.'

He read in silence for a moment, then said, with a laugh, 'I see that you might enjoy this, although I am not sure your mama might not wish you to read it. It is all about those poor girls who behave as Rose did the other night, and suggests that a decent wage might prevent them from indulging in such conduct.'

He looked mischievously at her over the top of his paper. 'Yes, McAllister, I will continue to further your education. You may read it.' And he handed the newspaper to her across the table.

It took McAllister all her will-power not to wrench it from his grasp and to see and devour her work in one go. Somehow she managed to keep her self-control, opened it at the right page and began reading it slowly, as though she had never seen it before, although she knew every word by heart—because it was written from the heart.

She had just read the last paragraph when the kitchen door opened and Matey entered, far earlier than she normally did, to stare at the unlikely scene before her: Dr Neil characteristically leaning back in his wooden Windsor armchair, McAllister sitting on her stool, reading the paper, the used coffee-cups and the empty biscuit plate sitting between them.

'Well, well,' she said reprovingly, looking at the unfinished grate and thinking of all the other duties which McAllister should have performed by now. 'You are up early, Dr Neil, and are keeping McAllister from her work.'

'In a way, Matey, in a way,' said Dr Neil, lazily catching at her hand and pressing it as she passed him. 'McAllister's first duty is always to the Master, and so I commanded her to make me a pot of coffee. You must not reprimand her for doing as she was told.'

'And I suppose that you will inform me that you instructed her to drink a cup with you, as well,' said Matey drily. 'And I can only say that the Master will not like it if his breakfast and lunch do not arrive on time, because he serves his maid coffee, engages her in chit-chat, and encourages her to read disreputable papers when she ought to be blackleading the range, or scrubbing the kitchen floor.'

McAllister leapt to her feet. 'I will start work at once,' she said, casting a wistful eye on the *Clarion Cry* which she was leaving behind. Fortunately she had managed to read quickly through her own piece, which looked really professional, but she wondered what J.D. was thundering about on the editorial page. And then there were the letters. J.D. had told her on her last visit, when she had handed in the column she had just read, that there had been a large number of letters about Vesta's contribution and he would be publishing some of them in the next issue.

She finished the blackleading—a truly nasty job which she was glad to be done with early in the day. Dr Neil had left the kitchen, to finish his toilet, presumably. Matey was bustling about, doing some of the chores which McAllister had neglected while drinking coffee with him, and on opening the biscuit tin she complained bitterly that Dr Neil would eat them out of house and home if he continued to run through biscuits at his present rate—a judgement which amused McAllister, but also made her feel vaguely guilty.

Later that day, in the early afternoon, Matey was instructing McAllister in how to knit—something which had been left out of her previous education. Matey watched her, dark head bent over her work, hands busy, having mastered the basics of the task with what Matey thought was surprising speed.

She was not sure what she felt about the rapport which was springing up between her treasure and his now not so new maid. On the one hand he seemed much improved since her advent. When Matey had ventured a favourable comment about his midnight drinking having stopped, he had simply said, 'You must thank McAllister for that,' and so her influence seemed to be a good one. On the other hand, however, who and what was she? The mystery of her origins occupied both Matey and Dr Neil in quite different ways.

Almost as though she knew that Matey was thinking about her, McAllister looked up and said, 'I would never have thought that I would enjoy knitting so much, and the ladies' sewing circle, too.'

'So you will go again next week?' Matey asked.

McAllister nodded vigorously. 'Oh, yes, I want to help to make things for the big bazaar Mr Sands was talking about, to help those who live here in such misery.'

'Yes,' said Matey encouragingly, 'we hold it every year, and we usually make quite a large sum to give to the various charities connected with the Church.'

'I was thinking. . .' said McAllister slowly. 'When Miss Purdue showed us those baby clothes—the little dresses and nighties for the children of the poor fallen girls in the home on Callendar Street—they seemed so stark and plain. Would the circle mind if I embroidered some rosebuds on their bodices after the other ladies had made them up? And perhaps she might agree to allow the circle to make some fine ones in lawn to sell at the bazaar and I could do some white Swiss eyelet embroidery on them. Mama taught me how to do that when I was quite small. But I think that the poor girls might like something pretty, too.'

Her face was so earnest that Matey felt a lump in her throat. She thought that McAllister had never seen misery before, and that her response to it was a warm and loving one—and practical, too. Perhaps the fallen girls might behave better if they were not constantly reminded how different they were. She would support McAllister's idea to prettify the baby clothes; it might make the poor things feel happier and that someone really cared about them.

'No reason why I shouldn't suggest it,' she said briskly. 'But you would have to keep to your promise to do it, you know. No backsliding.'

'Oh, I always keep my word,' said McAllister, equally

brisk. 'Mama and Papa were always most particular about that.'

Matey, like Dr Neil, thought that McAllister might have been spoiled and pampered in her old life, but she had certainly been exposed to many good principles of conduct, even if she was headstrong.

'You can do an errand for me this afternoon, McAllister,' she said. 'One that I think that you would like. The housekeeper at the rectory said that they have a splendid display of late June roses this year and offered to let me have some. Would you like to take the trug from the kitchen cupboard and go and collect them for me?'

'Oh, yes,' said McAllister, jumping up; she liked walking and doing things rather than sitting about, even if she did enjoy knitting and plain sewing more than she had ever thought that she would. 'Do I need to change?'

She was wearing her afternoon uniform and Matey thought that she looked charming in it; it was not surprising, after all, that Dr Neil had a soft spot for her. She wore a black cotton frock with a very full skirt and frilly lace-edged petticoat underneath it, just showing. Her black stockings were finer than her morning ones, as were her buckled shoes. Over her frock she wore a spotless white apron decorated with lace; it had a little white top, similarly adorned, and perched on McAllister's lustrous blue-black curls was an elaborate white cap, lace-trimmed, with long white streamers.

'Oh, you will do very well as you are, child,' she replied. 'No-one will object to such a pretty uniform. Don't be too long, and try not to dawdle on the way there and back. Remember that Dr Neil is entertaining two of the doctors from the hospital and Mr Sands, the curate, to dinner tonight, and I shall need you back to help me—there will be a lot to do.'

McAllister nodded. Hooray! Freedom, if only for a short time, and she would have a chance to speak to Rose, whom she had not seen since their evening out together up West. Matey had told her that Rose had not returned home until the small hours, and the housekeeper there, Mrs Parker, a middle-aged widow, had almost turned her away, but had relented, although Rose had lost her next three half-days off as a punishment.

More of a punishment, perhaps, than Matey realised, McAllister thought, seeing that Rose would lose three free suppers, and some spare cash besides.

She found the trug in the outhouse, not the kitchen, and cleaned it before trotting off towards the rectory, which was quite a long walk from Vetch Street, through a rowdy street market where an organ-grinder and his monkey were performing, and a Punch and Judy man stood on the corner, and Sally-Anne—no longer McAllister now that she was out of the house—for all of her advanced years stood and watched Mr Punch for some time before she guiltily remembered what she was supposed to be doing.

She trotted off again, through a really insalubrious area known as Bligh's Corner, after some landlord, long dead, and she unconsciously quickened her pace a little so as to arrive in the relatively respectable square where the rectory stood, next door to St Jude's church where Dr Neil's household worshipped every Sunday.

Sally-Anne reached the gates and walked up to the rectory, an eighteenth-century building which had once been beautiful, but like the area around it had gone to seed badly, although Dr Neil had told her that it was elegant, if shabby inside. She had never visited it before, and looked around her with interest, remembering to go to the kitchen entrance. She had almost forgotten herself by walking to the big front door, and giggled inwardly at the shock that she would have given Mrs Parker if she had done so.

Rose answered the door, looking rather crushed. 'Ow, it's McAllister from Dr Neil's,' she called into the kitchen, unceremoniously. 'Ow are yer, McAllister? Got home safely, did yer, that night we spent up West?'

'Eventually,' said Sally-Anne, a little coolly.

'Thought as 'ow you would,' said Rose. 'Ave a good supper, did yer?' And she gave a grotesque wink.

'Yes,' said Sally-Anne truthfully, if deceitfully. 'Mrs Parker promised Miss Mates some roses, and I've called to collect them.'

'Don't keep the gel on the doorstep, you gaby,' said Mrs Parker. 'Tell her to come in.' And Rose led Sally-Anne into a large and airy kitchen full of the smells of a good afternoon's baking, its windows giving a splendid view of lawns and flowerbeds, full of blossoming rose-bushes. The rector, the Reverend Mr Hallam, was a bachelor, and his garden was his only passion—his ministry quite wilted before it.

Mrs Parker unpinned the large white apron she had worn to bake in. 'Mind you look after the tarts, Bailey, while I collect some roses for the gel here to take to Miss Mates. What's your name, gel?'

'McAllister,' answered Sally-Anne, remembering to do her servant's bob.

'Well, you come with me, McAllister. I hope you've got more sense than Bailey here. You don't look it, though Miss Mates speaks well of you.'

Mrs Parker bounced into a garden shed, came out with a pair of secateurs. 'A dozen and a half red ones should do, I think. Ena Harkness,' she added. 'Hold your trug out, gel.' And she cut a dozen and a half splendid blooms and laid them reverently in Sally-Anne's trug.

'Oh, what a lovely garden,' said Sally-Anne, looking around her as the last bloom was placed on her pile.

'Like it, do you?' said Mrs Parker, pleased. 'A Yankee, aren't you? Do you have gardens in America?'

'Yes,' said Sally-Anne respectfully, thinking of her mother's splendid garden, but she also thought that St Jude's garden was an oasis in the wilderness.

'Sit down before you go,' said Mrs Parker kindly; she thought McAllister a great improvement over Bailey, so soft-spoken and pleasant. 'It's hot today. I was thinking of giving Bailey and myself a rest and having some lemonade. I'll bring you a glass when we've finished cooking—which shouldn't be long if Bailey has done as she was told. I know Miss Mates won't mind you having a rest before that long walk back. She's a kind soul.'

Sally-Anne sat down on a wooden bench, the trug at her feet, and drowsed a little in the sun. She was feeling tired, what with all her hard work and the walk, and writing for J.D. after her long day was over. Miss Mates had said not to dawdle, but surely she wouldn't mind McAllister having a little rest and a long, cool drink? Mrs Parker's lemonade would be highly welcome when it arrived. . . She dozed off.

Dr Neil arrived home in the middle of the afternoon. His round had been long and arduous, and he was thinking how pleasant it would be to see and tease McAllister and ask her to serve them all some home-made lemonade.

But the little house was quiet, and the reason was plain. Matey was seated on her own in the parlour, darning, and there was no sign of McAllister.

'Lost McAllister, have we?' he said, tossing his soft

grey hat on to the sideboard. Not for the first time Matey noted that his first thought was of his maid.

'I sent her to St Jude's Rectory to collect the roses which Mrs Parker promised me,' said Matey, looking at the clock. 'I thought that they'd make the parlour look nice for your dinner party tonight. She really ought to be back by now.'

'To the rectory?' said Dr Neil, struck. 'You let her go there on her own, through the market and across Bligh's Corner? It's not really a safe route for a pretty girl like McAllister.'

'Oh, come, Neil,' said Matey, speaking to him as though he were eight again. 'She's getting on for twenty-one years old, and perfectly capable of looking after herself.'

'Oh, no, she's not,' said Dr Neil grimly. 'She's a regular babe in the wood in the East End, however knowledgeable she might be in her own world—wherever that is.' He had sunk into his armchair, but jumped up. 'I'll go and collect her, or meet her on the way home. There's only one route she can take.'

Matey opened her mouth to remonstrate with him, but forbore. Best to say nothing, perhaps—and she watched him pick up his hat and dash off to save McAllister from any dragons she might meet between Vetch Street and the rectory.

Sally-Anne was still seated on her bench, the empty lemonade glass beside her. The rose-filled trug was at her feet. She had her back to the entrance of the garden and was looking across it at a small orchard whose fruit never found its way to the rector's table, always being pilfered by the small street arabs of the district. She did not hear Dr Neil come up behind her until he said, 'So there you are, McAllister. I was fearful that I might find you down another alley.'

She turned towards him. He had removed his soft hat and the sun was gilding his hair.

'So you came to rescue me,' she said, teasing him for a change. 'But, as you see, I don't need a knight errant this afternoon.'

'No,' he agreed, 'but all the same I shall walk you home. I need you to help Matey with my dinner party and I shall make sure you arrive in the kitchen in one piece.'

'I shall not,' said Sally-Anne grandly, 'reproach you, Dr Neil, for rescuing me merely to ensure that I shall carry on skivvying for you. On the contrary, I am wondering how I may reward you. . . I know. . .' she said, and bending down, picked up the most beautiful of the blooms. 'A favour for my knight,' she said, and handed it to him.

Dr Neil bent down to take the bloom from her, and as their hands met his heart gave a great lurch. The piquant face looking up at him was alive with mirth.

He swallowed and the world steadied again. 'Come,' he said. 'I accept your favour, my lady, although I may not wear it on my sleeve as a true knight should. And now work awaits us both. We may not dally here among the roses in Arcadia—more's the pity.'

'Yes, indeed,' said Sally-Anne, rising. 'I must peel the potatoes for Matey, and you must take evening surgery and be ready for your guests.'

Dr Neil carefully replaced her recent gift to him in the trug, before taking it from her, and watched by Rose, peering interestedly from the kitchen window, they set out together for Vetch Street.

Oddly, Neil's suspicions about McAllister's presence in the East End, dormant since his rescue of her, were revived by his sudden awareness of how much she was coming to mean to him. It was almost as though he was trying to erect walls around his heart to protect himself from his softer feelings.

'Still enjoying your masquerade, McAllister?' he offered, and although his voice was soft there was a sting in his words.

Sally-Anne—she would not be McAllister again until she reached Vetch Street—bit her lip. She thought that he had stopped his baiting of her, had accepted her, if not exactly for what she claimed to be, but as herself.

'I'm sure I don't know what you mean, sir.' And her voice was a parody of a servant's showing dissent, a politeness which verged on the impolite.

'You know perfectly well what I mean.' He gave a little laugh and tightened the hand he had placed on her arm—Sally-Anne had not offered to take his; that was not a servant's right. 'I live in fear every evening, McAllister, that I shall come home to find that our unlikely treasure has flown the nest, tired of playing with us.'

Sally-Anne wrenched her arm away from his hand, stopped, and turned to face him, regardless of interested spectators. 'I am not playing,' she informed him fiercely, 'and I shall not leave you without due notice, however inconvenient.'

'Three months' notice,' he said, and his voice was kind again—her high spirits always amused him. 'I shall demand my full pound of flesh, McAllister, be sure of that. I warn you, the Master will not lightly lose such a hard-working and decorative part of his household.'

This was a declaration of sorts, however lightly made, and one which Dr Neil had not thought to make to any woman in any form, and before Sally-Anne could take in its full meaning he rapidly continued, 'And now let us stop providing entertainment for the passers-by. You look ready to dance with rage, and although we might collect a few pennies from them in return for our providing such a spectacle I hardly think that we could put it on as a permanent entertainment!'

He tucked her arm in his again, so firmly and gently that without actually fighting him off she had no alternative but to walk on by his side.

'Oh. . .' began Sally-Anne furiously, and then caught his twinkling eyes, and one raised eyebrow—— He was waiting, she knew, to see how she would react.

And she began to laugh, her temper draining away, and for the first time she realised that he was frequently doing something which no one else had ever succeeded in doing before—he was defusing her rage. The famous high temper which no one, not even her formidable papa, knew how to cope with, once she was on fire, was being controlled by a man whose outward-seeming was mild and pleasant, although beneath Dr Neil's bland exterior she was beginning to sense a will as strong and resolute as her own.

What on earth would Mama and Papa say if they knew? How did *he* do it, when they couldn't? Jared Tunstall, who manipulated billions of dollars, made and broke men at will, whose power was legendary, had never managed in a clash of wills with the daughter he adored to overcome her, once she had made her mind up, or decided on a course of action.

And even when, in the end, he had sent her to London, to her uncle Orrin, after one last, disastrous, raging tempest, he had managed her physical transference from the United States to England, but her will had remained unbroken. She had refused to give an inch.

So why could Dr Neil, with a few words and a

sidelong look, lance her indignation so easily, compel her to reassess herself and life? She looked sidelong at him, walking along beside her, his unspoiled profile presented to her; but the other scarred side did not matter, because it was Dr Neil who mattered, not his face. . .

Sally-Anne stopped. Oh! She had read of Cupid, the little god of love, and of his wicked darts piercing the heart at the moment of understood love, and she had laughed a little at the idea; but one of them had struck home at last, and she knew that on the two previous occasions when she had previously and disastrously thought herself in love it had not been love at all. . .

This, then, was love. So sweet and strong that merely to be beside the loved object, to feel his hand on her arm, was enough. No! No! It wasn't! She wanted more, much more, than that. She wanted to please him, to see him smile, and tease her by calling himself the Master, and pretending that she was his slave.

And—oh, she also wanted—no, desired—to stroke his smiling face, to run the tips of her fingers gently along the dreadful scar to show that she loved every part of him, to. . . For the first time in many months she contemplated the uncontemplatable, and thought that it might not be so with him, even though her heart began to thud uncomfortably at the very idea.

She had stopped without thinking, stopping him as well. He turned his lazy smile on her, and asked, 'What is it McAllister? Not another swoon, I trust?'

'Yes—no,' she said idiotically. 'It's nothing. My heart missed a beat. . .' And oh, that was yet another lie, for it was not nothing, it was something. Sally-Anne Tunstall had found her true love at last.

CHAPTER NINE

Of course, Matey was not best pleased that she had taken so long to come home—or so McAllister thought when the older woman came towards them after Dr Neil had let them both in. He thought that McAllister had been oddly subdued on the walk home, and had surreptitiously admired her face—even more beautiful, he thought, when pensive, even though in her early days at Vetch Street it had been her animation which he had admired.

Admired! What a word! It was love he was beginning to experience, and what a joke that was. How could he be falling in love with the beautiful cuckoo in his nest who was exactly the sort of pampered darling a poor doctor ought to avoid? When she had tired of her games she would take wing and fly away, and even if she stayed, how likely would it be that she could ever settle down as that poor doctor's wife?

He too realised that Matey was not pleased, but it was not their late arrival which was troubling her, but something else, as soon became apparent. She ignored McAllister, and said sharply to Dr Neil, 'You have a visitor. I have put her in the parlour; she insisted on waiting until you returned.'

'Oh,' said Dr Neil, staring at Matey. 'Is it Teresa Darrell?'

'Worse than that,' said Matey grimly. 'Lady Macleod. I told her you'd not be best pleased to see her, but she insisted on staying, as I said before.'

McAllister was fascinated. Another woman chasing

Dr Neil! Well, she wasn't surprised; he was eminently chaseable. And was this strange emotion she was experiencing jealousy?

Matey turned her attention to McAllister. 'You've taken long enough to do a simple errand, I must say. Never mind.' She took the flower-filled trug from Dr Neil, admired the blooms, adding briskly, 'Come along, McAllister; you might as well make up for lost time,' and all three of them walked into the parlour, Matey and McAllister of necessity, since it was their only indoor access to the kitchen.

A blonde woman fashionably dressed in half-mourning, wearing a violet gown, her hair dressed high under a huge picture hat trimmed with a bird of paradise in full flight, rose to meet them, or rather to meet Dr Neil. She threw a cursory glance at Matey, inclining her head slightly, made no gesture at all to McAllister, but merely stared inimically at her, offended by such youthful, dewy charm.

'Ah, Neil, there you are,' she announced. 'I thought that you would never come home, but I would have waited until the cock crowed.' An unfortunate allusion, thought McAllister nastily, who knew her Bible, and that the cock crowed after betrayal, and from what Matey had said this woman specialised in betrayal.

'I have my duties to perform, Lady Macleod,' he said sternly, face and voice frozen alike.

'Oh, not Lady Macleod, surely,' she said sweetly, putting a gloved hand out to him, and then proceeding to remove her gloves as provocatively as she could. 'Angela, always Angela, Neil.'

McAllister could not remember having seen her in her old life in high society, which was fortunate, perhaps. She was a violet-eyed beauty, her figure full and voluptuous, a regular fly-trap. McAllister's thoughts were growing nastier and nastier, but she could not endure the sight of the woman who Matey had said had trampled on Dr Neil and rejected him after he had sustained his war wounds and started his new career as a doctor.

She felt Matey take her by the arm and pull her rapidly away. 'Come on, McAllister. Work to do!' And her last sight of them was Dr Neil standing cold and upright, the scar on his white face angry and vivid, facing the lovely woman whose whole posture was that of a pleading Niobe—McAllister wondered where all these classical allusions were suddenly coming from, remembering that Niobe was famous for her tears, and for their power. Would they have the power to move Dr Neil?

Angela Macleod breathed a sigh of relief at the closing door—never mind that every word they uttered might be heard in the kitchen.

'You must know why I have come, Neil,' she said, and she held out her arms to him.

'No, Lady Macleod,' he said, his voice still relentless. 'I have no idea why you are here. And I must inform you that you are not welcome—not welcome at all!'

'Oh, never say that, Neil. Remember what we once meant to one another.' Her eyes brimmed with tears. 'And Hector is dead, Neil, dead these six months. Think what that means for us.'

'Yes, I know that Hector is dead. Stair told me so. It means nothing to me, madam.'

'Oh, Neil,' she wailed, the tears falling at last, great crystal drops. 'You do not know what my life has been these last ten years with *him*. As soon as we were married he took me off to Scotland, kept me there in virtual purdah, never let me out of his sight—his jealousy was manic. I thought of you every day, of how we could have been together, and now we may start again.'

'Start again!' He laughed and the sound was frightening. 'Do you remember what you said to me in this very room when I begged you to marry me and you told me that you were going to marry him? Shall I remind you of what you said?'

'Oh, Neil, do not judge me too harshly. I was so young and foolish and I did not know what I was doing.' She had crossed the room to stand before him, and the scent of her expensive perfume was in his nostrils—and it nauseated him.

'You knew very well what you were doing,' he replied, not giving her an inch of himself, wondering how he ever could have desired her. Maturity had given her extra beauty, but her predatory nature was written on her face. 'You were marrying a rich old man for his money and rejecting the crippled boy who had been your sweetheart since childhood, and whose engagement ring you wore. You were not made to marry a poor man and live in an East End hovel, you said.'

'Ah, but you need not do that now, Neil,' she answered him feverishly, seeing him slip from her. 'I am a rich woman; he left everything to me, and so he should have done, after all that I sacrificed for him. And now we can be together again, and enjoy the life we were always meant to have.' And she put her arms around his neck and tried to place her mouth on his.

Dr Neil stepped back so swiftly that she almost fell; he seized her by the shoulders and held her from him. 'Do you think to wipe out what you said and did, and ten years' loneliness, so easily? I worshipped you, Angela, thought that I was coming back to you, and when you left me, you left me with nothing. My life is here, and I have no intention of sharing it with you, not if you offered me an Empire, let alone a castle in Scotland and the fortune of a man whom I despised and who I warned you would treat you badly. You are ten years too late with your offer of yourself. And I have half a mind to take you at your word, give you what you seem to want and turn you out of my house after I have finished with you.'

Her eyes glittered, and, mouth twisting, she flung away from him. 'Oh, you were always a fool, Neil, always—a fool to think that I would be content to live on nothing with a younger son and a fool to reject me now that I can give you the life which you ought to be living.'

She had begun to pull on the long suede gloves which she had earlier stripped from her beautiful hands. 'But I suppose that you are consoling yourself after the fashion of a fool who lives in the slums. Does that pert chit you were escorting home satisfy you, Neil? You used to be more fastidious, used to be above servants——"We must not exploit them," you told Hector once—how we laughed over that!'

Neil strode to the door, opened it, and held it open. 'I must ask you to leave, Lady Macleod. Your insults to myself I can stomach; those you choose to demean an innocent young girl with are quite another thing. Miss McAllister is in my home under my and Matey's protection. You forget yourself.'

Angela, Lady Macleod, who had once been Angela Deverill and whom he had thought that he had loved more than life itself, picked up her parasol, an object as lovely and useless as she was.

'And that is your last word, Neil? Remember, I shall not come to you again.'

'My pleasure, Lady Macleod,' he said curtly. 'I do

not wish to see you again. Pray take your leave; you have outstayed your welcome these past ten years.'

She was by him and was gone, the door closing behind her, this time for good. He had thought that he had done with her long ago, had assumed that she had lost the power to hurt him.

He did not know, indeed, which hurt him the most—the memory of the bright young girl she had been, or the knowledge that now, having sold herself to a rich old man, she had come, once that man had died, to try to buy him for herself.

In the kitchen Matey and McAllister had been compelled to hear every brutal word—neither Dr Neil nor his tormentor had kept their voice down—bustle about and bang pots as they might. McAllister wanted to go in and do something, anything, to stop such a harpy from hurting him.

She knew that he would be hurt even though she hoped that he had stopped loving such an undeserving, self-serving shrew, because anyone would be hurt by such a scene.

Once the outer door had banged shut, Matey said, violently for her, 'Good riddance to bad rubbish! Thank God she's gone,' and the unwonted strength of her language betrayed the depth of her feelings. 'She hurt him dreadfully when he came home from Africa, crippled and his career in the army over, just when he needed her loving support the most, and now she has the gall to chase him again, when I hoped and prayed that he had finally recovered from her brutal treatment of him.'

'She's very beautiful,' was all that McAllister could say to that.

'Handsome is as handsome does,' snapped Matey, who as an ex-children's nurse had a fund of such sayings. 'And by that maxim, McAllister, she's as ugly as sin and high time Master Neil realised it.' He had reverted to being her youthful charge, as he always did when she was worried about him, and McAllister uttered a fervent inward Amen.

There was silence from the other room. Usually when he was giving one of his little dinners he came into the kitchen while they were preparing it, joked with them, had his hands smacked smartly by Matey when he lifted saucepan lids and tried to peer into the oven; but today he stayed away.

'Take him some tea,' said Matey, who was rolling pastry for a raspberry tart. 'I'm worried. He shouldn't be on his own.'

How the British depended on tea—but it seemed a good idea. McAllister bustled in her turn, made the tea and carried the silver tray through into the parlour, to find Dr Neil at the sideboard, looking grim, the whisky bottle in his hand. She thought that he'd not started to drink, but might at any moment.

'Tea's better for you than that stuff,' she said pertly, as pert as the chit Angela Macleod had called her. She did not know that Neil's anger and disgust with his old love had been fuelled more by her unpleasant reference to McAllister than anything else she had said to him.

But for a moment he looked thunder at her impertinence, then put the bottle down and began to laugh.

'No use supposing that you didn't hear all that passed, McAllister,' he said. 'Neither of us kept our voice down. Tell me, what should I have done? Run off with her and the money which she sold herself for?'

McAllister did not quite know how to answer him, and said slowly, 'I suppose that at some time or other we all sell ourselves for something.'

Dr Neil stared at her, took the tea-tray from her

hands, put it on a side-table. 'What a wise child you are becoming, McAllister. Is it living in Vetch Street that is changing you?'

'Or the people who live here,' she said, greatly daring, but she would say anything to keep his mind off the bottle.

'I don't want her, you know,' he said, pouring the tea in an amber stream into his cup. 'But she revived old memories, and sometimes memories hurt more than the acts which created them.'

'I know,' said McAllister, closing her eyes against her own unwanted memories.

'You do?' he said, putting the teapot down. 'Yes, I believe you do, McAllister. But surely you have no dreadful memories, so young and fresh as you are?'

'They are one thing we all have,' she replied, opening her eyes. 'Our ideas of what is dreadful may differ.'

For a moment Dr Neil was silent, then, 'Come and sit by me, McAllister.'

'Should I, Dr Neil?' she said, but gently.

'Perhaps not, but I command it. The Master commands it, his slave must obey.' And a hint of his normal happy, teasing manner to her was in his voice.

McAllister sat down, opposite him, in one of the Maplewood dining chairs.

'You have only brought one teacup with you, McAllister, so we may not share the tea as we shared the coffee earlier today.'

'Matey will expect me back to help her.'

'I suspect Matey sent you in deliberately instead of coming herself,' was his only answer to that. 'You know that I nearly broke my word to you about drinking just now, McAllister.'

'Yes,' she said, and to lighten the situation added, 'And had you done so I would have dropped all the dishes for your dinner party tonight over your unfortunate guests to show that two can break a promise!'

That did the trick, didn't it just! 'Oh, I'm glad that I behaved myself, then,' he said, his face clearing suddenly. What a fool I am, he thought, still to mourn for a lost past and a girl who existed only in my imagination, the reality being so different, when I have this ardent, hardworking. . .child. . .to keep me company, so different from the mercenary beauty who has just left. I should be running up a flag to celebrate her going, not behaving like a weak boy myself. And he looked at McAllister sitting primly before him, hands in her lap, the face beneath the lace cap so enchanting that Angela Macleod, née Deverill, and all her works, flew away forever, and he knew again where his heart now lay.

His face betrayed him to McAllister. Her own heart thudding dangerously, the atmosphere between them charged, she rose. 'I really must be going to Matey, Dr Neil. I am neglecting my duties.'

He rose, too, and they stood, face to face.

'No,' he said slowly, put up his hand to brush back a lustrous curl which had strayed from its bonds. 'No, McAllister, don't go.' And he put up his other hand to clasp her face, gazing ardently into her blue-black eyes, and his intention was suddenly plain.

He began to drop his head to find her parted lips, and McAllister, who was prey to the most extraordinary and conflicting emotions, one part of her welcoming a kiss from Dr Neil, whom she loved, a kiss which she knew would be passionate, the other part hating and fearing being held or touched by any man, including him, said breathlessly, 'No, you shouldn't. You must not; Matey. . .' She pushed at his chest, fear and love fighting for mastery in her.

Something she said, perhaps Matey's name, the lack

of privacy for the two of them in the small house, although they had both kept their voices low, stopped him.

He stepped back, smiled wryly, and said, 'I wasn't consoling myself after Angela Macleod, McAllister. You do believe me. That. . .kiss. . .would have been truly for you, no one else.'

What could she say but, 'I believe you, Dr Neil, and I really must go, or. . .'

'Matey will think that we are doing what I was about to do.' He laughed softly. 'Oh, you are a witch, McAllister, a very witch, designed to turn any man's head. Even *she* saw that. Yes, you may go.' And lightly, now that the danger was over, 'The Master commands you to go.'

'And you promise not to drink Matey's "nasty stuff"?'

'Yes,' he said, 'and will you keep my guests safe from flying pots and food?'

'Agreed,' responded McAllister gaily, and then in a flash was back in the kitchen, Matey's shrewd eyes on her. Their interchange had been soft, not loud, and McAllister wondered how much Matey had heard, and whether she approved or not—and did not care.

Full summer, the heat of late July was on Vetch Street. The dead flies on the fly-papers which hung in every room bore witness to that. Even so, one naughty specimen, avoiding the fate of its fellows, buzzed around McAllister's head.

She was engaged in dressing a doll for the bazaar which loomed nearer and nearer. The doll had been given in all its naked glory by one of the poorer parishioners, a relic of better days, and McAllister had undertaken to make its trousseau. She had finished the sewing part, and was now knitting its little coat. When that was finished the doll would be ready for sale, and it would be all her own work. She had already embroidered a dozen little nighties for the babies of the fallen girls, decorating them with tiny pink rosebuds and pale green leaves.

Since Angela Macleod's visit her rapport with Dr Neil had grown stronger and stronger, although he had never touched her again. Her duties over, she played chess with him in the evening, or childish card and board games with him and Matey, laughed, talked and read, in some odd way enjoying herself in this hard life more than she had ever done before in her old soft one.

Late at night she kept up her journal and wrote her column for J.D., and on her last visit he had offered her a post on his editorial staff, a full-time one, when she had finished her East End stint, as he called it.

'But not yet,' he had said. 'Your work is still creating interest, and the women of the Fabian Society are talking of following it up with a scientific examination of the social and economic condition of the women in the poorer parts of London, carrying on where Booth in his great survey of poverty left off.'

'No one. . .' began Sally-Anne passionately, thinking of all that she had seen since arriving in Vetch Street—the poor creatures in Dr Neil's surgery, and the even poorer ones who could not afford to go there—and of Dr Neil's own selflessness letting people off their bills, so that only the small income he still received from an aunt's legacy allowed him to keep going at all, when he could have been revelling with Stair. 'No one who has not lived among them knows how hard their lives are, how wretched their condition, could imagine what they suffer. Anything that I can do to help them, any words I write which may soften their lot, is little enough.'

Like Dr Neil, J.D. thought how much she had

changed and was still changing. The flighty girl she had been was graver, and her compassion was real because the suffering of which she spoke was no longer an abstract thing to her.

This afternoon, however, all that was far from her mind. She was on her own: Dr Neil had been called out some time ago to attend a woman in childbirth, and Matey had gone to visit an old friend in St John's Wood, and she was the sole mistress of the doctor's house in Vetch Street.

A little earlier the mother of Dr Neil's surgery boy, who carried out the doctor's errands on the bicycle which lived in the outhouse, had come to say that Eddie had broken his arm and would not be fit to carry out his duties. She had been crying, for the money Eddie earned was precious, and McAllister had not known what to say, only that she was sorry and would inform Dr Neil when he had returned.

McAllister finished the right front of the coatee, as Matey called it, cast off, and looked again at the half-grandfather clock with a sigh. Half-past three. Dared she make herself a cup of tea in Matey's absence? Of course she dared.

She was just lighting the gas on the tiny ring when the knocker on the front door sounded a veritable tattoo. Irritably—she really wanted that cup of tea; she was growing as bad as the British—McAllister turned off the gas ring, blew out the match, and walked to the front door, grumbling to herself, Hold your horses, I'm coming, I'm coming, when another urgent series of knocks sounded.

She opened the door and there was Rose, dirty and dishevelled. She said urgently, 'Ow, McAllister, Dr Neil says to send his boy wiv his emergency bag and some towelling, and quick about it.'

McAllister stared at her. 'Where is he?' she said practically, and then, 'Oh, shoot, I can't send the boy; he's broken his arm today.'

'Doctor says to be quick,' repeated Rose, 'and he's in our Buildings. One of them upstairs is avin' a bad time, and 'er only fourteen, too.'

McAllister hopped up and down gently, her reaction the common one of a child to worrying news. 'Oh, dear,' she wailed, 'he must want his bag urgently to send for Eddie,' and then, irrelevantly, 'Why aren't you at work, Rose?'

'Turned off, wasn't I?' said Rose. 'For slippin' aht at night. The missis caught me, and that was that.'

McAllister made up her mind; if Eddie could not cycle to the Buildings then why should not she? After all, she knew where he was, and although it was a man's bicycle, not a woman's, she could surely manage to ride it. She began to pull off her apron. 'I'll go,' she said, and ran to the surgery to collect the bag, and to pick up the roll of towelling and a pair of scissors which Dr Neil kept for emergencies.

She dragged the bicycle from the shed, placed the bag and the towelling, a little insecurely, in the basket at the front and somehow managed to throw her leg, encumbered by her heavy skirts, over the high framework, so different from the shape of the one on which Papa had taught her to ride.

'Ow, McAllister, that don't look safe,' panted Rose as she wheeled herself and the bike into the road, preparatory to setting off for the buildings.

'Never mind,' called McAllister, 'needs must. . .' and wobbled down Vetch Street, praying that she arrived at her destination in one piece, the balance of the wretched thing being all wrong, especially with the overloaded basket at the front. Behind her Rose followed her at a wheezing trot, keeping up with her, until she suddenly mastered the antiquated machine, and sped away, feeling like a Swiss mountaineer with his St Bernard dog, setting off on his errand of mercy.

CHAPTER TEN

DR NEIL COCHRANE was engaged in one of the worst tasks a doctor had to face: attempting to save the life of a young girl and the child she was trying to bear, after earlier neglect and mismanagement from the moment the birth had begun.

He had cleared the small, fetid room, in which five persons lived, of everyone but the girl's grandmother, who seemed to have some idea of how to help him—the girl's mother was a defeated, apathetic creature only just over thirty herself. The grandmother was capable of fetching water from the tap in the courtyard, if nothing else.

Pulling out his watch, he stared at its unkind face. Would Eddie never come? Rose should surely have reached Vetch Street by now and Eddie been sent on his way by Matey or McAllister after being summoned from his nearby home.

A face peered round the door at him. His patient, a girl whose age was uncertain—he judged her to be about fourteen or fifteen—was at the moment quiescent, her face as grey as the linen on which she lay, her eyes closed. Her pains, which had started long before a frightened Rose, acting as an amateur midwife, had thought to send for him, had stopped—a bad sign.

He impatiently waved the face away; he wanted no useless, interfering spectators, and the impatience was as much for his own continued failure as for the uncaring curiosity of the woman who had looked in—life was cheap in the Buildings.

The old grandma who was holding the girl's hand looked across at him as he walked to the window to stare down into the street to watch for Eddie. He really should have had the sense to bring his emergency bag and the roll of towelling with him, but Rose's terrified urgency had sent him on his way with all speed. He could not have visualised such a desperate situation as the one which he had found.

And then he saw McAllister. She had mastered Eddie's cycle and came around the corner as though she were taking part in one of the bicycle races which had recently become such a popular spectator sport.

'McAllister! What the devil. . .? Where's Eddie?' He watched her swing an indelicate leg over the top bar of her man's bike, displaying a neatly rounded calf which would normally have engaged his interest, but in the cruel circumstances failed to register.

She pulled the bag and the towelling from the carrier, hitched up her skirts to show yet more leg—still unheeded—and dashed into the Buildings. He could hear her frantic progress up the uncarpeted stairs and along the top corridor until she threw the door open.

Panting, her hair coming down, her face red with the effort of riding at speed, she thrust the bag at him, saying breathlessly, 'Rose said that you wanted this. Eddie couldn't come, he's broken his arm, so I came instead.' She hung on to the towelling and the scissors, and then looked around the dismal room to find a clean surface on which she could put them.

Fascinated, Dr Neil, who had opened the bag and was beginning to pull out strange-looking forceps and a bottle of chloroform, watched her lift up her black skirt to reveal a spotless white petticoat, from which she cut a large square which she placed on the grimy table, having first cleared to one side the used cups and plates covered in half-eaten food.

McAllister, coughing slightly against the stench of the room—Dr Neil was hardened to it—laid the towelling and the scissors on the clean square, and said briskly to Dr Neil, 'Is there anything in your bag which you might need urgently? If so, you can give it to me to keep clean and I can hand it to you when you want it. Dr Bodkin of New York General told Papa once that surgical instruments should be kept absolutely spotless. Do we have any boiling water or carbolic soap?'

She knew very little about surgery and nothing about childbirth, but she had a fund of common sense, and the moment she had pushed through the useless, wailing women downstairs, and seen the squalid room in which Dr Neil was working, she had begun to dredge up what little she knew in order to help him. She hoped that she would not disgrace herself by fainting, or by being unable to help him through fear or disgust of what she might be seeing. At the moment the girl on the bed looked comatose, but she supposed that would not last.

'What do you think you're doing McAllister?' asked Dr Neil as she walked towards him, just at the moment when the girl began to moan and thrash about, her pains suddenly returning in full force. 'You can't stay here. It's not a fit place for a young girl to be.'

'And it's not a fit place for a young girl to have a baby,' snapped McAllister, who had just seen that his patient was little more than a child, 'but she's having one, all the same. Surely even an amateur nurse would be helpful.' She looked at the grandma, who although willing seemed full of the resigned acceptance of disaster which had ruled the women downstairs.

'I don't want a nurse who might scream or faint when matters become difficult, or would swoon at the sight of blood,' said Dr Neil, a little frantically, trying to care for his patient and send McAllister away at the same time.

'You are really wasting your energy on me,' said McAllister severely, 'when you should be concentrating on your patient. If I promise not to shriek or have hysterics, will that do? As for the sight of blood, that has never overset me.'

'Oh, very well,' he said wearily; he might have known that it was useless to argue with McAllister—her tongue was as long as her will was strong. 'Make sure that the old grandma keeps up a constant supply of hot water to keep the instruments clean. You may cut the towelling into large squares, and then you can come and be my nurse—and God help you, McAllister, if you hinder me by starting to have fine lady's vapours. Things are bad enough here without that!'

McAllister, for once, did as she was told. Dr Neil's face was nearly as grey as his patient's, and she did not wish to distract him, but to help him, rather. The towelling prepared, she made a neat pile of it, and then went over to the large bed, on which four or five persons normally slept. The girl was now writhing and moaning faintly, barely conscious of what was happening to her.

She saw McAllister, though, and caught at her hand.

'That's right,' said Dr Neil encouragingly. 'You hold on to McAllister. And McAllister, you can keep Effie here steady for me while I take another look at her. Put that pillow under the small of her back so that I can lift her legs. Yes, that's right. Now we can have a look inside.'

McAllister swallowed when he bent between the girl's extended legs, and Effie shrieked aloud, throwing herself about, trying to avoid his gently probing hands.

'Hold her steady,' he commanded. 'She'll not hurt

herself then.' And the internal examination over, he said to McAllister, 'Lay her down. She'll be quiet for a moment, I believe.' Which proved true. The girl had fallen half-conscious into McAllister's arms.

'Now fetch me some towelling, wet it in that bowl of water and hand it to me. . .'

Trembling and obedient, McAllister did as she was bidden. She was already feeling faint, as much from the stale heat of the attic room as for any other reason. Dr Neil wiped his hand on one of the pieces of towelling.

Effie was lying quite still, her eyes shut, her swollen stomach seeming too large for her otherwise immature body.

'What's wrong?' whispered McAllister bluntly. 'I didn't think childbirth was normally as difficult as this.'

Dr Neil discarded the towel, throwing it into a packing-case, checked that his patient was not needing immediate attention, and drew McAllister into the far corner of the room where their conversation could not be overheard.

'I suppose, McAllister, if you're going to be of any real use to me——' He was interrupted by Rose bursting in, a Greek chorus of depressed-looking women following her.

'Ow, McAllister, yer got 'ere safely, then. Can I 'elp, Dr Neil?'

'Yes, Rose—and the rest of you, out! This is not a raree show. And you, Rose, if you want to be useful you may keep everyone away, run any errands I may require, and take over from, or help McAllister, when I tell you to. You can help the old grandma to keep up a supply of hot water.'

He bent over the bed once again. He had spoken in the voice of the army officer he had once been, expecting instant obedience, showing McAllister a man far removed from the one she had now known for over two months.

'Now,' he said, after inspecting Effie again, and taking McAllister out of earshot, 'listen carefully to me, for I don't want to repeat myself later when things get difficult. Effie here is in a bad way for several reasons. She is weak for lack of good food, she has plainly suffered from rickets, her body is not yet sufficiently mature for her to carry a child successfully to term, and on top of all that her baby is coming in quite the wrong fashion.

'A normal baby arrives head first to make childbirth as easy as possible—and even that would have been difficult for her, given her narrow pelvis——You do know what and where a pelvis is, I hope, McAllister?'

Yes, McAllister did know all about pelvises, but had the sense not to spark back at him that, of course, she did know to what he was referring.

'But this baby is coming feet first, which is very bad indeed, and makes a successful delivery very difficult. Had I been sent for much earlier I would have tried to turn the baby—but now. . .it's too late. First she was on her own with Rose and some of the women, then they sent for the midwife, who didn't turn up, and only after that did they think to come for me. So, we have a long, hard task before us.'

He had said 'we', which heartened McAllister enormously but also meant that she must try to justify his confidence, and not let him down; he must not think her a fine lady only playing at life—she meant to do her share, and yet try not to hinder him.

'Listen to me carefully,' he continued, his face grave. 'I want you to measure out an ounce of chloroform in the jug you will find in my bag. With the chloroform we can ease Effie's pains at this stage. You must only give her an ounce every hour, and you will only start when I tell you, and stop immediately I order you to. You understand me?'

She nodded mutely, and while she did as she was told he went over to the bed where Effie had begun to writhe and cry out, and her pains, which were erratic, had started again—that they were so erratic was another bad sign, Dr Neil quietly explained.

'Sit by her,' he ordered. 'Let her take your hand, stroke hers; it will comfort her a little, and when I tell you give her the chloroform——Good—that's the way. Now, when she is fully dilated, which will take some time, I will tell you to stop. That way, we shall save her a great deal of pain, and she can husband her strength for when she needs to push the baby out.'

The trust which had shown on Effie's face, before the chloroform-induced unconsciousness, was now repeated on McAllister's as she looked up at Dr Neil. Effie's fear had disappeared a little under his quiet comfort, and it had the same effect on McAllister. She thought suddenly that she had taken Dr Neil for granted, that she had not fully realised either his hard work or his dedication, and for the first time understood the impulse which had caused him to leave the cushioned life of a younger son of a good family and become an East End doctor instead.

Before, she had understood his choice in a theoretical fashion; now she was seeing what that choice meant, and how hard he tried for his poor patients, and for such little return other than the simple and offered faith of the poor, suffering girl on the bed.

Later McAllister was to remember that afternoon spent in the stifling attic as a kind of nightmare punctuated by Dr Neil's barked commands to her and Rose; she had ceased to exist for him except as a pair of willing hands and legs. He had ordered Rose to stand by and cut more squares ready for when Effie entered the second stage, and would be conscious and suffering again. 'Wet them, Rose,' he said. 'We can give them to her to suck on when she needs to push.'

Was this what love led to, McAllister thought more than once during the long afternoon: this agony, this terrible suffering? Had her mother gone through this four times, once to produce herself? Were all men and women born in such pain? Reason said, Not always, for otherwise mankind itself might come to an end.

Or were the acts which produced this end so far away from them in time that somehow the temporal distance anaesthetised reality?

Sally-Anne, for thinking this she was Sally-Anne again, not McAllister, Dr Neil's acolyte in childbirth, had never seriously considered such things before, but living among the East End poor she was beginning to ask questions not only about her own, previously pampered life, but about life in general, and the stunted lives of those around her in particular.

One of the defeated-looking women, sullen and grimy, came in once with cups of tea for them all. Dr Neil drank the foul-tasting stuff gratefully; he had now taken off his tie, and the sweat stood in pearls along his forehead. When he walked over to hand his empty cup back, his limp was very pronounced and the scar on his cheek red and angry.

The woman took the cups, gave the figure on the bed a dispassionate stare. 'I did say as 'ow she ought to 'ave 'ad Mother 'ampton,' she observed.

'Did you so?' barked Dr Neil. 'Seeing that Mother Hampton was dead-drunk under the table at the Jolly Waterman when Rose Bailey went for her, a fine job she would have made of it.'

He looked at McAllister for the first time since she had begun to help him, and saw her strained white face, the eyes enormous in it.

'Would you like a rest, McAllister?' he enquired. 'You could let Rose take over for a little.'

McAllister knew that if once she stopped her ministrations she would never get up again, and her reply was as firm as she could make it. 'Thank you, but no. I shall go on as long as you do, Dr Neil.' She would show him that there was no chance of her giving way to a fine lady's vapours!

Nevertheless Dr Neil encouraged Rose to help; he said that he really needed two pairs of hands now that Effie was fully dilated. He ordered McAllister to stop giving her chloroform and the two girls worked busily side by side. Once conscious again, Effie began to scream, pain taking her over, and only McAllister's soothing hands, and Dr Neil's voice, urging her to push with each pain, stopped her from becoming a mindless howling thing on the bed, unable to help herself.

Rose supplied McAllister with the damp towelling squares, and she alternately wiped Effie's forehead, and gave her the towelling to bite on when the pains came strong and fast.

'Now,' said Dr Neil fiercely, for the baby had suddenly decided that, whatever position it was in, it was going to be born, 'give her the chloroform again, McAllister; the baby is ready to be delivered.'

He ordered Rose to take one of Effie's legs and lift it on to her shoulders, and McAllister the other, to make it easier for him to help the insistent baby on its way. 'And when you need to give her more chloroform,' he said, 'hand the leg you are holding to Rose—you may take them both on your shoulders if you will, Rose; it's important that she doesn't regain consciousness during the actual birth.'

He bent down, preparing to lever the baby into the world with his special forceps without either crippling it for life, and killing it, or the mother, or both of them.

McAllister really did think that she was going to faint this time, not through shock or disgust, but sheer physical exhaustion, except that the will which her family deplored kept her on her feet. And when Dr Neil commanded her to give Effie chloroform again while he finally manoeuvred the little body out the relief she felt was almost overwhelming, enhanced by the sudden strange joy she felt at the sight of the tiny purple baby boy.

Effie, spared the final agonising pangs of the actual moments of birth, recovered so slowly that McAllister feared that she had overdone the chloroform. She looked even more ghastly after the birth than before it, frightening McAllister. Dr Neil's attention was, for the moment, on the baby, and it was left to McAllister to wipe the mother's livid, sweating face, only the perspiration on Effie's face was cold, not hot.

Dr Neil had the baby upside-down and was smacking him to make him cry—having been born, he no longer seemed to want to survive in the harsh world outside his mother's warm body. He had damaged the baby's shoulder during birth, but not so much, he thought, that it would be a cripple.

The baby finally gave a feeble and pitiful squawk, quite unlike the enraged roars which McAllister had been told that her sturdy brothers had made on entering their privileged world—and which she had undoubtedly made herself—but at least he was breathing.

Dr Neil, cradling him in his arms for a moment before handing him to McAllister to care for, wondered not for the first time on such occasions whether he had done the baby a favour by enabling him to live. With no acknowledged father, a child mother—if the mother survived, which he was beginning to doubt—and an attic in a tenement as its home, his future seemed uncertain, to say the least. But he was not God, to decide such matters, only a competent and caring doctor, and his duty to humanity and to his Hippocratic oath—to save life, not destroy it—left him no choice.

He laid the naked red scrap briefly in Effie's arms, and said abruptly to McAllister, 'Let Rose do that while you take the baby from me and find something to wrap it in. We'll leave bathing it for the moment; I must take care of Effie and the afterbirth.'

The afterbirth! And hold the baby! She had never held a baby before that was not a fat, well-dressed, sweet-smelling thing, but not one of them had ever given her the strange sense of fulfilment which the pitiful scrap of humanity in her arms, wrapped in the square which she had earlier scissored from her petticoat, did.

As she cuddled him, seeing his tiny face, his perfect little hands, a great surge of emotion swept through her. Never mind the narrow life that he had been born into; his tiny presence seemed to make all the suffering and pain his birth had caused worthwhile.

Except that while she was loving him, gazing wonderingly at his blind eyes, Dr Neil said suddenly and hoarsely, 'Quick, McAllister; put the baby in the drawer over there and bring me as much towelling as you can.' For earlier, the grandma, who had left them some time ago, had pulled out a drawer from a deal tallboy, and put a noxious blanket in it, ready for the baby's birth.

Once again she leapt to it, put the baby down regretfully, and carried the towelling over to the bed, to see a dreadful sight. As was often common after breech births, the afterbirth had not come away as it should have done, and Effie had been so torn during the birth, Dr Neil told her later, that she had started to bleed, and then the bleeding had turned into a violent haemorrhaging, the passage of the afterbirth completing the damage already done to Effie's poor little body.

Effie, Dr Neil, Rose, McAllister and the bed were covered in blood. Dr Neil made vain attempts to stifle the bleeding, his own face now as grey as the bedlinen had been before it turned red.

'Oh, Gawd, she's goin',' shrieked Rose.

'No!' said Dr Neil violently. 'No, I won't have this. I thought we'd won this time.' And McAllister remembered his silent distress when he had come home after losing a woman in childbirth not long after she had arrived in Vetch Street.

But the battle was in vain, and McAllister, like Dr Neil and Rose, had to watch while all their efforts to save Effie were useless, and slowly her life leached away with her blood, leaving her white and drained on the bed, only the shouts of her now motherless baby breaking the silence of the room.

Two great tears ran down McAllister's face. She neither sobbed nor wept aloud as Dr Neil sighed, closed Effie's eyes, pulled up the sheet, and rose to walk to the window, to look out of it, at nothing, McAllister suspected.

She could only imagine what he must be suffering. Rose had begun to sob gently, not at all like her usual wild self, and someone must tell the poor mother downstairs that she had a grandson, but not a daughter.

CHAPTER ELEVEN

DRESSING the doll, after her experience with Effie, took on a different meaning for McAllister. Since the baby's birth and its mother's death her whole view of life seemed to have changed abruptly, as though someone had shaken a giant kaleidoscope and she saw the whole world and herself in a different light.

She was not even sure any more who she was—Sally-Anne Tunstall, the rich American heiress, or the humble servant McAllister, whom Dr Neil, Matey and the East End knew—except that, like Sally-Anne Tunstall, McAllister had never been humble.

She was, perhaps, an amalgam of the two, and her masquerade, begun, she now knew, almost as the game Dr Neil had called it, had, in turning into something more serious, changed her as well.

Dr Neil, coming into the parlour where McAllister was permitted to knit and sew, caught his breath at the sight of her with the doll. She had finished knitting and sewing all its little garments, had arranged its fine hair, and was now busily engaged in slipping them on.

He had caught a glimpse of her tender expression once before when he had handed her Effie's baby to hold, and later when she had bathed it before they had left the Buildings. Since then, since the whole-hearted and selfless manner in which she had helped him, and had comforted him after Effie's death—he remembered her saying gently to him when he had railed against Fate and his own incompetence, 'Don't, Dr Neil, don't. I know that you did your best, and you said yourself that the poor thing had little hope of surviving the birth'—his attitude to her had changed.

The raillery with which he had spoken to her in her early days at Vetch Street had changed its nature. From being a little bitter it had become increasingly affectionate, as Matey had shrewdly noted. He had adopted his slighting manner, he knew, to protect himself from the attraction which she had possessed for him from the first moment that he had seen her.

He could not allow himself to fall in love with a girl so obviously a part of the world of wealth and consequence which he had abandoned. It was foolish. Like Angela she would not want a poor doctor, and sooner or later would tire of her play-acting and retire back to that world—he wondered why she had left it, and what she thought that she was doing here in the East End, so far from her family and friends.

At first he had thought that her ebullient nature, the evidence of her having been loved and indulged, would mean that her response to life in and around Vetch Street would inevitably be shallow. But, as day after day she tirelessly pursued her harsh and relentless duties, never complaining, other than by the occasional wry joke about following such a demanding routine, and then, in this latest episode, showing such selfless devotion and practical compassion, his judgement of her had changed. She seemed to be maturing before his eyes.

Her sturdy common sense, the downright attitude to life which never ceased to surprise him, the constant loving references to a papa and a mama who sounded remarkably practical themselves, even if they had spoiled their beautiful daughter, informed him that she came from a background very unlike any that Dr Neil had ever encountered.

Perhaps it was because she was American, but all this supposition failed before the one fact that mattered to him: he had come to love her passionately, wanted to fulfil that love, and he did not know what to do about it!

He remembered with affection how she had refused to allow him to send for a cab to take her back to Vetch Street.

'No,' she had said, with her usual fiery spirit still dominant, even after the long and tiring hours which she had worked with him. 'You always walk home, I know, after your work is over, and I shall do the same.' She had laughed, looked at him with some of her usual mischief on her face, erasing for a moment the memory of what had so recently passed. 'You seem to forget that I am your skivvy, Dr Neil, not a fine lady to be cosseted.'

Her temperament had not changed, that was plain, but her moral nature had, as his had changed after he had discovered the wretched and hopeless poverty of the homes from which the soldiers who had served him had come. After that he could never feel the same again about his own fortunate life. He was sure that McAllister was undergoing the same experience.

She held the doll up, her work with it finished. 'There,' she said gaily. 'Salute the Master, Belinda, although I warn you that he will not be your master for long. You will find a new one at the bazaar, I hope.'

He put out a hand to take the doll from her, to admire her exquisite handiwork, and when, in the doing, her hand touched his, a shiver of something which she had never thought to feel again passed over her.

That Dr Neil was similarly affected was plain to her. And her pleasure was mixed with fear—but less so than she had expected.

'A most convenient baby, this,' he remarked lightly,

'seeing that she never cries, or does anything to provoke her parents—whatever they do to her.' He was trying to exorcise the wave of desire which had swept over him when McAllister's blue-black eyes were fixed so earnestly on him. He was so conscious of her that everything about her was vividly present to him.

He almost felt, as well as saw, her curls, which, as usual, had escaped from the bonds which confined them, clustering on her hairline, falling on to the beautiful oval face, the lips, so rosy and tempting against the pure complexion of her face. When she laughed he saw her teeth, not only shining tributes to American dentistry, but also to her remarkable constitution. Professionally, he had seldom seen anyone in such a perfect state of health—that alone was sufficient to mark her out in Vetch Street.

His passion, his arousal which the mere sight of her had provoked, was so strong that he wondered that she could not feel it too; it seemed to hang, a living thing, in the air between them.

Dr Neil tried to calm himself by a grave examination of the doll, as though it were one of his patients, holding the tiny wrist to take the pulse, only to see the laughter on her face, and for that to provoke him to further inward excesses. He wanted to undo the shining blue-black hair, to kiss the parted lips, to unfasten the high collar of her cheap black dress to find the exciting treasures beneath, to reveal the splendid breasts which strained against the cloth, to stroke them, to. . .

Desire had become a physical pain. The months of living in close proximity to her were taking their toll, combined as they were with his previous ascetic life.

He handed the doll back to her, avoiding the touch of her work-reddened hands, tried to say something stupendously dull, wondered wildly whether running upstairs and pouring cold water over himself might stop this unseemly conduct. 'I see that you have become a valued member of Mr Sands' ladies' sewing circle.'

'Oh,' said McAllister demurely, 'he may organise us and look in occasionally, but he does not exactly take part, you know.'

'I could hardly imagine him sewing a fine seam,' murmured Dr Neil, 'despite his ladylike proclivities.'

'That is very unkind of you,' said McAllister severely, but her severity was a mock. 'But I do know what you mean. We had a clergyman like that at home, and Papa naughtily called him Miss Nancy. Not to his face, you understand, and he did make up for it by giving lavishly to the church. . .'

'Before or after he lost his fortune?' asked Dr Neil wickedly.

'Who, Papa?' said McAllister, who had forgotten the whoppers she had told about her papa's bankruptcy, but, remembering them now, recovered herself rapidly. 'Oh, before, of course. It was such generosity which helped to bring it about,' she added helpfully.

'No doubt,' murmured Dr Neil, who was finding that this interchange, far from dowsing lust, was fuelling it, so that he had a terrible desire to fall on his knees before his skivvy, crying, 'Be mine, McAllister, be mine, immediately,' like a hero, or perhaps a villain, in a stage melodrama.

Instead, he said prosaically, 'I thought that you were determined to avoid all such bread-and-butter occupations, McAllister. What brought about this change of heart?'

McAllister, who had put the doll down, and was now fetching out her work basket to embroider pansies on some fine lawn dresses made for the bazaar by the aforesaid ladies, said, 'I didn't mean to become involved, you know, but Matey has been so kind to me—when not slave-driving me, you understand—that when she asked me to accompany her I had not the heart to refuse, and strangely, after I began to work for the bazaar, I found that it was most rewarding.'

The look that McAllister gave him when she said this was so killing that Dr Neil decided to remove temptation by removing himself. He made for the surgery, saying, lying in his teeth, 'I have some work to do, McAllister. You may bring me a pot of tea at four o'clock. Please do not ply me with biscuits; I have no desire to set you a bad example by pigging myself.'

McAllister cuddled her doll when he had gone. Ever since she had held the baby she had found herself treating the doll in the same way.

And I never liked dolls when I was a little girl, she thought with wonder. How strange! Mama was always a little put out by my preference for boy's play and toys, and that grew worse after she married Papa and had three boys for me to play with.

She remembered Rob, the eldest boy, named after her mama's father who had died in Arizona, saying to her one day, after she had been caught riding bareback at her uncle Orrin's ranch in Wyoming, 'What a pity you weren't a boy, Sally-Anne; we could have had such fun together.'

She had been just fifteen at the time, and had agreed with him heartily. She had not at all looked forward to being a débutante and wearing fancy women's clothes, and not being allowed to climb trees, and accompany Papa, who always, said her mama despairingly, let her do exactly as she pleased.

And now what pleased her was loving the doll, and sewing and embroidering baby clothes, and looking after Dr Neil—particularly looking after Dr Neil—and what would Mama say to that? Or Papa. For Papa, too, had wanted her to be a proper young lady after she had reached eighteen, and, for the first time, remorse struck her, for what had happened once that magic date had been reached, and for what had happened after that, culminating in. . .

She clutched the doll to her heart, and told herself to think of poor dead Effie whose fate had been so much worse than her own, and that should teach her to count her blessings as her dear aunt Nella had always said.

And how strange it was that, after all these months of resolutely not thinking about her old life in the States, she should begin to remember it with such pleasure!

J.D. had told Sally-Anne Tunstall that if it was inconvenient to visit him she could always post her column to him; he had seen her growing more and more responsible as the weeks went by, and he was no longer so worried about her safety.

The previous week she had posted it on Tuesday, having written it the day after Effie's death in a white heat of sorrow and indignation.

She had called it 'Death in the Buildings', and had based it not only on the tragedy she had witnessed, but had also written of the temptation for young girls to make money by selling themselves than by working long hours for poor pay, and had followed that by writing of women's disabilities in a world where care in childbirth was minimal, and how only the kindness of humane doctors made it possible for them to have any skilled treatment at all.

She was always careful never to write anything which might betray where she lived and the identity of those whom she wrote about, while stressing that the column was based upon her experiences and verifiable fact. Not having to visit Fleet Street meant that her afternoon and evening off could be genuinely relaxing, and she usually spent the time knitting, sewing or reading, with only the occasional foray up West.

Matey had gone out, not to return until late at night, leaving Dr Neil's tea in the larder on a plate carefully positioned under a fine gauze hood to protect it from the ubiquitous flies; he had said not to leave him supper, for he might visit the local evening market where prepared food of all kinds was on sale, from oysters to whelks; he was partial to shellfish, he said.

McAllister thought that when it was cooler, in the early evening, she might walk towards St Paul's to see the sights there, and was content to sit, her feet on a tapestry-covered tuffet, finishing off her embroidery for the bazaar; she was astonished to find how much she was looking forward to it.

Dr Neil also had his evening off from his practice on Wednesday, but after lunch he had vanished into the surgery, on the pretext that he had work to do there, but in reality to escape McAllister's siren call, which had unconsciously grown stronger over the previous week.

He thought that he had heard the house door close: McAllister must have left for a stroll, or perhaps even a visit up West, and it would be safe for him to leave the surgery where he had been reading Mr H. G. Wells's scientific romance *The Time Machine*, and return to the comfort of his armchair.

He entered the parlour, only to discover that he was not alone, after all. McAllister had gone out, but only to speak to Rose, who had managed to obtain a new post as a maid-of-all-work, and, her half-day off also being Wednesday, had come to ask McAllister to go up West with her again.

McAllister had apologised to Rose for refusing her invitation—she had sewing to do for the bazaar, she said—when the front door had banged shut behind her and she had been compelled to run round to the back and come in through the kitchen.

Breathless, she entered the parlour, to see Dr Neil arrive, his novel in his hand. They had not been alone together since their conversation on the day on which she had finished dressing the doll, both of them avoiding disturbing contact with the other, for their own good reasons.

Hearts thumping, they confronted one another.

'I thought you'd gone out, McAllister,' said Dr Neil inanely.

'Oh, is that why you thought it safe to come back to the parlour after your arduous work in the surgery?' said McAllister dangerously, casting a sarcastic eye at the half-read novel in his hand.

'Now, now, McAllister,' said Dr Neil unwisely. 'It's not for the servant to reprimand the Master.'

'It is, if the Master is telling whoppers,' replied McAllister grimly, her heart bumping with a combination of fear and excitement, as she continued to be provocative. And why was that? Was it annoyance that he had been avoiding her, as she had been avoiding him?

'I was not telling "whoppers",' said Dr Neil with dignity. 'What an unpleasant word. American, I suppose?'

'Oh, you suppose, do you?' sparked McAllister. 'And what is wrong with American words? Most of them were good British words first, and you haven't had the sense to keep the best ones, but have left it to us to do that for you.'

'And when do you start singing "Yankee Doodle",

McAllister?' said Dr Neil, provocative in his turn, but oh, she looked remarkable when she was all fired up, as he supposed she called it, and despite his resolution to have as little to do with her as possible he could not resist continuing to tease her.

'Better than singing boastful tunes like "Rule Britannia" as though you Brits weren't beaten hollow by us poor rebels,' was her riposte to that.

'Only because the French were obliging enough to do a lot of your fighting for you,' said Dr Neil, who as an old soldier had a grasp of military history.

'Oh, pooh to that,' said McAllister, wondering how this ridiculous conversation had started, and how it would end. 'Trust a Britisher to blame someone else for their own lack of success.'

'Wellington and Marlborough to you, miss,' said Dr Neil, his grin growing wider.

'And what are they, Dr Neil? Railway stations or public schools? Let me remind you that we Yankees have won all our wars, which is more than you can say.'

'Only because you Americans insist on fighting among yourselves,' said Dr Neil, and began to whistle 'Dixie',' 'which means you can never lose. . .so there!'

This came out so comically that they both began to laugh together, Neil putting his book down, and McAllister whooping into the apron which she had thrown over her head at his last sally, as though she were truly the skivvy she pretended to be.

She dropped the apron to show him her laughing, scarlet face, tears of amusement in her eyes.

They were by now close together, and the devil, who had got into both of them, whispered in both their ears; McAllister had meant to ask, Now, how did we arrive at that? and Dr Neil, who had meant to say something provocative to her, decided to do something provocative instead.

He took her laughing face by the chin, tipped it up, bent and kissed it. He decided that he liked what he had done—and did it again.

McAllister, still beset by that strange mixture of desire and fear which gripped her whenever he began to make love to her at even the lightest level, found herself shivering, but allowed him to continue, and when the next kiss found her lips she responded to him, timidly, it was true, but still a response.

Desire, long reined in, had Neil Cochrane in its grip. The longed-for mistress of his heart was in his arms at last, soft and apparently willing, and if her lovemaking was as fiery as the rest of her, what delights might he not taste?

His arms around her, he began so gently that although McAllister was already feeling stifled, and the fear of men which had beset her for so long had begun to tighten its grip on her, she not only allowed him to kiss and fondle her face and neck, but let him undo her hair, so that it tumbled about her shoulders, as magnificent in its abandon as he had imagined it in the long nights when he had been unable to sleep.

She tried to tell herself not to be afraid, for was not this Dr Neil, whose gentleness and compassion she had often witnessed, even if his tongue was sharp? McAllister knew that she must truly love him, for that could be the only reason why she could allow him, a man, to touch her at all. And oh, she wanted to touch him, but a strange timidity, so unlike her, was controlling all her actions.

Dr Neil was not in any way surprised at McAllister's reaction to his lovemaking; he expected such modesty from a well brought up young girl, and her arms around his neck, her timid responses, fluttering though they were, told him that she felt for him what he felt for her, and further inflamed his own passion, while warning him to go gently.

But going gently was difficult, to say the least, for his active mind was giving way to the essential basic desire for a man to possess the woman he loved and who loved him, and his kisses and caresses grew more and more urgent.

For McAllister it was torture. The war between desire and fear was consuming her utterly. She willed him to continue, but instinctively needed him to stop. Oh, this could not be happening—that she loved him so, and yet could not bear him to caress her! Her trembling gave him the impression of her own passion being fuelled, which in its turn led him on to further, and deeper caresses.

And then, his right hand, rising to undo the buttons of her high-collared black dress, his other arm unconsciously straining her to him, closer and closer so that she could feel his arousal brought on a memory so dreadful to McAllister, a memory which she had fought against for months—and fear suddenly won the battle.

She was stifling, she was being crushed, overwhelmed, and the hard man's body against her was not Neil's but that of the man who had. . .who. . .had. . .and panic ensued, all-enveloping panic, uncontrollable.

McAllister began to scream, to fight him off, shrieking, 'No, no! You are not to! Don't! You are hurting me! No-o-o! Stop, please stop!'

Dr Neil hardly knew what was happening. One moment he had McAllister in his arms, soft and willing, making relatively innocent love to her, and while her response had been gentle, rather than passionate—

which was to be expected—there had been nothing to show that she had not welcomed it.

And suddenly he had a maenad in his arms, fighting him, screaming, striking at him, the tears running down her face which fear had made unrecognisable, pushing him away, and when he let her go, for very decency's sake, because he saw no way to calm her unless he did, she sank on to the sofa, still sobbing and crying, her face hidden in a cushion, her whole body heaving and shaking.

'McAllister, don't be frightened. Dear God, McAllister, I shan't hurt you. What is it? What's wrong?' For, after all, he had done nothing to bring on such an astonishing reaction, for behaving as though he were trying to rape her. . .

Rape her. . .!

He was suddenly a doctor before all else, remembering other women he had seen, and tried to examine, victims of a brutal assault, who had been unable to bear a man near them, let alone a man attempting to make love to them, and a score of odd things about her behaviour, hardly noticed at the time, fell into place.

'McAllister,' he said hoarsely, falling on his knees beside her, trying not to touch her, for that might bring on her violent struggles again. 'Tell me what's wrong; I promise not to hurt you,' he repeated. 'It's Dr Neil, McAllister; you know that you can trust me—I. . .love you, McAllister, truly love you and want to help you.'

It was finally out, the declaration which he had never thought to make to any woman, after Angela, but the huddled figure on the sofa was not placated.

'No, you can't love me.' Her voice, muffled by the cushion in which she had hidden her face, was so despairing that it almost broke his heart. 'You can't love me. I want to love you back. . .and I can't, I can't, I'm so afraid. . .and so ashamed.'

She looked up at him, her face so blotched and swollen that despite himself he put out a hand to comfort her, only for her to let out a frightened cry, trying frantically to burrow into the sofa to avoid any contact with him.

All the months which Sally-Anne Tunstall had spent trying to erase the memory of what had happened to her, her refusal to remember any part of it, were as nothing. To be once again in the arms of a man, even one whom she had welcomed, not one who was attacking her, and whom she hated, had undone the self-control which she had so rigorously exercised.

Immediately after it had happened just the sight of any man, even kind Uncle Orrin, had been enough to make her feel faint, and nauseous. She had conquered that by an effort of the will which had once been almost her enemy, so strong was it, but had, in enabling her to live calmly among so many enemies in male form, become her friend. She had almost thought that she had recovered completely, until, once in Neil's arms, the memory of the rape inflicted on her had struck her down.

She had thought, wrongly, that she could allow the love which she had begun to feel for Dr Neil to express itself, only for her deepest instincts to take over when in beginning to make love to her he had unwittingly reminded her so strongly of what. . .*he* had done to her. Even now she could hardly bear to remember him, what he had done to her. . .his very name.

Dr Neil was speaking again.

'What was it, McAllister?' he said, his voice hardly recognisable, love mixed with anger at the wretch who had violated her. 'Were you attacked. . .?' He hesitated, barely able to say it; the word was a violation in itself. 'Raped?'

She could not speak; her throat was in spasm. She nodded, swallowed, began to whisper yes, could not, would not say it, said instead, 'Oh, I am so ashamed. I am soiled. . .and I. . .when you touch me. . . I cannot . . .oh, I cannot. . .I wish I were dead. I cannot make myself. . .and who would want such a. . .thing. . .?' And the sobbing began again, and to see her so defeated—remembering how gallant she had always been, even in the alley when she had attacked her assailant with her shoe—overwhelmed him. Realisation struck him. She had cared nothing for the man who was attacking her then; her despair now was because she could not bear the caresses of the man whom she loved, and she knew loved her.

Oh, how doubly difficult it was for them both. It had been tricky enough for him to help the women to whom he had no commitment even though he felt the deepest pity for them, but to help McAllister, whom he loved so dearly—how was he to do that?

'Oh, McAllister,' he said softly. 'You are not soiled. And the man who attacked you should feel shame, not you. You are hurt, I know, and unable to believe in any man's decency, but try to believe that whatever happened to you I still love you; you have not changed for me, it makes no difference, no difference whatsoever—except that I want to kill the man who hurt you.'

No difference? How could he believe that? How could she believe what he was saying? Of course it made a difference. She could no longer bring to the man she loved her untouched innocence, and, worse than that, she could not bear his lovemaking because it reminded her so bitterly of what had been done to her. He would not want a spoiled thing! And now she was frightened of *him*—Dr Neil, who was so kind and good, and had already been so badly damaged by life. . . She tried to control herself, but the will which had driven her for so long was broken, whether forever, or temporarily, she did not know.

Dr Neil rose. Useless at the moment to try to touch her, to convince her that what he felt for her was love and a pity so enormous that it was almost unmanning him. Like McAllister he was discovering that it was easy to bear the grief and pain of others when you were not emotionally committed to them. He had felt distress and pity for the sufferings he had seen about him, but they had not struck home to his heart as seeing McAllister brought so low had done.

He must let her cry herself out. He suspected that perhaps McAllister, always so gallant in facing life, as he had now seen on several occasions, had tried to suppress, to crush down the awful memory of what had been done to her, had refused to give way to grief, to shed healing tears, until in his arms something had reminded her so strongly of what had passed and broken the barriers her will had erected. And once broken, once the grief and tears had begun, it would take some little time for her to recover, although now that she had faced what had happened she might do so more quickly and easily than she would have done had she continued suppressing her memories, and refusing healthy grieving.

'Let me fetch you some water,' he said gently to the distressed figure on the sofa after a little time had passed. She had stopped crying and lay there rigid, her face averted from him, her whole body rejecting him and the cruel world.

He left her to go to the kitchen, began to run the tap, then heard her rise, to dash from the parlour—not, he hoped, to leave the house; but, going after her, he saw her mounting the stairs to her room, to be away from him, simply because he was, for the moment at least, no longer Dr Neil, but only another member of the sex which had betrayed her.

He drank the water himself, the puzzle of McAllister half-resolved, for there were still some pieces missing to explain the mystery of her presence in Vetch Street.

CHAPTER TWELVE

SALLY-ANNE TUNSTALL, beloved daughter of Senator Jared Tunstall, arguably the richest man in the USA, and his dear wife Mary, niece of Orrin Tunstall, the American ambassador, society beauty, heiress, spoiled child of fortune, who had once thought that the world was her ball to play with, sat on her bed in an East End attic, dressed in her skivvy's clothing, grieving because she could not consummate her love for a poor doctor who had renounced the world over which she had once reigned.

For the first time in her life she faced the truth of her past, clear-eyed as her formidable father's daughter ought to be, devoid of pride and love of self, and inspected what had brought her to this pass. One thing, and one thing only, she knew beyond a doubt. Unless she could face that past, she could not bury it. She had evaded it long enough. . .

'So, here I am, Uncle Orrin,' she had said gaily, 'your naughty niece, exiled because she was silly enough to fall in love with a poor man who was only interested in her money. How many of the men whom I meet in London society will be after that same money, do you think? Only, they will have something to offer for that money, will they not? Titles and lands, and a position in the world. They will buy me for that. Terry Rourke sold me for enough dollars to buy himself and his true girlfriend a small business.'

Her bitter disillusionment was plain in her voice, her

uncle thought. They were in his study—his office, he called it, American-style. Now in his early sixties, he was still a big, handsome man, his shrewd common sense a byword. He was not as clever as his half-brother, Sally-Anne's father, but he shared the same intensely practical outlook on life.

'Now, my dear,' he said, 'no need to take on so; you are young. You have the sense, I am sure, to avoid those who wish to exploit you. . .'

'Especially after my recent unfortunate experience,' she remembered saying lightly, trying to disguise her profound hurt. 'Tell me, Uncle Orrin, shall I always be regarded as my father's heiress, never seen for what I truly am?'

He answered her in his usual calm manner, which was easy for him, thought Sally-Anne, for was he not one of the lords of the world and a man to boot? What did he know of the pains and penalties of being a female? But she responded to the kind note in his voice when he said, 'Now, my dear, you are a clever girl and a brave one. Life is not easy for any of us, and despite what people think can be hard for those of us who have the luck to be well endowed with this world's goods. Use the common sense which I know you are blessed with, and little can go wrong.'

Well, she had shrugged her shoulders metaphorically at that, and oh, how she wished that she had heeded him, instead of going on what she now saw clearly had been her wilful way.

Who had she been trying to impress? Her mother and father, or the young man who had made her his easy prey? Terry Rourke had been her father's chauffeur, a handsome, black-haired Irishman, with a lively, impudent face, quite unlike Dr Neil's. She thought that he had put her off handsome, impudent men for life.

How it had happened she did not know, but back there in New York he had begun to pursue her, and she had found ever-increasing opportunities to talk to him; he was so gay and lively, quite unlike the rather stiff young men whom she met in New York and Newport society.

He had taken her out one day, her and Mama, and when he had handed her out of the big Daimler, her papa's pride, he had slipped a note into her hand, inviting her to meet him when his duties were over, and go out with him—perhaps for a ride on the Brooklyn Ferry.

Sally-Anne loved a dare, and Terry Rourke's appeal had been frank and animal—he had excited her, and it had been simple for her to lie to her mother, to set out to go to a girlfriend's home on the following afternoon and meet Terry instead.

'I never thought that you'd have the guts to come,' he had said. He was well dressed in imitation of those whom he served, was clever and determined to make his way in life: he would not be Jared Tunstall's chauffeur forever, that was for sure. He had already decided not to seduce Sally-Anne—that would be too dangerous—but to manoeuvre her and her father into a position where he could be bought off.

His plan was simple. He would persuade her that he loved her, ask her to promise to run away with him if her father refused his consent to their marriage, and, when he finally asked her father for her hand, threaten him with the prospect of his daughter's elopement—he and Jared Tunstall both knew how self-willed his daughter was, and that any threat from her would not be idle. On the other hand, for a reasonable sum, he, Terry Rourke, would consent to be bought off. He was shrewd enough to know that to be too greedy with Jared Tunstall might lose him everything.

Sally-Anne had known nothing of this—only that standing with him on the ferry that day was sheer enchantment.

'Freedom,' she had said, shouting into the wind, glad to be rid of chaperons, lady's maids, and, yes, fond mamas and papas. Together they had done all the things that she had wanted to do and never been allowed to: gone to Coney Island, licked lollipops on the front there, enjoyed herself in funfairs, and ridden on the Big Wheel.

He had always been the gentleman with her, and if, at times, he had regretted what he would ultimately do to her, because he had begun to care for her more than his plan demanded, he could not let that deter him. Jared Tunstall would, he knew, ruin an employee who stole his daughter away from him. But, 'I love you, Sally-Anne,' he had said one day, giving her the lightest of butterfly kisses. They had wandered into Central Park, and Sally-Anne had pretended that they were simply another happy pair of young lovers. 'Are you prepared to risk everything for us?'

She had looked deep into his black eyes; for six weeks she had enjoyed, in the brief times they had spent together, the happiest and most carefree days of her life, surreptitiously stolen, with the help of a willing friend, from her guarded life, the life of a rich heiress.

She had lifted his hand and kissed it. 'You know I am, Terry.'

'And, if I asked your father for your hand, you would support me? Say that if he refused to allow us to marry you would even run away with me? You know that he will be angry with me, of course, but he will be angry with you a little.'

Sally-Anne had lifted her head proudly. 'Oh, Terry, what does that matter? If he does not approve, why, I am ready to leave with you. So long as I love you, I wouldn't mind being poor, and I don't want his money.'

Terry Rourke had thought cynically that Sally-Anne Tunstall had no idea what being poor meant, and he wanted Jared Tunstall's money, or some of it, at least.

'That's the spirit, my darling,' he had said, 'so long as you are prepared for storms. . .'

Her trust in him had been absolute. But it had all been a trick, a dreadful trick. He had gone to her father, and what happened she never quite knew.

Afterwards Jared Tunstall had said to her mama, 'It was a question of a little hustler meeting a big one, and if it weren't that he has hurt Sally-Anne so badly I could almost admire the swine for his gall. He knew that I would never let him marry her, and, besides, he has a girlfriend of his own, so when I offered him money to go away and leave her alone he stood me off as much as he dared, and collected a big enough stake to marry his girl and start a small business, which, he kindly informed me when he left, he intends to turn into a large one, one day.'

When her papa told Sally-Anne of Terry Rourke's betrayal—she never saw him again—she had not believed him, at first.

Finally, 'But he said that he loved me,' she had wailed.

'He loved my dollars more,' Jared Tunstall had replied, hard for once on the daughter he had always indulged. 'And you lied to me and to your mama and poor aunt Nella again and again in order to be with him. I thought that you had more sense, Sally-Anne. Couldn't you see how flash he was?'

'Oh, you're so cynical,' she had flung at him, head

up; she was never down for long. 'And I shall never forgive you for tempting him away from me. He loved me and I loved him.'

Jared Tunstall had not meant to tell his daughter of Rourke's sweetheart, but, seeing her obduracy, he had done so.

'I don't believe you,' she said, white to the lips.

'Believe me,' said her papa. 'Time you grew up, Sally-Anne. Your mother is right—I've spoiled you.'

And that had been that. True love had never existed, except in her imagination. But she would not be put down; she would not. She had hated the pity she thought that she saw in her mama and papa's eyes, and when her papa had suggested that she might like to spend a year in London with her Uncle Orrin, be presented at court, meet his old friend the Prince of Wales, now King Edward VII, again, she had agreed with alacrity—she, who had hated being parted from her mama and papa.

She would show them. She would, she hoped, find her true love there. There must be many in London society so rich that her inheritance was not a temptation to them; it could not be made up only of rogues and fortune-hunters.

The American Princess, for that was her nickname, was an instant and stunning success. She was rich, beautiful, clever and amusing, and her wit became renowned; she was featured in the picture papers, in the scandal sheets, and everyone of consequence was reported at one time or another to be going to marry her. And if there was something wild and desperate about her London career which disturbed her uncle and aunt a little there were few to criticise. Everyone from the King and Queen down seemed to love her.

When she appeared at a ball people stood on chairs to see her. It was Lillie Langtry all over again, the old ones said wisely. She was introduced to the novelist Mr Henry James, and took tea with him at his home, Lamb House, in Rye, and he thought that she was all the beautiful American girls he had written about rolled into one!

And then she had met Havvie Blaine, or, more properly, Havelock Torquil Roderick Blaine, Marquess of Blaine, heir to the Twelfth Duke of Innescourt, the most handsome man in society, the most run after by every girl from the age of sixteen upwards, and most of the married women, too, said the cynics.

Who else but the American Princess was good enough for Havvie? From the moment that they were introduced it was plain that they were meant for one another.

Sally-Anne could not believe her luck! Love, the oldest title in England, after the Crown's, of course, and all for her. She lived in a dream of love from the moment that he had bowed over her hand when she had been introduced to him by Daisy Warwick at Warwick Castle, and murmured, 'Not an American Princess, surely, but a true one,' and later that evening, dancing with her for the third time, he had said into her ear, 'And can a princess stoop to a mere marquess?'

'An American Princess can stoop to anything,' she had replied gaily, 'because we don't need to stoop. We are all equal, you know, in the land of opportunity.'

Well, they had said she was witty, and Havvie frequently got the benefit of the wit—as well as the beauty—and, of course, the future benefit, if all went well, of her money.

For what no one knew was how strapped for cash the Blaines were. If necessary, Havvie Blaine would have married a one-eyed dwarf to restore their fortunes, but luck was with him—he had Sally-Anne Tunstall in his sights, and the hope that she and her papa might not enquire too carefully into the Innescourt means, and if they did, why, transforming the daughter of a vulgar American robber-baron into Great Britain's premier duchess was surely worth a dollar or two.

Sally-Anne had no idea that Havvie Blaine was Terry Rourke all over again, and even her uncle Orrin was deceived by Havvie's name, his charm, and the feeling which he seemed to possess for his niece. So that when, one evening, Sally-Anne, radiant in pink and silver, a fortune in pearls around her neck, the mere sight of which made Havvie salivate internally, was gently led by him into a conservatory—at the Keppels' this time—and proposed to, there was only one answer which she could give him, and that, of course, was yes.

'Yes,' she breathed, 'oh, Havvie, yes,' and if, when he kissed her, with the perfect decorum with which a well brought up young peer should treat a single girl—even one who had promised to be his wife—she did not feel quite the surge of passion which she had expected, she put that down to her inexperience, and his tentative handling of her, which would change with time, she knew.

Oh, they made the handsomest of couples, Havvie and his American Princess—the latest Yankee heiress, unkind gossip said, to buy herself a title and a place in English society. Her manners, as well as her looks, were rather better than most, it was agreed—which was fortunate for the Blaines.

It was to be the wedding of the year. Papa and Mama, informed, were coming over, the lawyers had gathered to draw up the marriage settlement, everything seemed set fair.

Except, even before disaster struck, Sally-Anne had begun to awaken from her dream of bliss. After all, before he had proposed, she had not seen so very much of Havvie, and she had been so flattered that it had not struck her how banal his conversation was, and how limited. And if she had heard nothing of the gossip about his private life before she accepted him, certain ladies he had discarded, both married and single, took care that she overheard quite a lot now.

Even then, all might have been well. Wearing Havvie's ring, a diamond heirloom given to all Blaine brides, laughing, talking and playing with him as the London season began, Sally-Anne persuaded herself that she was as happy as a girl could be, Terry Rourke's betrayal wiped out and forgotten. She would see Mama and Papa again soon, they were coming over well before the wedding, and what bliss to greet them as the future Marchioness of Blaine, beautiful blond Havvie by her side, eager to meet them—or so he publicly said—his private comments were somewhat different—more to the effect that he could swallow Sally-Anne and her dollars, but her parvenu papa was quite another thing!

So when, on that fateful afternoon, enchanting in pale amethyst, unpinning her huge straw picture hat, crowned with a bouquet of early spring flowers, she was told that she had a visitor waiting to see her—'A Mrs Greville. Most insistent, Miss Tunstall,' the English butler said. 'She was adamant that she would wait for you, however long you were in returning'—she thought nothing of it.

She and Havvie had been to a flower show. 'And you are the fairest flower of all,' he had said, and presented her with a spray of pink carnations.

Mrs Greville sat quite alone in her aunt's drawing-room. Her aunt and uncle were out at some official function. She rose as Sally-Anne entered.

She was tall, in her early thirties, and had once, it was plain, been a great beauty; but time, and grief,

Sally-Anne thought perceptively as she moved to greet her, had worn her down.

'You do not know me, Miss Tunstall,' she began abruptly. 'And I must thank you for consenting to see me. What I have to say, though, may not, I fear, please you.'

This bewildered Sally-Anne, but for once her intuition was acute. Dulled since meeting Terry Rourke, it had inconveniently come to life again, and was telling her things about life—and Havvie—which she did not wish to know.

'But you feel that it is necessary to speak to me,' she said gently, wondering why this woman, whom she did not know, wished to say unpleasant things to her—but of what?

'I must,' said Mrs Greville. 'It is my duty, to myself, and to my children. You know that I am Mrs Honoria Greville?'

'So the butler said.'

'You have not heard of me from any other person?'

'No,' said Sally-Anne, still bewildered.

'No? Then I must inform you. I have been Havelock Blaine's mistress since he was turned twenty-one, nine years ago. I was married then, but I had left my husband because of his cruelty. Havvie and I are exactly of an age. We could not marry, but he has kept me in comfort ever since we became lovers and he fathered my two children. He. . .promised me marriage, should my husband die. Six months ago my husband broke his neck on the hunting field. Havvie did not offer me marriage, after all; he offered it to you, instead. I ask you to break that pledge you made with him so that he may marry me, the mother of his children.'

Sally-Anne, suddenly pale, stared at the woman before her. She had known that, beyond a doubt, Havvie must have formed liaisons, had mistresses—few young men of his rank and class arrived at the age of thirty innocent. What she could not have thought of was this sort of permanent liaison, almost a marriage.

'Oh, I am so sorry,' she said. 'But. . .'

'But what?' exclaimed Honoria Greville proudly. 'I have every prior claim; even you must see that.'

Sally-Anne did not know what to say, what to think. That Havvie could so lightly do this. . .'But he asked me to marry him,' she said feebly. 'He loves me now.' And, saying it, thought, No! And can I want him, a man who can do this?

'Loves you?' Mrs Greville began to laugh. 'Oh, no. He does not love *you*, believe me. He loves your dollars. You see, he does not intend to cast me off, not at all. We are, he says, to continue as we are, only your money will make my life more comfortable, he says. But it is not enough, Miss Tunstall. I have, in effect, been his wife for nine years, and now I wish to be his wife in truth. But no, he does not love you.'

'I don't believe you,' said Sally-Anne, white to the lips now. Whether she wanted Havvie or not after this revelation was one thing; to learn that he wanted her only for her money was quite another thing.

'Believe me,' said Mrs Greville, and there was almost pity in her voice. She had opened her handbag, rummaged in it, produced a letter. 'Here, read this, see what it says.' And she handed the letter to Sally-Anne.

'No,' said Sally-Anne, trying to hand it back.

'No?' said Mrs Greville, her lip curling. 'Are you afraid to read what the man who loves you says about you?'

To call a Tunstall afraid was almost, as Sally-Anne already knew, enough to raise the devil. She opened the letter, drew out a blotted sheet of paper—Havvie, she was well aware, was not the most fluent letter-writer in the world. But what she read was fluent enough.

'My dearest Honoria,' it began, and then went on to enquire lovingly after her and the children. But it was the second paragraph which did Mrs Greville's work for her.

> I am really impatient with you, my dearest. You know perfectly well that you, being penniless, and myself, being little better, cannot marry. And you know, too, that you need have no fear of losing me when I marry. How could she compare with you? Like all Americans she is both greedy and gullible—greedy for a title and gullible enough to think that I could love such a raw provincial chit as she is. Were it not for Papa's dollars I would not look at her twice!
>
> No, she may give me her money and my legitimate heir, and that is all. My heart is always yours, even though the laws of God and man rule that we may never marry.

Sally-Anne thought that she was going to faint. Havvie Blaine, for all his name and lineage, was no better than Terry Rourke. As with Terry she meant nothing to him, except as a means of extorting money from her papa. Sally-Anne Tunstall was a thing to be handled, used, of value only as an avenue to her papa's wealth.

'Why are you doing this?' she asked hoarsely. 'When I refuse him——' and Honoria Greville noticed the when—no mention of an if '—he will not marry you.'

'I think he might,' said Mrs Greville.

'No,' retorted Sally-Anne, 'not Havvie Blaine. He will marry for money, and if not me then another. He wishes to have it all. The money—and you.'

'Well, at least he will not have you,' said Honoria

Greville, reading the girl before her aright. Sally-Anne was not at all what she expected, and she was almost sorry for her.

'I think that you had better go,' Sally-Anne said—and she remembered with pride that she had not given an inch, had shown no emotion as her life had crumbled around her. For, whatever else, she would not marry Havvie Blaine now, and she would lose no time in informing him of that fact. Let some other heiress finance his illicit family. Sally-Anne Tunstall would rather drop dead at his feet than accept him after this.

But oh, she thought, tearlessly watching Mrs Greville leave, how could I have been so deceived—and twice at that. . .?

CHAPTER THIRTEEN

Greedy and gullible! Greedy and gullible! The words rang again in Sally-Anne's head as they had done that afternoon in her aunt's pretty drawing-room once Mrs Greville had gone.

For what reason the woman had done it Sally-Anne did not know. She could not really think that Havvie would marry her, once Sally-Anne jilted him—which she must, for in the face of that letter could she believe a single word he had said, or written, to her? And she could not believe that he would marry Honoria Greville, might even throw her off if he knew what she had done, which was to lose him his heiress.

She knew what she must do. She was her father's daughter, after all. Pride—and honour—demanded one thing of her. Cost her what it might, she would break off her engagement, and if it meant social ruin, so be it. She could not build her life on another's pain, or on Havvie's lies. He had looked into her eyes too often, told her that he loved her too many times for her ever to believe him again.

He would marry another heiress, she knew that quite well, almost certainly one who would take him for his title, regardless of his character and conduct. Maybelle Foy, the daughter of one of her papa's rivals, had, she knew, almost caught him before she, Sally-Anne, had arrived on the scene. Well, she could have him and welcome to him.

Once in her suite of rooms she sat down at a little Louis Quinze escritoire, its pale grey panels painted with carnations and pinks, and wrote a short letter to her faithless lover, asking him to call on her urgently at the embassy at eleven the next morning. She could not face him before then; nor would society approve of a private evening visit.

Then, pleading a headache and fatigue, she cancelled her outing for the evening, and went to bed. But not to sleep.

Eleven o'clock the next morning saw her immaculately dressed in a pale grey and pale pink creation, a great froth of fine lace at her throat and at her wrists. She did not know it, but pallor had conferred an almost grave beauty on her, so that Havvie Blaine, arriving on the minute, thought, not for the first time, that he might be selling himself for dollars, but that he was getting more than dollars in return.

He did not love her, but she would make a remarkable duchess, and the fact that she had inherited more than her share of her papa's famous shrewdness was a bonus which would assist the Blaines and make their future secure.

She received him alone, a privilege granted to her because they were so soon to be married.

'My love,' he said, 'what was so urgent that you had to summon me so soon after we parted yesterday afternoon? And I was sorry to miss you at the Keppels's thrash; I hope that you are recovered? You do look a little pale.'

His manners to her had always been impeccable, which made what he was shortly to do all the more shocking.

'Oh, Havvie,' Sally-Anne murmured; this was going to be even harder than she had thought—and she had said nothing to her uncle Orrin—she could not, not until her engagement was irrevocably over.

'I have asked you to call,' she said, 'to tell you that, after all, I cannot marry you. It would not be fitting. You do not love me, and I, I fear, was in love with love and not with you. Far better that we should part now, before all the arrangements go too far, and we are bound by them, and not by our desires.'

Havvie stared at her, his handsome face as ashen as hers had been when she had read his letter. 'I cannot believe that I am hearing you aright, my darling. What has happened? Yesterday afternoon we parted in such love and friendship—and now—now—you say that you do not wish to marry me! Only consider what you are saying. I am sure that you are only feeling a young girl's modest misgivings at the approach of marriage. Let me reassure you. . .'

Like the Player Queen in *Hamlet*, thought Sally-Anne dully, he protested too much. He flung down his soft hat and cane, crossed to where she stood, took her hand.

She rejected it, and said sorrowfully, 'Oh, Havvie, I wish that I could believe you. But I know only too well that you do not love me, that you are marrying me for Papa's dollars, and that I cannot bear. I thought that you loved *me*, and not my money.'

'But I do love you,' he said, impetuously for him; he had always been measured with her, one of his charms for a girl who tended towards impetuosity. 'How can you not believe me? Have I not given you sufficient proofs? I have always held back, my darling, from being too ardent, fearing to frighten you.'

'You are not telling me the truth.' She was measured, too. 'You know perfectly well that it is not me whom you love, but Mrs Greville, and the two children who are your responsibility, and, knowing that your heart lies with them, and not with me, I cannot marry you.'

She had thought to do it in a civilised fashion, not

confront him with her knowledge of what he had written about her, but he was persistent; he could see his prize and her dollars slipping away. Many heiresses could give him dollars, few could offer him the appearance and manner of a lady—it was that which had attracted him after the cruder charms of such as Maybelle Foy.

'How can you say such a thing?' he exclaimed. 'And who has been filling you with canards about Honoria Greville? I own that I had a liaison with her, but you must know that all such young men as myself have an . . .experienced life before they marry. But I have given her up, and in any case she has meant nothing to me for years.'

Sally-Anne closed her eyes, thought of his letter, dated that very week. He was determined to lie to her to the very end. But it would not serve him.

'How can you say that, Havvie? You have no intention of giving her up, and, in honesty, I cannot urge you to do so. You have a duty to her and to your children. I cannot overlook that—nor what you truly think of me—which is very different from the soft and loving words you have used to me so often.'

'Nor what I truly think of you,' he echoed; he was no fool. 'And what is that, Sally-Anne, and how do you know that?'

He was across the room in a stride, caught her cruelly by the shoulders. 'What do I think of you, and how do you know?'

Sally-Anne was suddenly frightened. 'Let me go!' she exclaimed. 'You are hurting me, Havvie. Suffice it that I know that your true opinion of me is scornful in the extreme.' And before she could stop herself she came out with it. 'Greedy and gullible, I believe. You cannot want such a person for a wife, and I certainly do not want a husband who thinks that of me—even before marriage.'

He did not let her go, and said hoarsely, 'Honoria Greville. I might have guessed,' and then he uttered a string of oaths, so oddly at variance with his usual smooth and civilised manner and appearance that Sally-Anne shivered and tried again to pull away from him, but he held her more tightly than ever.

'You cannot believe the word of a jealous woman, my darling,' he said. 'Reconsider, I beg of you. Together, we can build a happy life, I am sure of it.'

'It was not Mrs Greville's word,' said Sally-Anne, goaded unwisely into further indiscretion, still trying to break free, 'it was your handwriting—the same that told me that I was the light of your life and that you loved me dearly.'

'You are determined, then?'

'I must be, I am. Please let me go, Havvie. You are hurting me.'

'Irrevocably no? You are determined to humiliate me?'

'I must; I have no choice,' said Sally-Anne. 'I cannot marry a man who secretly despises me. I could have done that back in the States.'

'Oh, you might do anything, back in the States,' he jeered. 'You are all savages there.' He let go of her, and stepped back. 'Say it, then, Sally-Anne Tunstall; let me know the worst. Remember, I can make you a duchess one day. Surely that is worth paying a little for!'

'You want me to pay too much.' She was pulling off the beautiful antique ring. 'There, my Lord Marquess. There is your ring. Do you believe me now?'

'Oh, I believe you,' he said, his handsome face transformed through rage and spite into something quite different. 'I believe you. You speak of payment, Miss

Tunstall, and I shall certainly take mine now. You owe me something for the humiliation which you are about to put on me.'

He leaned forward again, and caught her to him, savagely, all his perfect manners gone. 'Payment, indeed,' he repeated. 'And if I may not have you permanently, then a little temporary use would satisfy me, I think.'

Sally-Anne was helpless before him. She was not a small girl, was reasonably athletic for a woman, but there was little she could do to fight off a determined man, particularly when she was neither mentally nor physically prepared for such a brutal assault.

He bore her down to the carpet, his face hard against hers, one hand pulling up her skirts, and when she still struggled struck her a blow which left her half stunned on the floor, for him to do as he would with her.

She could not believe what was happening to her. Frustration and lust tore at him, and so he tore at her. She tried to scream, but he put his hand across her mouth, and when, pulling herself free for a moment, she panted at him, 'Stop, Havvie, stop; you will regret this later,' he replied,

'Not I; I shall remember this with pleasure, you American whore.'

And there, on the carpet, the worst thing of all happened to Sally-Anne Tunstall, and there was nothing she could do about it, nothing. She tried to distance herself from it all, as Papa had once said that the Indians did, but it was useless; he hurt her too much, and, what was worse, took pleasure in her pain. . .

And then it was over. He stood up, face scarlet, looking at her and speaking to her as though she were the whore he had called her. 'I've had better tarts,' he said, and, walking to the door as she struggled into a sitting position, trying to restore her ruined self, for at some time she must leave the room and face her shattered world, he flung her his final insult. 'Try explaining *that* on your wedding night, Sally-Anne Tunstall, and tell your husband who it was who was there before him.'

He was gone. And even Terry Rourke had not shamed and handled her so. She wanted to vomit. She tried to rise to walk, but her legs would not let her. He had been careful not to tear her dress, but everything else seemed to be ruined irrevocably, not the least the inward psyche of Sally-Anne herself, which seemed to have been raped more than her body, if that were possible.

Somehow she got herself out of the room, and up the stairs before anyone appeared to speak to her, tore off her clothes, and then hid the betraying underwear in a Gladstone bag which she later threw off Waterloo Bridge after she had left the embassy, pretending to go with Laura Parslow on her European tour, but actually having hired herself out to J. D. O'Connor, and gone to the East End.

But that had all been in the future that morning. That, and the discovery that she could not bear a man near her in the early days after the rape; so she had feigned an illness, explained as the consequence of her breaking her engagement with Havvie, which, of course, had caused an immense furore inside and outside of society, and Mama and Papa had put off their visit to England, and sent her loving letters, for she had written that she had discovered that she did not really love Havvie at all, had merely been beglamoured by his appearance, name and title.

Which explanation, she was sure, had deceived neither Mama nor Papa, for both of them had written saying that if she needed them they would come at once after all. No, she had not wanted that, not Papa's shrewd eyes on her; she had shivered at the very thought. Later, perhaps, when she had recovered a little.

What had really caused her, in the end, to escape from her life as an American Princess was overhearing her English maid talking with one of the senior parlourmaids. She had thought that the woman had liked her, but the comment she had caught had been to the effect that spoiled children like Miss T. got what they deserved! It was probably the Marquess who had jilted her, and not the other way round. 'Useless,' she had jeered, 'like all spoiled rich girls. Never done a hand's turn in her life, and wouldn't know how!'

Sally-Anne sometimes thought that her career as a housemaid had been sparked off by that remark as much as by anything else—that and discovering how hard life was in the East End, and her determination to write about it from the inside, rather than as a privileged outsider looking in.

And now Havvie's cruelty had wrecked her true love for her, for she was unable to bring to Dr Neil either an unspoiled body or a spirit which was prepared to accept his lovemaking. The bitter sobbing which had consumed her immediately after her coming upstairs had stopped. Instead slow, silent tears ran down her face, and she lay down on the bed, trying to forget, not to remember. The truth shall set you free, but oh, the truth of her past had not done that—it had simply shown her what a selfish, unthinking thing she had been that first Terry Rourke, and then Havvie Blaine could have exploited her so.

Self-knowledge had come too late. And with that thought her tears stopped. For it had come, and perhaps, but only perhaps, she could build on that. There was, almost in response to this, a tapping at the door, the knob turned, and he spoke.

'Let me in, McAllister. Please let me in. I need to talk to you.'

On hearing him, desolation struck harder. Sally-Anne sat up, the sodden sheet in her hand. Her handkerchief had been a useless rag long ago. She said nothing. He spoke again.

'I shan't go away, you know. Let me in, McAllister. I need you.'

That moved her. If he had said, '*You* need *me*,' then that would have been the end for him.

'You can't need me,' she croaked.

'Oh, but I do.' Silence, and then, 'We need one another, and I shall sit here until you let me in. Think how scandalous that would be, McAllister, when they find me starved to death outside your door on the top landing. Think how dear Matey will grieve!'

This poor attempt at humour produced a broken sob, but also the reaction he wanted. Sally-Anne had a flash of memory of him just before their abortive lovemaking, remembered how dear she had felt him, so dear that she no longer saw his scarred face, but only Dr Neil, whom she loved.

She rose, ran across the room, unlocked the door, and then swiftly retreated to the bed again—not to lie on it, but to sit on it, huddled against the end, one shoulder against the iron railings of its head, hands primly in her lap, feet side by side, her whole posture defensive.

The door opened, and Dr Neil came in.

CHAPTER FOURTEEN

DR NEIL SAW her on the bed, face swollen and unrecognisable, all her bright lustre gone. He swallowed, and said gently,'McAllister, may I sit beside you? I promise not to touch you.'

Sally-Anne shuddered, but nodded. She had recovered the sheet, and held it as a baby might, with both hands. One thumb stole into her mouth, for comfort.

Dr Neil swallowed again as he sat down on the bed, not too near, not too far away. He knew the symptoms she was displaying. They were classic, and whatever had been done to McAllister had been so severe and unwanted that unless she was cured soon she would be stricken for life, all her bright spirit running to waste.

'Who hurt you, McAllister?' he enquired. 'It would help you if you could bring yourself to talk about it.'

Tell Dr Neil? Oh, no! She could hardly think about it herself. How could she tell him what Havvie had done, and said? She shook her head at him. Humpty-Dumpty was quite broken, soiled in the dust, and not Dr Neil, nor anyone else, could ever put her together again.

'Try to tell me, McAllister. I'm a doctor. You were . . .raped. . .were you not?'

'Yes,' she whispered, avoiding his eyes. It was the first time that she had ever told anyone of what had happened.

'And not too long ago. Not long before you came here?'

The thumb had crept out of her mouth. She looked at

it, and thought contemptuously, What a baby I am, a cry-baby. She put it in her lap, and, her voice a thread, said, 'Yes, oh, yes,' and then, 'I did nothing to provoke it, nothing. . . We. . .were. . .not. . .loving at the time. Not at all. Quite the opposite.' She stopped, and Neil waited patiently, not attempting to touch her, thank goodness. She stole a look at his face. He did not appear to be judging her, either.

'I was surprised. I suppose I trusted him, and then . . .oh, I can't tell you, but. . .he hurt me so, and I am unclean, so unclean. Who would want me now? The only consolation I have is that he did not make me pregnant. At least I was spared that.'

She knew that she had pushed her dreadful experience away, had refused to be broken, had tried to pretend that it had never happened. She had held her head high, kept up her indomitable front. She had been fiery Sally-Anne still, and then fiery McAllister, and a few moments' loving from a man she loved had undone her, had brought her not joy, but a trauma of the remembered pain and anguish which Havvie had inflicted on her. No good man, and Dr Neil was a good man, could want her after that.

Dr Neil knew that she was speaking the truth about what had happened to her.

'Your employer?' he said gently, not probing, remembering what she had said on the first day. He was still not sure that he believed that story, but in her misery was prepared to go along with her.

Sally-Anne nodded. She could not tell him about Havvie; neither could she *speak* the lie to him, not to Dr Neil, but she could not tell him the truth, for that would mean telling him who she was, and she could not tell him that, not here, not now; it would spoil everything between them if he knew that she was the spoiled and pampered American Princess.

'McAllister,' he said, and oh, his voice was so kind. He could not want to be kind, could not love the tarnished and ruined thing Sally-Anne Tunstall was, but she looked at him all the same.

'I love you, McAllister,' he said. 'Believe me when I say that to you. And nothing you have told me makes any difference to that. Believe me when I say that I would never hurt you. Hold my hand, McAllister. Hold my hand.' And he put his hand out to her, warm and loving on the counterpane between them.

That wretched thumb was in her mouth again; it left her mouth and she watched the hand it belonged to inch its slow way across the counterpane towards his, almost as though it had nothing to do with her.

As it stole towards him, Dr Neil made no move, did not move himself or it, when she put her own hand on his, but let it lie lax, so that she felt no threat from him. And so they sat, side by side, for some time, the afternoon sun gentle on them, through the attic window.

Once or twice, Sally-Anne shuddered, and then, as he made no move, she looked at him, and gave a watery smile.

'There, that's not so bad, is it?' he said, giving her the smile which always transformed his ruined face.

Sally-Anne nodded. He might call her McAllister, but since she had fled from him she had become Sally-Anne again. Could she trust him? Dared she trust him, or any other man, ever again? Her own strong and unthinking rejection of him had shocked her as much as it had shocked him.

Emboldened, Dr Neil inched towards her. He pulled his hand gently from hers, and, still gentle, put his arm around her to hold her by the shoulder. He felt her grow rigid at his touch, made it so light that she hardly knew that it was there.

'Trust me, McAllister,' he repeated.

Oh, she did want to trust him, but. . .but. . . But she did not pull away, and when he moved nearer still, holding her as though she was infinitely fragile, and turned her so that she was fully in his arms, her head on his shoulder, he did it so slowly that Sally-Anne felt not fear, but reassurance.

How long they sat unmoving Sally-Anne never knew. All she knew was that she was turning into McAllister again, Dr Neil's pert and lively maid, and that this was the haven which she had unconsciously been seeking in the months since Havvie Blaine had assaulted her.

She could feel the strong beat of his heart, the warmth of his body, smell the masculine scent of him, and still she was not frightened, for this was Dr Neil, was it not, and why should she be frightened of him?

'You see how easy it is, McAllister,' he whispered suddenly, and he kissed the top of her head, 'when it is love that lies between a man and a woman, and not hate and fear.'

The kiss had been such a butterfly of a thing that she did not reject it, and when he bent and kissed her cheek she did not reject that either. She even thought that she might like to sleep like this, held in one strong arm.

But Neil had other ideas. If he was to save her from a lifetime's retreat from life and love he had to move her along the right road as quickly as he dared and as quickly as she would let him. Some gentle lovemaking on this first occasion to prove to her that she was not repulsive to him because of what had happened to her, and that all men were not brutes, was in order. The rest could wait for another day.

He kissed her again, on the forehead this time, and

whispered in her ear, 'Kiss me back, McAllister. On the cheek, if you like. The Master promises not to bite.'

This even brought a ghostly chuckle; Dr Neil's being the Master again was enough to bring McAllister back, she thought, if only to provoke him to further jokes. Still she could not bring herself to touch him, until, turning his head, she saw the scar, and without thinking leaned forward to kiss that, a butterfly kiss like his, to show him that she loved him—and his scar.

Time stood still in the attic room while they exchanged the most innocent of kisses and embraces, and McAllister faced her future, the bruises slowly disappearing from her wounded spirit under the healing power of true love. Dr Neil—she could not think of him as Neil—was careful to hold her in such a way that she felt no restraint, although his own self-control was slowly beginning to slip.

Holding her in his arms, warm and loving, feeling her fear drain away, was beginning—shamefully, he thought—to rouse him. Oh, this is wrong, he reminded himself fiercely, when all she needs is mild affection and the ability to trust, and if I go too far it will only be to betray her again—or so she will think. But oh, I love her, and if truth be told I want to prove that love in action.

He dared not pull away, even though he did not want her to feel his changing body, but at this point one of her gentle caresses touched the corner of his mouth and before he could stop himself his mouth was on hers, and restrain himself as he might it was a lover's kiss, not a friend's.

McAllister did not reject it, but answered it. Something was beginning to happen to her; as love began to drive out fear, the tension in her body relaxed, and the feelings which she had experienced when Dr Neil had first begun to make love to her, earlier that afternoon, returned again.

His restraint, exercised for so long, paradoxically excited her, because she felt no fear of him. So that when his mouth closed on hers she responded passionately, and a great wave of love and affection for him, and for his patience, engulfed her, and carried her away.

She raised her left hand to stroke his scarred cheek and on impulse kissed it again, saying, 'Oh, my love, my poor love; you were hurt even more badly than I was.'

On Dr Neil this had an effect even more erotic than any more intimate caressing of his body might have produced. He possessed just enough self-control to continue his gentle stroking of her, but both his arms now held her, and almost without her willing it McAllister's crept around his neck, and unconsciously they sank, from their sitting position, on to the bed, to lie with McAllister's head on the pillow, Dr Neil's by her, he careful to lie still, to do nothing which might suggest any kind of bodily union. They lay half entwined like this for some time, occasionally exchanging kisses.

By now Dr Neil was in an agony of desire, the loved one in his arms, so near and yet so far——But not so far as he thought, for McAllister suddenly wanted more from him than he was giving. She felt herself dissolving and the nearness of him, his gentleness after Havvie's remembered brutality, was having its effect on her.

She gave a little cry and turned fully towards him, inside his arms, pulled his head towards her, and began to rain kisses on him. To return them he, too, moved, and he was now above her, and for a second she felt fear again, only for him to murmur into her neck, 'Don't be frightened, McAllister, I won't hurt you,' and he began to kiss her throat, exposed above the white blouse she was wearing, while his right hand stroked her breast through its cloth.

At what point McAllister's fears finally disappeared beneath his loving patience, and they began to make love in earnest, neither of them could have said. He said huskily, 'Let me, McAllister,' and began to unbutton her blouse, 'I want to stroke you, McAllister, and not your clothes,' and she made no effort to stop him, and when he bent his head to kiss the breasts he had fondled with his hands the cry which she gave was one of pleasure, not fear, for now it was Dr Neil loving her so carefully that the flood of pleasure was almost on her from that alone.

No, he would not hurt her, and now she wanted to be him, to be part of him. Her hands moved to unbutton his shirt, and, that done, she not only wanted to stroke the golden down on his body, but to see that body, to see *him*.

And, quickly now, the irrevocable moment was approaching, when his passion, which she could feel hard against her, would demand fulfilment, and in doing so might destroy the fragile palace of love which they were building together.

Only, both their minds, their tortuous, questing minds, the busy intellects which glorified them, but tormented them, had been consumed, if only momentarily, in the fires of passion.

McAllister no longer knew herself, nor Dr Neil either; if he demanded fulfilment, so did she; the desire to be one, not two, had overcome them both. And as proof in the healing power of accepted love her hands undid him, as he undid her, until, naked together, he lifted himself to enter her, and if for McAllister there was a moment of trapped fear it disappeared when she was truly his, and they were, at last, one thing, moving together in harmony in an experience quite unlike the shock and terror which she had felt with Havvie, and had always feared would happen to her if she ever made love again.

Dr Neil had not meant to consummate his love for McAllister, but having begun to heal and reassure her he had started something on its way which was beyond his control, or McAllister's either. They had lived in proximity for weeks—nay, months—they had shared in the coming of life and the going of death, had suffered and exulted, and finally they offered their shared love as a sacrament, he crying out her name, and she his, in the blessed joy of fulfilment.

Time started again as they lay panting, their hearts beating as one.

'Oh, forgive me, my dear love,' he said at last. 'I had not meant that, only to reassure you. Oh, I am as bad as the man who ravished you.'

She put her hand on his mouth. 'Oh, no. Never say that. I wanted it too, so much, so much. The other was violation. It was not like loving you. . .not like that at all. . .' She could say no more, only after a moment when he did not answer, 'Please don't reproach yourself, my darling, when you have given me back to myself again.'

And, after that, she still in his arms, they slept a little, two tortured spirits, who in finding each other had found love and peace together.

McAllister awoke to find him above her again, put her arms around his neck to draw him down to her, but he shook his head.

'Too late, I fear. Matey will be back soon, and—oh, what would she say to me for seducing you as I did? We must return to the world, I fear, but first——' And he kissed her cheek, so gently that her tears flowed again, only they were tears of joy, not pain.

'First?' she whispered.

'Will you marry me, McAllister? I must call you that. It is McAllister who is dear to me, not Sally-Anne. Can you bring yourself to marry a poor doctor, be his wife, and share his burdens? It is little enough I have to offer you—apart from my love, that is.'

Now was the time to tell him who and what she was, but she could not spoil this magic moment; it was McAllister he loved, not Sally-Anne Tunstall, and she would not ruin her perfect afternoon. Later, later, she would tell him—of the embassy, Papa and J.D.—but for the moment it was enough for her to be the wounded girl whom he had healed.

'You have offered me more than anyone has ever done before,' she said. 'For it is McAllister the poor servant whom you love, and that is sweeter to me than any fortune you can offer me, Dr Neil. Of course I will marry you. I want to share in your work, not live in idleness.'

Dr Neil was pulling on his clothes, hiding his scarred body, the scars which she had embraced in their mutual passion. 'You? Idle?' he said, thinking of the tireless girl she had been. 'I mocked you one night, my darling, for working so hard, remember. I thought that it would soon pass, and it did—for you to work harder still. Yes, you may share my life, and live a little more easily, I hope.'

He kissed her again, almost shyly, as though they had not so recently been as intimate and close as a man and woman could be. 'Come, we must dress. There will be other times, my love.'

CHAPTER FIFTEEN

'Not with the Parslows?' said the American ambassador incredulously. 'You are telling me, Warrender, that my niece is *not* travelling with the Parslows? Why, I know for a fact that she left here to go with them, and half a dozen trunks went with her.'

'Nevertheless,' said Jordan Warrender, one of his senior counsellors who had recently been travelling in Europe, ostensibly on holiday, actually on a tricky diplomatic mission, but who had looked up the Parslows on finding them in Venice, 'she is most definitely not with them. Cried off at the very last moment, Mrs Parslow said. Fortunately, and by pure chance, I had said nothing that could lead her to assume that we thought that she was travelling with them—as arranged.'

Orrin Tunstall reverted to being a Westerner, as he often did in moments of crisis. His smooth speech was saved for English society and the Court of St James. 'Godammit, feller, where in Hades is she? She's been sending me postcards—how's she managed that, hey?'

Jordan Warrender sighed. He had had a few hopes for Sally-Anne Tunstall himself, had been sorry to see her go. He had read her banal cards with more interest than they deserved.

'Oh, I bearded Miss Laura, on the quiet,' he hastened to add. 'I know you want no scandal. She confessed that Sally-Anne had written them on old ones Miss Laura had collected on earlier trips, and Miss Laura had posted them for her, to deceive us. No,' he forestalled his superior, 'she has no idea where Miss Tunstall is. Talked vaguely about work—she didn't know what—that Miss Tunstall had hinted she was going to do.'

'Work!' grunted Orrin, unkind for once about the niece he loved. 'That, Warrender, will be the day. She's done nothing but play for the last two years. I thought better of her once.'

Warrender proved his mastery of diplomacy by looking enigmatic as the ambassador continued to fulminate. 'Good God, feller, she could be anywhere, and a regular Babe in the Wood at that. Caught by two swindlers already; what's she doin', eh? Tryin' to find a third? Yore duty, feller, is to find her, and discreetly. If not it'll be for me to tell her lovin' papa that his baby daughter is lost, and what's the bettin' he'll be over here on the fastest boat runnin', to cut my throat for me if anything's happened to her?'

A fortnight after Orrin Tunstall's unwelcome discovery of his niece's absence, Sally-Anne sat writing her journal at midnight. She had just finished an article about pawnshops, the meat of which had been supplied by Rose, who had come round again and invited Sally-Anne to tea at the Buildings. 'To see the baby,' had been the bait, and so she had had tea with the Baileys and the baby, whom Mrs Bailey had adopted—a piece of altruism which staggered Sally-Anne, who thought that Mrs Bailey had enough to do on too little with her own brood.

'Couldn't let it go to the Home,' Rose had said briefly. 'Like to die there——' As Dr Neil had agreed, after the funeral of the little boy's mother, attended by Sally-Anne, Matey and Dr Neil. 'What's one more mouf to feed?'

Common sense said otherwise, but the unheeding

kindness of the very poor took little account of that, Sally-Anne had found. Now she was writing in her journal that she would tell Dr Neil who and what she was on the coming Saturday, after the bazaar was over. 'For,' she put down, 'I want to go there as humble McAllister who keeps the house clean, dressed the doll and made and embroidered the baby clothes, not as the American Princess doing the gracious, ladling our Papa's money, not one penny of which I have earned, smiling and patronising those not so fortunate as myself, and then leaving them to go home to the embassy—to forget them!'

When Matey had returned on that fateful afternoon, Dr Neil had told her that he had proposed to McAllister, and that she had accepted him. Earlier he had tried to hint to McAllister that she ought, perhaps, to inform her family, but she had been deliberately obtuse. She wanted so much to remain with him on the terms which had always existed between them, did not want the wealth and consequence of her real life to come between them before it needed to.

Matey was not surprised by their news, was pleased by it, in fact. McAllister's influence on her treasure had been so good, he was quite transformed.

'And I am still your maid,' McAllister had said gaily to him, but, of course, she was now less and less of a maid and more a member of the family, working side by side with Matey in cheerful equality, living and playing with them in the evening, and when Dr Neil spoke of the wedding day again she said that she must write to her uncle at least, before anything could be arranged, and let him think that she had done so.

The bazaar drew nearer and nearer—and what a strange thing, McAllister thought, to be such a central part of her life, and she and Matey worked together now, in that, as in everything else, and Matey's liking for her grew daily, for the eyes McAllister turned on him were always so full of love, and he was easy and happy with her, as he had not been since he was a boy before Africa and Angela Deverill's betrayal.

'Such a fine day,' said McAllister happily, serving breakfast to the three of them. She sat and ate it with them now, and oh, it was torture that in deference to propriety and Matey they had not made love again as they had done that golden afternoon, always to be remembered. But their eyes and looks made love for them, and spread happiness around them, and their talk was always of the future they were to spend together.

'The Master commends his slave for the quality of the breakfast as well as the weather,' said Dr Neil, catching at her hand and pressing it as she walked by.

'You may thank me for the breakfast,' McAllister said, sitting down to attack her own meal with vigour, 'but the weather—now that, alas, is beyond me. If it were not, you may be sure that I would have arranged a better climate for the Brits than the Lord has seen fit to give them.'

'Witty as well as useful,' said her lover appreciatively. 'I can see, Matey, that breakfast conversation is always going to be lively when Mrs Dr Cochrane is at table, if it resembles McAllister's, that is!'

McAllister looked at him from under the long dark eyelashes which had won his heart from the very first moment when he had seen them, on his sofa, adorning the unconscious girl he had carried in from the street.

'And you are both ready for the bazaar, I see,' he said, for he had already watched them carry through the packing-cases filled with their work, ready to be transported on Mr Hanson the grocer's small cart, due to call at Vetch Street at ten o'clock, for them to start setting out the stall.

'Sands tells me,' he observed, 'that some grand rich people, relations of his, have promised to come along to buy—to ease their consciences, one supposes, they having so much, and the poor devils whom the bazaar is to benefit having so little.'

'All grist to our mill,' said McAllister cheerfully, never thinking that Mr Sands's grand relations might prove to be Nemesis, arriving in group form, to smoke out Miss Sally-Anne Tunstall, American heiress and the ambassador's niece, the Marquess of Blaine's one-time intended, AKA—also known as—in the language of American police reports—Miss Sally-Anne McAllister, skivvy and Dr Neil's fiancée.

On the contrary, all seemed set fair, and when they had loaded the packing-cases on to the cart Matey and McAllister set off for the church hall, to lay out the stall, to have everything ready for the afternoon's visitors, Dr Neil having promised to come along to help them. 'Try to keep me away,' he had whispered, 'although it is exquisite torture for me these days, my dear McAllister, to have you so near, and be unable to stroke every bit of your delectable body. I only wish that your uncle would hurry up with his consent; I doubt whether my resolution to behave myself can hold out much longer.'

'You are being very naughty,' McAllister whispered back, pretending to be severe, 'and the only thing that I can say in your favour is that I am in nearly as bad a way as you are, and know exactly how you feel—but be patient, it cannot be long now,' for she knew that once the bazaar was over, and she was at last able to tell him the truth, they could go ahead with their marriage plans, the only delaying thing being the time it would take Mama and Papa to cross the Atlantic.

And suddenly she knew how much she longed to see them, to introduce him to them, and to tell them how sorry she was for her wild behaviour over Terry, and for her conceited folly over Havvie. Except, of course, she could never—ever—tell them what that folly had led to—even if, looking back, she could now honestly say that she had done nothing to provoke it, that she could have expected anger from Havvie at her changing her mind, but never that he would do as he did.

And even now, after Dr Neil's healing influence, daily exerted, for although he could not make direct love to her he was able to let her know in a thousand different ways how much he loved her, and how precious she was to him, she still felt the odd shudder of shame and fear.

But it was a happy McAllister who arranged the stall with Matey, joked with Mr Sands, and then in the afternoon after lunch walked with Dr Neil and Matey to the church hall.

At first, the afternoon was as much a pleasure as McAllister thought that it might be. Wealthy ladies, doing a little charitable slumming, as well as a few shopkeepers' wives, bought the pretty baby clothes, and the doll she had dressed went for a fabulous price, to be given to some little girl more fortunate than those for whom the money was being raised.

Dr Neil, with many a joke, helped them, made change, and once went out to return with lemonade and glasses for all the ladies who were so busy manning the stalls, Mr Sands helping him—the rector being a vague benevolent figure who came in and blinked at them all, said, 'I am sure, ladies, that you will all gain treasure in heaven for your noble work here today,' and went out again.

Such a modest occasion to make a girl like Sally-Anne Tunstall, used to kings and courts, happy, but it was, she discovered, true happiness to hold her future husband's hand, drink the lemonade he had brought her, and watch her work being praised and, more to the purpose, sold.

Afterwards, she was to wonder what might have happened if Mr Sands's grand party had not turned up. As the afternoon wore on he began to look unhappy, muttered to Dr Neil that he might have supposed that his cousin James would forget to come—he lived a busy life, after all.

He had promised, Mr Sands said, to bring some friends with him, but by four o'clock there had been no sign of them, until, suddenly, there was an immense bustle outside, and Mr Sands, rushing out, came back to announce triumphantly that Cousin James had arrived—'Better late than never' being his unoriginal version of the truth, and the Hon. James Sands and his friends processed in to salve their consciences by buying bookmarks, needlecases, embroidered handkerchiefs and even some of the exquisitely embroidered baby clothes on offer.

McAllister, happily unaware of who made up the party, watched these inhabitants of the world in which she had lived since she was eight years old stare and chatter as they made their way through the doorway, Mr Sands bowing and scraping at them as befitted a poor relation to whom they were doing a favour, the rest of the bazaar's patrons staring at these strange beings, male and female, as though they were visitors from another planet, perhaps one described by Mr H. G. Wells.

Dr Neil muttered in her ear, 'I never thought poor Sands such a flunkey; even to persuade them to buy our knick-knacks this is surely excessive.'

McAllister could not but agree with him, and had to

stifle a grin as he led them around, the women staring, and the men, manifestly bored, dragged along to accompany wives and girlfriends who would, that night, describe their visit to the East End in terms that would do justice to a journey up the Amazon.

And then her smile froze on her face, and she saw Dr Neil's change. His face changed because his brother Stair was one of the party, escorting the young heiress to a beer barony in Milwaukee, which was as much as such a penniless man as himself could aspire to, especially as his title was a mere baronetcy. But walking along beside him, sucking his cane, and looking ineffably bored as he escorted his new marchioness, née Miss Maybelle Foy, the meat-packer's heiress from Chicago, was none other than Havvie Blaine, of unblessed memory.

The mere sight of him was enough to make McAllister's toes curl. She retreated round the stall; she had been at the front, helping a customer to choose something from what remained unsold.

Stair saw his brother and came forward to greet him, Havvie still at his side, his wife picking up and putting things down as though they were contaminated—she had not married Havvie in order to slum it, as she later said.

'Neil! What are you doin' here? Hardly your line, hey? Sellin' baby clothes, old thing, and Matey——' he turned his bright eyes on his old governess and nurse—'still with him, eh? Gets the cane out to you, does she, Neil? Haw, haw!'

His feeble wit amused his party, if no one else. 'This is my parish, Stair,' said Dr Neil, 'and, seeing that I live here, such occasions as this deserve my support. All for a good cause, and I hope that you and your friends have come here prepared to spend.'

He moved round to the front of the stall, pulling McAllister with him. For some unaccountable reason she had bent down to inspect the floor, hoping, though Dr Neil did not know this, to escape the attentions of Havvie and his friends, all of whom had known her well in her old life.

Dr Neil would have none of it. 'Come on, McAllister,' he said good-humouredly, 'do your bounden duty. The Master commands you,' he then murmured, for her ears alone.

There was nothing for it. McAllister, clad in her shabby bottle-green dress enlivened at the throat by a bit of cheap lace, her serviceable shoes on her feet, her hair simply tied up in a knot on top of her head, her hands red raw from hard and constant manual work, resignedly straightened up, to meet the gaze of Havvie and his friends.

Recognition came slowly, but, as she had feared, it came, and when it did so Havvie's cruel eyes ran up and down her body. And there was no doubt that Stair Cochrane had recognised her as well. He looked from her to his brother, his mouth open, about to speak. The American Princess had disappeared from view months ago, and here she was, in an East End church hall, wearing shabby clothes, in the company of his brother and his old nurse.

Havvie forestalled him. His expression wicked, he continued the stare which seemed to strip poor McAllister of her clothing, a stare so cruel that Dr Neil immediately saw its import and began to bridle at the sight, putting out a protective hand to his beloved, to feel her tremble beneath it. A second or two later, Maybelle, her attention drawn from what was on the stall to what stood beside it, also recognised Miss Sally-Anne Tunstall.

'Well, well,' drawled Havvie Blaine, at last, 'what have we here? If it isn't the oh, so charming Sally-Anne—missing from our midst to turn up in the East End—and in fancy dress, too!'

His derisory gaze swept over her, and then over Neil, who, at the jeering note in Havvie's voice, and the addressing of McAllister by her correct Christian name, had suddenly stiffened. 'And the good Dr Neil Cochrane with her, the saintly refugee from the best society, who prefers the company of the dregs to that of his equals—well, well, well!'

Dr Neil was so shocked—both by Blaine's manner and the cavalier fashion in which he spoke to them both, that his normal composure left him, and he could think of no more to say than, 'You know Miss McAllister?' and his voice was incredulous, so incredulous that Havvie's eyebrows shot up in gleeful, unholy delight at the prospect of yet another opportunity to humiliate the girl who had jilted him.

'Know her?' His voice carried every shade of innuendo in it. 'Of course I know her—as what man does not? Very well indeed. I think you would say I know you very well, Sally-Anne, wouldn't you?' And the smile he gave to the frozen victim of his indecent amusement was pure poison. 'Miss McAllister, is it now, Sally-Anne? A strange setting for the Tunstall heiress, all this——' And he swept his hand around the shabby room, noting the protective arm which Dr Neil had placed around Sally-Anne's shoulders.

By his side Stair Cochrane's grin and Maybelle Blaine's inimical stare were equally hateful at the sight of the suddenly stricken expression on Dr Neil's face. He took his hand from Sally-Anne's arm, gazed first at Havvie, and then at McAllister, and said, in a hollow voice, 'The Tunstall heiress?'

'Didn't you know?' Havvie's grin grew broader. 'Allow me to present, since you seem to be in the dark about your companion, Cochrane, Miss Sally-Anne Tunstall, the American Princess, niece to the American Ambassador, heiress to Senator Jared Tunstall, of whom, even you, Cochrane, shut away as you are, have surely heard. The American politician and robber-baron, the biggest and richest rogue in the States, and she so free with her charms before marriage that marriage to her was neither necessary—nor desirable.'

Afterwards Neil Cochrane thought that he should have struck Havvie down then, but shock at learning who McAllister really was had him in its grip, and he let the shameful accusation go by. He heard Maybelle Blaine titter, saw McAllister's—no, Sally-Anne Tunstall's—stricken face.

All of the courage, the new-found confidence which Dr Neil had given her, with his love, drained away from Sally-Anne at the sight of Dr Neil's face when Havvie told him who she was.

She put up her hands in a gesture reminiscent of the one which she had made in the attic, when she had been still fearful of him and of all men, but the gesture was as much for Havvie as for him.

'Please, please, Havvie,' she said hoarsely.

Both men looked at her, and the expression on Dr Neil's face struck her to the heart. Oh, why had she not told him who she was straight away? Why had she waited—to be confronted with this?

'Oh, I like that,' said her former fiancé softly. 'Oh, yes, I do, indeed. What do you want of me, Miss Sally-Anne Tunstall? More of what you had before? The virtuous doctor not satisfying you? Tut, tut. . . Go home, Sally-Anne, and I'll think about it, so I will—if you ask me nicely again, that is. . .'

Sally-Anne put up her hands again, could barely look at Dr Neil. Why did he not speak, stop Havvie? But Neil's world lay in ruins about him, as he thought of all the lies which McAllister had told him, and listening to Havvie began to wonder where the truth lay. All of his suspicions about women since Angela Deverill's treatment of him came back with a rush, and he could not tell whether McAllister was registering shame or guilt.

He swung on her, said, 'He's telling the truth?'

'Yes.' Sally-Anne thought that she was about to faint. 'That I'm Sally-Anne Tunstall, yes. But not the rest, Neil, not the rest. He's lying about that. He's the one who. . .hurt me.'

Havvie's wicked eye was on Dr Neil again. It was as though everyone else in the little hall—Mr Sands, the curious spectators, Havvie's party—did not exist—only the three of them left in the world. Oh, was not this delightful, to hurt again the girl who had rejected him, the girl who when all was said and done would have been a greater prize than the vulgar woman he had married for her money? Sally-Anne deserved punishment for forcing him to do that, if for nothing else. And by her expression the wound he was dealing the pair of them now was a mortal one.

'So innocent,' he jeered. 'But can you believe her, Cochrane? Did she put on her pretty act for you? Show you her little deceits? The bashful, wounded virginity, such coy shrinking to inflame the passions even more—as I know to my cost—and then, when she's finished with you, rejection. Using her money and her charms to trample on you, to humiliate an ex-lover.'

Neil was ready to knock Blaine down, had come out of the trance which had held him silent under Havvie's insults to the girl he loved—but he saw Sally-Anne's face, and read there only guilt, not the shame which gripped her.

'No, Neil,' she said, swaying, 'he's lying. How can you let him say such things about me, before so many? Are all men liars and cowards?'

'Do but look at him, sweetheart. He knows, doesn't he, that I—and possibly others—was there before him?' Havvie said.

Neil broke on that, and on Sally-Anne's cry. She had put her hands before her face, and by now the whole room was watching them, although most could not hear what was being said.

He pivoted, and despite his lameness, his sedentary life, he was still a powerful man, and he knocked Havvie Blaine flying, for him to be caught and steadied by Stair, who fended his brother off with one hand.

The women standing on the edge of Havvie's party shrieked and Maybelle Blaine cried viciously to the distraught Sally-Anne, 'Haven't you done enough damage to poor Havvie, Sally-Anne Tunstall, without egging on another of your lovers to attack him?'

Another of your lovers! Sally-Anne's paralysis cracked. She advanced on Maybelle, her hands clenched into fists, as she had advanced on her little brothers, sometimes seriously, sometimes in play. 'You lie, Maybelle. You know you lie. I'll teach you to tell the truth. If no one will fight for me, I shall fight for myself.'

'No,' said Neil; both *Dr* Neil and McAllister, his love, had disappeared. He caught Sally-Anne's wrist in his hand with such strength that she cried aloud. Ignoring Havvie Blaine, Stair, the astonished Mr Sands who could hardly believe what he had been hearing, and all the other spectators, he dragged her across the room and through a side-door by the small stage, into a long corridor. Still holding her, he locked the door behind them, then released her wrist to take her by the shoulders and pin her against the wall.

For some reason she had snatched up her bag as he had dragged her by the stall; she remembered seeing Matey's grieving face, Matey's hand on his arm, Matey saying, 'No, Neil, no. Think what you are doing,' and Neil ignoring her.

His face was ashen and he was shaking. 'You lied to me,' he said, his voice thick with passion. 'Not once, but many times. I thought that you were telling lies, but, by God, not such lies as you told. The poor girl with a dead father and mother, ruined in the Depression. Such a touching story, Miss Sally-Anne Tunstall——' and he spoke her name as though he were striking her with it '—and all a lie. Lies, all of it. And the rape—was that a lie too, to catch the silly doctor? Why did you do it? Did it amuse you? If you lied so badly about yourself, how can I know that you did not lie about your innocence? God forgive me, Sally-Anne Tunstall, I have spent my life avoiding such flytraps as you plainly are. The American Princess—even the poor doctor has heard all about *her*, and then you came into my home. . . Did it amuse you to seduce the poor doctor after the noble Marquess? Do you like playing games with men? Does it feed your vanity? Is that why you refused to name a day for our wedding?' And he shook her at the end of each question.

Sally-Anne's world had collapsed about her. Half an hour ago she had been in a heaven of love with the enraged man before her. And why did he believe Havvie, and not her? Oh, they were all the same, men, even the best of them. Her hope of happiness was gone, all gone, and if she had to bear a little of the blame for not having told him immediately who she was, then surely that was not a thing to hang her with. Could he not trust her a little, just a little? Was Havvie's word worth so much more than hers?

Up went her head. If she was to be betrayed yet again, then she would go with banners flying, trumpets braying, and no tears to speed her on her way.

'Do you—did you—love me so little, Neil, that you believe him without question, and me not at all?'

'Oh, my sweet cheat, but he knew you, didn't he? Knew your little deceits. He knew that you weren't a virgin when you came to me.'

'He knew because he raped me,' she answered him, head still high. She remembered Havvie's last words when he had left her that afternoon, and knew that what he had said was true. In taking her virginity he had taken away her power to convince any man of her innocence, even the man before her who had said that he loved her. 'I told you the truth about Havvie. I lied to you about who I was because——'

He interrupted her, savage again. 'The truth, Miss Tunstall? Do you know what the truth is?'

What could she say? She had lied to him because she wished to evade the unpleasant truth of her life as a rich heiress, to try to make a new life free of old ties and old mistakes, where she would be loved as McAllister, who had nothing. And how right she had been to lie! For look what had happened, once he knew who she was. . .

She flung her head back. She was her father's daughter again, the daughter of the predatory pirate who controlled Wall Street, who was a powerful man in government as well as in the world of society, was King Edward's friend, who kowtowed to nobody.

'The truth, Dr Cochrane? Do you want it all? You shall have it. First of all my name is neither Tunstall nor McAllister. You fell in love with an illegitimate girl who carries her father's name by grace and favour, not by right—never mind that I was not meant to be illegitimate; that is what I am. And the first man who pursued me did so to gouge a small fortune out of my father, to marry his true sweetheart and set himself up in business. And the second man who pursued me did so to gain a large fortune, to spend on his long-term mistress and their children, and to laugh at the silly girl and her father who gave it to him. And when the silly girl found out and rejected him he raped her for her pains.

'And the third man who. . .said he loved me. . .' and her voice faltered at the words '. . .loved me so dearly that on hearing the slanders of my assailant he believed every word that he said, and none of mine. I loved you, Neil Cochrane, truly loved you, that was no lie, and I shall make sure I never love another man. And all the lies that I told you were to try to escape the lie that was my life.

'And what did you love? Tell me that. For sure, not Sally-Anne McAllister, but some doll of your imagination you took to bed to comfort yourself.'

He turned his ravaged face on her, and the ravage was grief, and she had never loved him more, doubt her though he might.

'How can I believe you, when all that I thought I knew of you was false. . .?'

'Try believing your heart, Neil. Or is that too much to ask? Let go of me,' she said fiercely, as his hands tightened on her shoulders. 'Unless you wish to do to me what Havvie did.'

He dropped his hands instantly, as though she had struck him. 'Was it a game for you, Sally-Anne? To trap Stair's poor brother and add another to your list of conquests?' And he almost groaned at the sight of her.

She had never looked more beautiful, standing there in her poor clothes, defying the world—and him.

'And if I had told you the truth, Neil, that day when Jem Higgins knocked me senseless, what would you have done then? Sent me on my way?'

'Better that than you should practise all your sweet deceits on me.' And his voice shook.

'My sweet deceits.' Sally-Anne closed her eyes, opened them to see him lift his hands to cover his face, his head bent, shoulders bowed, his world in ruins about him. 'Oh, I see, I see,' she said scornfully. 'You are determined to wallow in self-pity again, determined to think me a whore so that you can return to the bottle, and blame all women, and not yourself, that you are frightened to face life. So be it. I shall be a whore, and leave you with a whore's kiss.' And she leaned forward, pulled his hands away from his face, placed her mouth on his in a kiss of such passion that they drowned in it, and then, with a sudden twist, she was away from him, out of the arms he had placed about her, running down the corridor towards the outer door.

She turned and said, voice shaking, 'Goodbye, Neil, goodbye. Think what you will of me. Think that, for me, you were but a summer's play, but summer is nearly over. . . Goodbye.' And she was out of the door—and out of his life.

For a moment the paralysis which had struck Neil from the moment that Havvie had begun his assault on her reputation was on him again. Sanity returning, he ran after her, to find that she had taken the key out of the lock—and locked the door from the outside, against him.

Desperate to find her, to say—what? Anything to get her back again. He ran through the hall, the mockery of Havvie Blaine's party following him as he dashed out of the main doorway—no sign of her there—and then back down the alley at the side—and still no Sally-Anne.

Distraught at what he had thrown away—and, whether she was guilty or innocent, he only knew that he wanted her back—he ran towards Vetch Street like a man possessed, head bare, careless of curious glances and jeering comment at his headlong progress, reaching Vetch Street—to find that she was not there.

Her sewing basket sat on the kitchen table where she had left it, after lunch. And then he was up the stairs to her room, to find there her few poor possessions—but still no Sally-Anne. And he had no idea of where to go, and how to find her—nor of what he would say to her when he did find her, either at the embassy or anywhere else she might have gone.

He only knew that he had lost her, and she might be the liar, cheat and whore he thought she was, or the injured innocent she claimed to be—he did not care which, for whatever she was she had taken his life and his hopes with her.

CHAPTER SIXTEEN

'AND still no sign of her? No clue to where she might have gone?'

Jared Tunstall was distraught; his much adored daughter had disappeared, but as was his usual way no one could have guessed at his inner feelings. Only his wife Mary, always calm, and still, at the age of forty, a great beauty, could guess at the real distress which tore at him.

'Nothing,' said his brother Orrin. 'Nothing. We have been most discreet, you realise. I know that you would want no scandal attached to her name.' He hesitated; best not to tell Jared of what Havvie Blaine had been saying of her; he was fearful that if his brother knew he would do Havvie a mortal injury——Best perhaps to warn Mary Tunstall privately.

Jared and Mary Tunstall had arrived at last in London, summoned by Orrin when it became apparent that Sally-Anne could not be traced.

'Dear God,' said her father. 'What can she be thinking of? For all we know she could have been made away with.'

He rose, began to pace the room, stared at the butler who entered, and said to Orrin, 'Beg pardon, sir, for interrupting, but the housekeeper says that a young woman, claiming to be Miss Sally-Anne Tunstall, has arrived at the servants' entrance, and what is she to do?'

'Do?' said Orrin energetically. 'Send her in immediately, Baines. Have you seen her? You know Miss Sally-Anne.'

'Begging your pardon again, sir. Mrs Wren says that the young person does not look as an ambassador's niece should. . .'

'For God's sake,' said Jared Tunstall, beginning to feel a little hope at this news that his daughter might, after all, be safe. 'Send the girl in; we shall soon know if she's Sally-Anne. Surely the housekeeper can recognise her?'

'Mrs Wren is new, sir, since Miss Tunstall left to go on holiday,' explained the butler. 'But I will send the young woman in, if that is your wish.'

'English servants,' snorted Jared, to have his wife put her hand on his arm, while Orrin rose, saying,

'I will see her, and if it's Sally-Anne, which I suspect it might be, and not someone masquerading as her for some God-forsaken reason, I'll send her to you. You won't want me around.'

'My brother,' said Jared, wher Orrin had gone, 'is the truest gentleman I know; beats all these so-called aristocrats here hollow.' He resumed his tigerish pacing of the room, to stop only when there was a timid knock at the door, to call impatiently, 'Come in, come in.'

Clutching her battered handbag, graceless in her servant's clothes, Sally-Anne Tunstall advanced into the ambassador's private drawing-room to confront her mother and father, who stared at the strange sight she presented.

'What are you doing here?' was all that she could find to say. 'I thought that you weren't coming over until the fall.'

'Good God, Sally-Anne!' exploded her father. 'Your uncle Orrin tells us that you have been missing for months, not travelling with the Parslows as we thought, and when you surface again *you* have the gall to question *us*.'

Seeing them after so long, after all that had happened to her, it was as though they were strangers. She had not realised that they were so young. After all, Papa was only just forty-one, and Mama was younger than that, and they were both so handsome that it was a wonder—or perhaps not—that they were so faithful to one another, so much so that it was almost a joke, Papa having been a great ladies' man in his youth, she had discovered.

The sight of them made her feel old—old and soiled.

'I decided not to go with the Parslows,' she announced, as though she were saying the most reasonable thing in the world, but her lips were numb with fright, Papa was such a hard man to defy. 'I changed my mind at the last minute.'

'And that's it?' said her papa quietly; he was always at his most dangerous when he was quiet. 'You turned down Havvie Blaine at the last minute, too. You then disappear, frighten us all to death, and suddenly, without warning, reappear, wearing fancy dress——' this was an unfortunate echo of Havvie, to be sure '—and all you can say for yourself is that you changed your mind!'

'Yes,' she said, again, as though it were the most reasonable thing in the world, but she saw that her mother looked worried, and that doubtless Papa was behaving as he did because he had been worried about her, his darling, whom he had sent away from him, only to lose her in a foreign country—for that was what Britain was.

Jared Tunstall, enraged by his daughter's cool refusal to be intimidated in any way, advanced on her, his face stern as she had never seen it before, although his business rivals would have recognised it. He was obviously even more angry with her than he had been during the contretemps with Terry.

'By God, Sally-Anne, your mother said that I spoiled you rotten, and I think that she's right. Answer me! Where have you been? What have you been doing? Why did you not have the common decency to inform your uncle Orrin of where you were going, even if you no longer wish to oblige your mother and me?'

Perhaps what disturbed him most about his daughter was her uncharacteristic calm.

'I have been learning about life,' she replied. 'Life outside the bastions of privilege, rank and wealth. As I believe that you both did, when you were my age—if you can remember so far back—but I knew you would prevent me from doing so if I told you the truth.' This piece of insolence shot out without her willing it.

'I found it very illuminating,' she continued, and then, as her papa, his face now black with rage, advanced on her, his hand upraised, her mama's suddenly fearful hand on his arm, as she cried to him,

'Be careful, Jared,' Sally-Anne answered him almost indifferently—for after what Dr Neil had said to her nothing seemed to matter any more.

'Must we wrangle so soon after we meet again, Papa? I'm very tired. I should like to have a good bath—I haven't had one for weeks—and something to eat, before you begin to cut me up as though I were one of your business opponents laid out for you to hand them the *coup de grâce*.'

She thought that he was about to choke, or to strike her down, and that would be the end, the very end; but did she not deserve it, and more, for the way in which she was speaking to him? But for the life of her she could not behave as she ought when she stood among the rubble to which her life had been reduced.

Something in her expression, the hint of a mortally wounded animal inviting further hurt, touched the almost feminine intuition which was one of Jared Tunstall's greatest assets in the cruel game of life. He mastered his rage, dropped his hand, said, his voice as indifferent as hers, but the feeling beneath it deep indeed, 'I should have thrashed sense into you long ago, Daughter, as I would have done had you been a boy. You're too big now, more's the pity—and, in any case, I don't think it would answer at the moment.' For he had suddenly realised that she was at the end of her tether—for what reason he did not know, and neither did he care, only that he must go warily with her, lest he damage her beyond repair.

'The pity is, I wasn't a boy,' she told him, her voice still indifferent, her face calm, quite unlike any Sally-Anne her parents had ever known. 'But there it is. You must make the best of me, Papa. I will tell you what I have been doing later.'

If he was adamant, so was she. They stared at one another, and as her mama had so often said, and thought again as she watched them, they were so alike in every way except their sex that they might have been two sides of the same coin.

'At least tell me that you have come to no harm in your adventuring,' he said, and, wonderfully, his voice was pleading.

Her face broke into a mischievous grin that was pure Sally-Anne. 'Not since I left the embassy, no. On the contrary, I have been most carefully guarded and looked after.'

Her mother spoke at last. She had left the two of them to duel, not even acting as referee, waiting for them to tire, perhaps even to appeal to her. 'Leave off, Jared, do,' she said briskly. 'The child looks done in; let her have the bath and the food she asks for. She's not one of your junior clerks to be bullied.'

She advanced on her daughter, caught sight of the red and ruined hands holding the shabby bag, drew in her breath, and said, 'What on earth, Sally-Anne, have you been doing to, or with, your hands?'

'Working,' she said briefly, and turned to her papa, who was, for once, at a loss, both his women against him, Sally-Anne in an unlikely alliance with her mother, who had put a protective arm around her daughter's shoulders, which her daughter did not throw off impatiently in her usual brusque manner.

Something of his momentary, and unusual, lack of confidence where she was concerned penetrated her dulled senses; she said penitently, 'I will explain later, Papa, I promise. At the moment I could not boil water successfully.'

He had to be content with that. He watched them walk away. She was right. With that spirit and her inventive brain, she should have been a boy, and together they would have run the world. Bright though his three sons were, they had nothing on Sally-Anne, the daughter conceived in the purest love, out of wedlock, to bring him joy and sorrow.

She had her bath, which seemed to help, washing away her sorrows as well as the accumulated scum of living in a house where, for a female, baths were difficult—she remembered Dr Neil standing in the outhouse in the yard, pouring water over himself, the water running beneath the short door—all that she could see of him being his head and his bare feet. Shamefully, she had had a vision of his body naked, even before they had gone to bed together, her first intimation that she was beginning to feel more for him than she ought, for the vision had not frightened but intrigued her.

And later she had found that his body, scarred as it was, was better than the one which she had imagined for him, as a living and breathing man was better than a marble statue or painting, and her vision had lacked life.

How could she think of such a thing? She should try to forget him, but the memory of their afternoon together had the power to make her cheeks rosy, and so they stayed while she put on the plainest gown which she could find in the wardrobe which she had left behind, with her personal maid, when she had pretended to go with the Parslows. Her dress sense, as well as her character, seemed to have changed while she lived at Vetch Street.

Finally, when she was fastening the long row of buttons on a classic dark blue creation, her mother came in, her lovely calm as untouched as ever, as though missing daughters suddenly returning were quite a normal thing. Usually this calm annoyed Sally-Anne; today it soothed her.

'Come here, my child,' said her mama gently, seeing her struggle with the tiny miniature pearls. 'Let me fasten that. Your poor hands are making you clumsy. They look as though you have been blackleading grates!' Only for her to step back, the calm a little shattered, as Sally-Anne blushed to her hairline.

'You haven't,' she said faintly.

'Yes,' said her daughter. 'And scrubbed the floor, swept the house, and laid the fires, too. As well as carried in the coal, made the beds, run errands, carried out the slops. Everything. I'll tell you and Papa about it over tea, if I may.'

'There is something which I must say to you before we join Papa,' announced her mama. 'It is about Havvie Blaine. You were right to break with him if you decided that you had made a mistake in accepting him, but oh, my dear, your uncle Orrin tells me that he dare not inform your father of the dreadful things Havvie is hinting about you for fear of what he might do to Havvie. Your uncle thinks that your papa might even kill him.'

'What dreadful things?' said Sally-Anne, who knew what Havvie might be saying, for had he not said it to her, before his court?

'I can't tell you,' said her mama.

'Say it,' said Sally-Anne steadfastly.

'That you are promiscuous, and that he jilted you, not you him, because he found you out.'

Sally-Anne closed her eyes, and said, 'Papa could kill Havvie for all I care about him. Except that the Brits here are not so straightforward as we are, and might hang Papa for giving Havvie what he so richly deserves. I agree that we must not tell him, but he is sure to find out, you know. And I am more worried about what he thinks of me than of what he might do to Havvie.' And despite herself her lip quivered, and her face began to crumple.

Mary Tunstall looked at this greatly changed daughter whom she felt she hardly knew, but was sure that she was going to admire, as well as love. 'You are a good girl, Sally-Anne,' she said, 'and in a way that is your biggest cross. You have had to learn how wicked people can be.'

This was perceptive and she was rewarded by a brief display of her daughter's old impulsiveness, Sally-Anne kissing her mother fervently on the cheek before they joined Papa in the drawing-room.

'So, Sally-Anne,' he said, the three of them on their own, before the tea-tray, Uncle Orrin and Aunt Nella having tactfully found that they had other engagements. 'What have you been doing?'

Thankfully he seemed to have recovered himself, she noted. The worry over her disappearance which had caused his relief that she was safe to express itself in what she acknowledged was quite justified anger had abated.

'I know that I owe you both an explanation and an apology,' she said slowly. 'I am so sorry that I caused you such grief by acting as I did, by going off without telling anyone. When I left here, I never thought. . .' She hesitated, said shyly, 'That is something I have learned, I suppose—that in the past I never stopped to think before I spoke or acted. . .though, goodness knows, you both told me to, often and often.'

Both her parents were surprised at this admission, she saw; and, seeing, she was ashamed of her past wilfulness.

'And,' she went on, 'I was compelled to end my engagement to Havvie when I discovered that he did not love me at all. . .merely wanted Papa's dollars, and, worse, despised us, all of us, for being rich and vulgar Yankees. He intended to take Papa's money and use it to keep his long-term mistress and their children; he laughed at me behind my back. . .while he pretended to my face that he admired and loved me dearly. I shudder to think what kind of life I should have had with him. You could not wish me to marry such a. . .cur, for that is what he is, despite his title.'

She saw her papa's face change at this news, and went on rapidly, 'He took it very badly. . .' which was, she thought wryly, the understatement of this, or any year '. . .and I felt so dreadful. First Terry Rourke. . .

and then Havvie Blaine. . . I thought that there must be something wrong with me, and I had to do something to prove that I was not just a thing which other people used, of value only because you, Papa, are so enormously rich. You do understand?' she said, a little fearfully.

Thankfully they both nodded and her papa said gently, 'Yes, but, Daughter, why did you need to disappear?'

'To escape it all,' she said, her fiery pride suddenly back again. 'My reputation, your wealth, everything. I needed to be nobody, to find out how ordinary people lived. And then J. D. O'Connor, who edits the *Clarion Cry*, had asked me to write for him—almost as a joke at first—about women's lives. He suggested that I write about poor women, and the only way in which I could honestly do that was to go and live among them, and I knew that you and Uncle Orrin would never agree to that.

'So I got Laura Parslow to help me, and went to live in the East End, and the only work I could find, being such a fine lady and quite untrained, was as a maid-of-all-work, a skivvy, which I was by day, and wrote my column at night, when my work was over.'

'A skivvy?' said her papa, almost disbelieving, and she saw that Mama felt the same. 'On your knees, doing the dirty work, Sally-Anne?'

'Really, truly, a skivvy. Sixteen hours a day.' She held her hands out for them to see. 'And you need not worry about whether I was safe or not. I was in a doctor's house. Dr Neil—he's Stair Cochrane's younger brother—he works for the poor in an East End practice——' Her voice almost broke when she said his name, and her mama knew immediately that Sally-Anne was not telling them the whole truth about her

East End adventures. 'And his old nurse and governess is his housekeeper, a kind dragon who kept me in order. And I learned so many things,' she said, 'I am not sorry I did it, not at all, even if it was desperately hard work.'

She swallowed. 'I learned discipline, you see. And J. D. O'Connor liked my articles—he said they created a great deal of excitement and interest; I wrote under the name of Vesta. And Dr Neil and Matey—Miss Mates—taught me so much about. . .life. . .so much that is useful. . .and I learned how hard it is for most people to live even halfway decent lives. . .and now I am home again.'

She fell silent.

'And that's it?' said her papa, as he had done earlier, but in a different and kinder tone of voice altogether.

He rose from his chair, came over to her and took her hand in his. Like his wife, he had heard her voice change when she had spoken Dr Neil's name, but he said nothing of that. He bent from his great height to take her right hand into his own large one, turned it over to look at the scars and callouses hard manual labour had inflicted on its once pink and white delicacy. 'Were you a good parlourmaid, Sally-Anne?' he enquired gently.

'Miss Mates said that I was the best and most hard-working girl she had ever had,' she answered proudly. 'But it was very tiring at first, there was so much to do.'

'So, you were a good, hard-working skivvy; and the work that you did for the *Clarion*—was that worthwhile, too?'

'Oh, yes. J.D., Mr O'Connor, has invited me to join his permanent staff of reporters now that I think that my work in the East End is. . .over. I want to accept, Papa, I really do. I don't want to be a society lady any more, but I'm not quite sure whether I want journalism to be my life's work. I have thought about being a doctor, after seeing Dr Neil—he didn't start to study until he was about my age; but he's a man. . .' She fell silent.

She wanted to talk about him, but she could not. She could not forget his betraying, rejecting face.

Her papa was speaking again, his voice grave, his expression kind. 'I think I have been very wrong in treating you as I have done, Daughter, in the way I brought you up. You are too like me to be idle, to be a useless fine lady. I should have known better. You should have had a tough education. You need occupation to direct your energies. But I was so proud of my beautiful daughter, and I wanted to make up to you for the years we lost before I met your mama again; I wanted you to have the best of everything, and I thought that that was what I was giving you. I was wrong.'

'And you gave me the best!' For the first time she spoke with all her old unbridled fire and passion. 'You thought that you were doing the right thing. It is I who am wrong, not you.' Only to meet his shaking head. Oh, how she loved him, her strong and handsome father, not the ogre she had thought and called him over Terry—and to hear him admit that he was wrong!

Sally-Anne saw her mama's loving, watchful eye on them both, pulled her hand from her father's, ran to her mother to drop on her knees before her.

'You will not mind, Mama, if I take only a small allowance from you and Papa?' For she thought that to reject his money altogether might hurt him. 'And not live in high society, but earn my own living and try to do something worthwhile with my life?'

'And stay in England?' asked her mama, not wishing to lose a Sally-Anne who, for whatever reason, seemed to have changed so greatly since she had last seen her, as a spoiled, petulant and wilful child, thinking only of herself.

'For a little, perhaps; I don't know,' said Sally-Anne. 'To find out what I want to do.' She resolutely pushed away the memory of Dr Neil and the life which she had been going to share with him.

She stood up and faced them. Pain and love were mixed in equal proportions on her face. 'Please say that you will agree, will at least let me try to earn my own living, find out if I am strong enough to do so—not go back to being useless, merely a symbol of Papa's wealth, not really his or your daughter.'

Of course, they agreed, and if afterwards both of them also agreed that there was more to Sally-Anne's story than she had cared to tell them, about both Havvie and the mysterious Dr Neil—they had noticed that his name was constantly on her lips—they did not tell her what they had guessed. She wished to live her own life, and they must respect that wish.

Before she left them, she said one more thing. 'I have asked Uncle Orrin to tell everyone who calls for me that I am not "at home". I have no wish to resume my old life.'

Jared Tunstall thought that something more than hard work had brought his daughter fulfilment and a new maturity—and, with them both, a deeper beauty. He put his arms about her, held her to him.

'When Orrin told us that you were missing,' he said, 'I knew how much we both love you. And now that you have come back I want to tell you that. And of course you shall live the life which you have decided on—as Mama and I have lived ours—even if it means that we lose you.'

She had lost them, and found them again, and if she had had to love—and lose—Dr Neil in order to do so, then so be it. In life, she was discovering, gain and loss frequently went hand in hand.

Heads turned that night when Senator Jared Tunstall and his wife entered the ballroom at Devonshire House. At forty-one, six feet two and a half inches tall, with the face of a handsome pirate and the body of an athlete in tip-top condition, Jared was worth two of anyone's looks, and his serenely beautiful blonde wife Mary was no less remarkable.

It was easy to see that he was the Princess's father: her likeness to him was astonishing, as more than one person commented. Maybelle Foy, now Lady Blaine, tittered to her husband as they walked across the floor, after mounting the stairs.

'Your one-time intended's folks,' she said—she did not see him wince at the Americanism; she did not yet know him as well as Sally-Anne did.

He laughed, however, and said something derogatory about the Tunstalls to his little court of parasites. Later, in the supper-room with the tall Senator in earshot, he could not resist doing it again, with Maybelle egging him on, loudly drawling his opinion of Sally-Anne's reputation—or lack of it. 'Like her father's, more than a little dubious,' he announced.

Jared heard this, as he was meant to. He put down the plate he was carrying, spun round on his heel and surveyed Havvie leisurely. His clothes and his voice were perfect. A great mimic, he had developed for English society an accent which outclassed the Brits around him.

'So you,' he said, his mien so dangerous that Mary beside him, fearful, put a restraining hand on his arm, 'must be the Marquess of Blaine, seeing that you are escorting the former Miss Maybelle Foy, of Chicago. Do not expect me to congratulate you, madam, I am too busy congratulating myself that I am not the father-in-law of a man who can speak so demeaningly of any young girl in public. May I, instead, commiserate with you, Lady Blaine? You have made a bad bargain in marrying Havvie. It's becoming a family habit, I fear. Your father has brought off some very bad bargains lately.'

'You are insulting, sir,' began Havvie, scarlet.

'Oh, I take my cue from you, sir,' said Jared cheerfully. 'Be thankful we are not in the States. Were we so I should have been happy to kill you for speaking so of my daughter. As we are in England your punishment must take another form.'

'Oh, we are civilised here,' sneered Havvie, feeling safe in the crowd, although Tunstall's size and presence were intimidating, to say the least.

'Then I shall be happy to take a civilised and modern revenge,' said Jared gravely. 'Lady Blaine, I have spent the last week debating whether or not to ruin your father Hiram, and his syndicate, and provide the information to send them, and him, to prison for stockmarket fraud. Thinking that dog must not eat dog, even if my meal be only that of a mongrel, I had almost decided to spare him. Between you both you have changed my mind for me. I shall immediately take all steps to destroy your father's fortune so that you, my noble Lord Marquess, will have married your Yankee bride for nothing. All she will have brought you is her own ill-bred person. I wish you both joy of your poverty. There will be no American dollars for you to spend on mistresses and in night-houses where children are on offer, my lord.'

He had had Havvie Blaine investigated when he had heard of Sally-Anne's engagement to him, and her rejection of him had saved him, and her, a deal of pain and trouble.

He paused. He had spoken in so low a tone that only the few near to them had heard him. Maybelle Blaine flushed scarlet, and said shrilly, 'You forget yourself, Jared Tunstall. This is not Washington DC.'

'As well I know,' he said, 'or I might be tempted to thrash that cur beside you until he is senseless for what I hear that he has been saying about London of me and mine. I give you ten years, sir,' he said to Havvie, 'but you are in bad condition, I see, so sweeten your language in future, or it will be the worse for you.'

He turned to his wife, and said, 'Mary, my love, you will excuse me if I ask you to leave immediately. I have cables to send, and work to do. It is day in New York, and there is still time to ruin a man before dark.'

Maybelle, face ashen, was transfixed as she watched the Tunstalls leave. Of them all she was the most aware that Jared Tunstall's threats were never idle, and that her new husband had ruined her father, and themselves, with his loose morals, and looser tongue.

'Go after him, Havvie,' she almost shrieked. 'He means what he says. He will ruin us all. Apologise—anything—to stop him.'

Jared turned again, his face stone. 'Too late, madam; if you had defended my daughter when he slandered her . . .but now, if you both walked on your knees from here to Chicago, I would not change my mind.'

'Jared,' said his wife in the motor returning them to the embassy, 'was that necessary, or wise?'

'Both,' her husband said grimly. 'No one will ever dare to slander her again, and besides, I have the feeling—and you know that I am seldom wrong about such things—that that effete swine did our daughter a great hurt. I know her well, and how brave she is, and by God, for whatever he may have done he shall pay, and pay again. I don't think he'll badmouth her in future, but he will have learned his lesson too late.'

CHAPTER SEVENTEEN

SHE had gone. He had lost her. The house was empty and all that Dr Neil Cochrane had left was Matey's grieving, reproachful face.

'I'm surprised at you, Neil,' she said—he was not even eight years old to her now, more like five or four. 'Yes, I know that she deceived us as to who she is, but how could you believe a word Lord Blaine said about her, and she such a good hardworking girl? I remember him well. He was always a horrid little boy for all his pretty face, and now he's a horrid man. And you're not to start drinking that nasty whisky again. It's not like it was with Angela Deverill—if you've lost poor McAllister it's your own fault.' And it was cold tea and coffee, burned toast and chops and sniffs all the day long. He was no longer her treasure, but a naughty child, too old to be smacked.

She had seen salvation for him in McAllister, that was for sure, and if Neil was more doubtful, about that and about her, with Havvie's hateful words still ringing in his head, and his memory of her tortured face growing the more painful whenever he recalled it, the passing of time only accentuated the agony of his loss.

A night without sleep found him red-eyed and haggard. Midway through the next morning a footman and a supercilious lady's maid arrived to collect her few belongings, so that the last traces of her life with them had gone. On the day on which he had lost her he had sat for hours on the bed in the attic where she had lived during her time with him, and where they had shared their afternoon of love, and now, on the evening of the second day, he sat there again.

The evening sun fell low upon him. The empty room mocked him, emphasised the lost vitality of her presence. Everywhere he went in the tiny house he saw her: sitting at the table, sewing, on her knees, blackleading the grate, laughing at him as she handed him his cup of tea or coffee, and holding up the doll she had dressed for him to admire.

Guilty or innocent, it did not matter; he wanted her back, and he knew at last that, whatever he had felt for Angela Deverill, it was not this.

Earlier, avoiding Matey's compressed lips, he had picked up the whisky bottle and reached for a glass—anything, so long as he achieved oblivion, surcease from pain—and then he had heard her voice again, in the corridor at the church hall, mockingly telling him to retreat to it.

He had stared at the bottle in his hand, walked outside, smashed it against the outhouse wall, watched the liquor run down, dark against the brickwork, and returned to the house, almost reeled past Matey as though he had drunk all of it, and mounted the stairs to her room to remind himself of what he had lost, hurt though it might.

In the morning he would go to the embassy, fall on his knees before her, beg her to return, to forgive him—anything—because he loved her, and love, if it were true, not only conquered all, but accepted all—— 'Love is not love, Which alters when it alteration finds,' Shakespeare had said in his greatest sonnet, and he had discovered that for himself—but too late, too late.

He rose, paced about the little room, stared at the oak bureau, remembered it in his old room, in the nursery; it had come here with Matey—he remembered her showing him the secret drawer it held, quite capacious, and unthinkingly worked the mechanism which opened it——

To find it, not empty, but holding a leather-bound book, and, beneath it, a small pile of newspaper cuttings.

Neil picked up the book. It had 'Sally-Anne's Journal' stamped in gold lettering on the cover. The clippings, he saw, were all from the *Clarion Cry* and were the articles on East End life, written by Vesta.

A thousand questions clamoured in his head, and the journal held the answers to them all. The clippings were another, more puzzling matter. He stared at the book. The time for gentlemanliness had passed; in a moment he could learn the truth of her, and if to do so involved not behaving like a gentleman, then so be it. He wanted her back, regardless, but some part of him wanted desperately to know the real truth.

He flipped open the book whose pages were filled with her beautiful, careful script, which he had seen many times on the shopping lists which she had made up under Matey's instructions.

On the cover, facing the first page, was an inscription: 'For Sally-Anne, to keep her English adventures in, from her loving papa.' The writing was bold and strong and black. Feeling more than ever like a cur, Neil turned the pages—but it was all of her that was left to him—and, he told himself firmly, he would read just enough to discover the truth about her. . .and why she had hoarded the cuttings.

Later, much later, he put the book down, and the cuttings which he had picked up at the end of his reading.

Halfway through the journal he had jumped to his

feet—he was ready to rush out of the room, to find Havvie Blaine, to kill him for what he had done to her, and for lying about it afterwards. Common sense prevailed, tears pricked behind his eyes, he sat down again. He could not help her by attacking Havvie and creating an even worse scandal; that would be self-indulgent, merely seeking to exorcise his own guilt for not believing her.

He learned the truth about the cuttings, closing his eyes when he thought of her sitting in the attic, her long day done, painstakingly writing for O'Connor the articles whose brilliance and feeling told him of the intellect which lay behind her beautiful face and emphasised again what he had thrown away.

But the worst of all was to read what she had finally written on the night before the bazaar, the night before he had added himself to the list of those who had betrayed her—— It was the worst hurt of his life.

> I am so happy, as I never expected to be, knowing that he wishes to marry me, has not rejected me as soiled goods as so many would have done. He is so different from the others, from Terry and Havvie; he loves me truly for myself, which is the best thing of all, not because I am Papa's rich daughter, the King's friend.
>
> We are all going to the bazaar tomorrow. I have so looked forward to it, making all the things with Matey, and thinking of what we shall do with the money we make—which is stupid really, when I know that I could so easily give them so much more—— But that would be nothing, for what I have done with Matey has been done by me, and not by Papa, for that is what giving them his money would mean.
>
> And when we get home again I shall tell him the

truth—about who I am, and about Havvie, not the lies about being a governess, and Mama and Papa being dead. And I shall tell him about the journalism, too, for I want to go on writing, and I want nothing false and wrong to lie between us.

Oh, my darling Dr Neil, you will never know quite what you have done for me. Not only have you given me your love, freely, but you have made me able to face life again, without fear, be able to face Mama and Papa when I next see them, enabled me to love again, with all my heart.

This is the true, right end of my English journal.

Neil Cochrane, holding the book in his hands, could not even weep over it; he was beyond tears, his hand on the page on which his dearest love, whom he had sent away from him with scorn and mockery, had told of her love for him, and the hope and joy which he had given her.

All turned to ashes because he had not trusted her, or the love she had given him.

He never knew how long he sat there. Only, very late, Matey knocked on the door, and said, timidly for her, 'Neil? Neil? Are you all right? I am worried about you. Neil, answer me.'

He put the book on the bed. In the morning he would take it and himself to the embassy, to beg her to forgive him. He hardly dared hope that she would change her mind and marry him. In the meantime there was Matey to reassure—Matey who had always given him her love and support, whom he had taken for granted, as though her love and loyalty were simply his due. He was no better than Stair, or Havvie, in his lack of concern for the feelings of those about him, he thought. Charity began at home, and, though there were larger claims on him in the world outside, what was the worth of his work there if he ignored and hurt those nearest to him?

'Don't worry, Matey,' he said to her, leaving the room of many memories, putting his arms about her, seeing with new eyes how old she had grown, and that he was all she had, the last of the many children for whom she had cared in a long life of selfless service. 'I did not mean to be selfish. And you were right to reproach me over McAllister. I treated her abominably, but, God willing, I shall try to mend matters in the morning.'

'Tomorrow's always another day,' she said, trotting out one of her many sayings, and he neither smiled nor mocked at her, but went downstairs to eat the supper which she had prepared for him, because that was the way she showed him her love and concern, and the least which he could do was respond to it.

Jared Tunstall and his wife, splendidly dressed to spend the morning shopping—Jared to see his English tailor, Mary to examine the latest Paris models at a small shop in Bond Street where she was well-known to the staff—walked into the embassy hall to hear the sounds of altercation.

The butler was arguing wih a tall fair man, threatening to send for the footmen to turn him away physically if he persisted in demanding to see the person who was refusing access to everyone, and particularly to anyone answering to the name of Cochrane.

Sally-Anne's name floated across to them as they prepared to leave. Jared's eyebrows rose. He dropped Mary's arm, and walked over to where Baines confronted the visitor. He thought he knew who the tall young man might be. Two days ago, after his daughter had told him her story, he had immediately contacted an enquiry agent whom he knew to be trustworthy and told him to find out all that he could about Dr Neil Cochrane, Sir Alastair Cochrane's younger brother. The information had arrived by the first post that morning, and Jared Tunstall already knew more about Neil Cochrane than Neil Cochrane did about him.

He had read of a distinguished army career, of a decoration won on the field of battle for bravery, his invaliding out of the army, the fight against injury, and his selfless life as an East End doctor. And here was the man himself, scarred face, heavy limp, and impressive bearing, demanding to see Sally-Anne, but he gave away nothing of this, merely said, 'What is it, Baines?' and then to the intruder, 'And who the devil are you, sir? And what do you want of my daughter?'

Neil Cochrane knew immediately who it was who was speaking to him. This tall and handsome man, not so many years older than himself—he must have been a mere boy when McAllister was conceived—could only be by his manner, and his resemblance to her, McAllister's formidable father, so often referred to. And the beautiful blonde woman with him, although so unlike her, could only be her mother.

'You must be Senator Tunstall,' he said, 'and I am Neil Cochrane, Stair Cochrane's younger brother, lately your daughter's employer. I desperately need to see her.'

So, this was Dr Neil, so often referred to, thought Jared Tunstall, in his turn. His daughter's latest love—and why she had so precipitately left him, he was about to find out.

'Miss Tunstall particularly said that no one was to be admitted to see her,' said Baines plaintively.

'Then you may admit him to see me,' said Jared Tunstall curtly, immediately informing Neil where

McAllister got her logic-chopping ability from. 'Mary, my dear, you will excuse us for a moment. This way, sir.' And he indicated the library door to Neil.

Oh, thought Neil, following him, you could see at once what a man of power he was, for all his relative youth, and why Sally-Anne was what she was, her father's daughter in every way, so alike in will, intellect and temperament, he dared swear. The suppressed energy radiating from the man before him reminded him again of McAllister, who possessed all those traits which women were not supposed to share—and how difficult that had made life for her.

'Well, sir?' Tunstall was saying to him. 'Why do you need to see my daughter so—desperately, I believe you said?'

'I don't know what she has told you, Senator Tunstall, but until forty-eight hours ago she was my housemaid; I thought that she was penniless, and that we were to marry. She talked of an uncle whose permission she might need. I never thought that her uncle was the American ambassador! I love her dearly and, God forgive me, when unexpectedly Havvie Blaine came into our lives and lied about her I believed him, and not her. I debated whether to call on him to kill him for his slanders before I came here to try to see her, and ask her to have me back—if you think I would make her a suitable husband, that is. God knows, I have little enough to give her in a worldly sense. As for killing Havvie, I did not think that she would thank me for the scandal,' he finished simply.

'Oh, you have no need to kill Havvie,' said Jared Tunstall drily, pulling his watch out of his pocket to look at it. 'I should estimate that about three hours ago I ruined his father-in-law and started him on his way to prison, thus effectively ruining my Lord Marquess, too.

You say that you wish to marry her. She has said nothing of this to me, and as her father I really ought to know, I think, what she, and you, propose to do, even if in the modern fashion you do not choose to ask me for my blessing.' This last came out in true McAllister style, satiric and sure, another way in which father and daughter were alike. Had this self-contained man been as impulsive as McAllister when he had been her age?

'She said that you and her mama were dead—you died of grief after bankruptcy.' Neil saw Jared's mouth twitch. 'Yes, I know now that it was a whopper, as she says, and I also know now why she said it. I wish to see her to renew my offer of marriage, although. . .' and his voice trembled '. . .I shall understand why she refuses me, if she does.'

'You may be sure,' said Jared Tunstall, 'that if ever I do go bankrupt I should certainly die of grief, or of mortification at such a turn. She was right about that. Perhaps you would like my permission to address her. You are a man of good family, I believe, but of small means, as you said. I take it that you would like a handsome settlement on marriage?'

'God forbid,' said Neil fervently. 'Begging your pardon, Senator, but unearned wealth does not seem to have made McAllister—I mean Sally-Anne, you understand—happy.'

'No,' said Jared. 'But I think that you might indulge me by accepting a small one—if she accepts you, that is. After all, I am her papa. You think that she would manage as the wife of a struggling doctor, be able to cope with the work and the responsibility?'

'Cope with the work?' said Neil, a little astonished. 'You should have seen her as our maid! I have never known anyone work like it—and I discovered today that she had been writing articles for the *Clarion Cry* at midnight on top of everything else she did in the house. Being my wife will be a great deal easier than that.'

'So one hopes,' said Jared, amused at these revelations confirming what his daughter had told him two days ago. 'Well, you have my permission to approach her. Anyone who can inspire her to such industry deserves to win her, and you look as though you will be able to cope with her. She really needs a strong man by her side; I hate to think what marrying a weak one would do to her—and to him. She is a most determined child, you know.'

'Yes,' said Neil, almost humbly. 'But then, I'm determined, too.'

'So one hopes,' said Jared again. 'Stay here a moment and I will try to persuade her to see you—— For what it's worth, you have my blessing, but the decision is hers, of course.'

Her father had gone. He had not put any pressure on her to see Neil. Merely said, 'I understand that he is a worthy young man, quite unlike Rourke, or Havvie Blaine, and I think from what he says, and the manner in which he says it, that he cares deeply for you. But it is your decision, Daughter.'

Well, that was fair enough, and, twisting her fine lace handkerchief in her hands, she had said steadily, 'Yes, I'll see him, but I can't tell you what my answer will be. Two days ago, I never wanted to see him again——' And her lip had quivered as she spoke.

'And now you're not sure,' her father had said.

'Yes, Papa. Quite sure that I love him. Not sure what to do about it.'

Sally-Anne now opened the door to the library, and there he was, his face pale, so that the scar blazed on it—but what of that? He was Dr Neil, and she wanted to throw herself at him, and would have done so three months ago, but he, and Vetch Street, and Effie and Rose, and everything, had changed her.

As she walked into the room she saw Neil's eyes hard on her, registering her beautiful gown, her carefully dressed hair, and even though the gown was plain she looked like a queen of society in it, she knew, and she wished that she were wearing McAllister's shabby bottle-green shirtwaister again.

'Dr Neil,' she said, her voice quite steady, which surprised her.

'McAllister—no, Miss Tunstall,' he said. He was carrying something, a parcel, and she wondered what it was.

'Oh, McAllister,' she murmured. 'I shall always be McAllister to you, I think.'

Neil did not know what to say. He had rehearsed a thousand fine phrases, but now before this grave beauty none of them seemed to answer.

He held out the parcel to her. 'I have brought you your journal, and the cuttings,' he said. 'You left them in Matey's secret drawer. Did she tell you about it?' Which, he thought, was inane enough, in all conscience, to say to your true love with whom you wished to be reconciled.

Sally-Anne, McAllister, Miss Tunstall, the American Princess—which was she?—put out her hand, then coloured and drew it back, her face turning pale. 'I found the drawer by accident. I forgot that I had left them there,' she said, and then, 'Oh, Dr Neil, you didn't. . .?'

'Yes' he said, 'I was not a gentleman, McAllister, my darling—for you are my darling, and come what may, if the whole world separated us, you will still be that. I had to read it, a little of it, and if listeners never hear any good of themselves, then the little which I read shamed me forever. Even before it I wanted you back with me, was ashamed of what I said, and afterwards. . . And if, because of that, you never want to see me again—because, after all, I am no better than Havvie; I simply raped you in a different way——' And, having lapsed into complete incoherence, he fell silent, not knowing what to say, except to add humbly, 'I think that your father approves of my suit, but that is no matter. Oh, dear McAllister, I have stopped making sense. I have been out of my mind since you locked the door on me on Saturday, and I richly deserved it. . .'

He was so wild and different from the usually cool and sensible Dr Neil that Sally-Anne stared at him, saying nothing, because unshed tears were choking her, and he took this as a sign of rejection, and began to speak feverishly again. 'I really cannot expect you to accept me after the way in which I have behaved, and then was wicked enough to read your private book, and the cuttings are there, I knew that you would want them back, and I expect that you will wish to make a career in journalism, and why accept a poor doctor, no need to do that, you çan always live on your father's allowance and what a remarkable man he is, so like you, or earn your living by your pen. . .'

How on earth was she to stop him—her dear Dr Neil who was so distracted by love that all his sense appeared to have left him?

'Yes,' she said simply, breaking in on his torrent of words.

'Yes, McAllister, what do you mean by yes! That you can earn your living by writing? Or that you will return to being an American Princess, marry into the Royal family, perhaps?'

He was almost shaking with the intensity of what he

was saying. She crossed the room to him, put her hands on his lips, and said, 'Hush, my dear Dr Neil, hush. The servant wishes to say something to the Master. Yes, I will accept you, and it has nothing to do with Papa, or common sense, or anything else. For the last two days I have known what I lost when I left you and, while you should not have believed Havvie, I can understand why you did. It would be madness for me to refuse you through hurt pride when all I want to do is be with you, as I have just found out.'

And now she could not stop talking, and he had put the book down, and they were shaking in each other's arms, and he was kissing her, and she was kissing him, and really this would not do—they were in the embassy library, and anyone might come in, and, 'Dr Neil, we cannot make love here; it would not be proper,' she said breathlessly. 'Even if you do intend to marry me—you do intend that, don't you?'

'And you hush, too, McAllister—yes, you will always be McAllister to me,' he said. 'And yes, of course I wish to marry you, and do you think, my dearest love, that, as Matey would say, we have both been struck by the asylum mop, we are carrying on so wildly, and shall I ever be sane again? It is relief, I think, and we must marry soon, I cannot bear to wait, and you won't mind living in a little house in Vetch Street when you are used to this, will you?' And he waved at the magnificent room, and her whole luxurious life which she knew beyond a doubt that she was willing to give up forever.

'You and the little house are all I want, my darling, and a small allowance from Papa, so as not to hurt him and Mama, but not enough to corrupt us—perhaps to educate the children.'

'The children,' he said fondly, holding her at arm's length. 'What a girl you are, McAllister. Have you planned how many we shall have, and what schools they will go to? And, truly, no regrets?'

'None,' she said. 'None. I have been plotting all morning how to get you back again. I thought of going to Vetch Street while you were on your rounds, waiting for you, and begging you to take me back, as a skivvy, nothing more, just to be near you, however much you despised me, and hang all worthless pride, and then you came. And why are you not on your rounds, Dr Neil? Did you want me so much that you gave them up?'

They were beyond sense, and later, much later, when he met her mama and papa, who had not gone shopping after all, but were sitting patiently in Uncle Orrin's drawing-room, and later still when Uncle Orrin and Aunt Nella arrived, and they all had luncheon together, the lovers' happiness was so patent that Jared Tunstall thought that his wilful daughter had found her true love at last.

And no, there were never any regrets; the Princess had found her palace in Vetch Street.

The other exciting

MASQUERADE
Historical

available this month is:

THE ERRANT EARL

Marlene Suson

Alienated from his family, Stephen Kendall had fought for Wellington, but now he had to return home, for he had unexpectedly inherited his father's earldom. Tired, dispirited, and upset to find the estate in poor heart, Stephen knew he had yet another hurdle to face – his wife. Manoeuvred by the earl into marriage with their neighbour's daughter, Laura Milford, but in love with another woman, Stephen had badly botched their wedding night, and for six years man and wife had not communicated. What was in store for him. . . ?

MASQUERADE *Historical*

Experience the thrill of 2 Masquerade historical romances absolutely free!

Experience the trials and the tribulations, the joys nd the passions of bygone days with 2 gripping historical omances - absolutely FREE! Follow the path of true love nd bring the past alive. Then, if you wish, look forward to receiving a regular supply of 4 Masquerade historical romances, delivered to your door! Turn the page for details of how to claim more FREE gifts.

mps
MAILING
PREFERENCE
SERVICE